Red Zone
The Daniels Brothers, Book 2

By

Sherri Hayes

Red Zone
Sherri Hayes

Copyright 2017 by Sherri Hayes
Originally published by The Writer's Coffee Shop in 2012

e-book ISBN: 978-0-9985652-0-0
Paperback ISBN: 978-0-9985652-1-7

Cover Photo and Design: Sara Eirew Photographer
Layout Design: Riane Holt

Other Books by Sherri Hayes

Finding Anna series
Slave
Need
Truth
Trust

Daniels Brothers series
Behind Closed Doors
Red Zone
Crossing the Line
What Might Have Been

Serpent's Kiss series
Welcome to Serpent's Kiss
Burning for Her Kiss
One Forbidden Night

Single Titles
Strictly Professional
A Christmas Proposal

Summary – Red Zone

The only thing Rebecca Carson ever wanted to do was join the FBI. Now, that was in danger because of a situation, of which she'd had little control. So when her ex-partner and mentor, Travis Hansen, calls and offers her an opportunity to help him with a job, she jumps at the chance.

Gage Daniels has made a pretty good life for himself. As a professional football player, all he has to do is ask, and most things are made available to him. This includes women. A well timed smile is usually all it takes to attract the opposite sex, especially in Nashville.

When a stalker threatens Gage, the team owner calls an old friend to help protect his star quarterback. Rebecca must work to protect Gage while staving off his advances. The last thing she wants is to be another notch on a hot shot athlete's belt.

Dedication

This book is dedicated to my dad. Without him, I'd never have developed a love of professional football. We spent many hours watching football and yelling at the television together while I was growing up.

Acknowledgments

First, I'd like to thank my two beta readers. They saw this story in the rough, but were always there with encouragement and ideas.

Also, a big thanks to all of my Facebook and Twitter followers. They always rise up to the challenge when I post strange questions that seem to make no sense, and they've been a great support, always encouraging me to "write faster."

Chapter 1

It was late by the time Gage Daniels arrived home Tuesday night. He was tired and more than ready for a few days off. Too bad he had to report to practice the next morning.

He tossed his keys in the bowl he had sitting just inside the door as he made his way into the kitchen to get something to drink. He noted that everything seemed to be in its place. His brother and his girlfriend had cleaned up after themselves well after using his home this weekend. That was good. The last thing he wanted was to come home to a trashed house. Not that he could imagine Chris ever partying like that. No. That was Gage's style. At least, it used to be.

Reaching into the fridge, he grabbed a beer and popped the top before taking a large swig. He had spent the last day and a half in Los Angeles with his manager, Mel, at an underwear photo shoot, of all things. Gage didn't dispute he was a good-looking man, but why someone wanted to put him, a quarterback, in a pair of tighty-whities in a magazine was beyond him. He didn't get it.

Mel had set everything up, so at least the previous day's shoot had gone smoothly. That morning had been another story. For whatever reason, his manager scheduled an interview with some magazine he'd never heard of. Apparently they were big in Europe or something. He said it would be good for Gage's image. Although after the interview, he wasn't exactly sure what image they were trying to promote. The woman conducting the interview had pawed at him the entire time.

"What do you like to do when you're not playing football?" She reached out to caress his thigh, her tone filled with innuendo. He knew he had a reputation as sort of a player, but come on! He was supposed to be there on business, not to get in her pants. Business was business. He didn't like mixing the two. Even if he had, there was no way he would have gone for a reporter, no matter how attractive. That was just asking for trouble.

"Swim." He'd kept his answer short, hoping she'd take the hint and move on with another line of questioning. No such luck.

"Hm. Anyone in particular you like to swim with? A girlfriend perhaps?" Her fingers glided suggestively against his arm this time. He leaned back in his chair, away from her. It didn't work. She compensated by leaning in, her top dipping low.

"Surely you don't like to swim . . . alone."

By the time the interview had finished, the woman was practically in his lap. He'd politely excused himself and retreated to the car waiting out front to take him to the airport. The magazine was taking care of the lunch bill anyway, so it wasn't as if he had to stick around to pay.

To make matters worse, someone had recognized him on the plane, and he'd spent the entire flight signing autographs and answering questions. Normally, he didn't mind. Really, he didn't. He loved his fans, and it was part of the job. After his disastrous lunch, however, he'd just wanted to be left alone.

Turning around, Gage spotted an envelope on the counter. How he'd missed it before was a testament to how tired he was, since it was lying there in plain sight. He picked it up and carried it with him upstairs to his bedroom. As much as he was dreading it, he had tapes for this coming Sunday's game to look over.

He booted up his laptop and logged into the team's private account. In the old days—not that he'd been around for the old days, since he'd only been playing professionally for five years—the players would huddle around a single television in one of the conference rooms to watch footage of the other team. He'd done that in high school, and that had been bad enough. This way was much better. Everything he needed to prep for the following day's team meeting was accessible through a website and could be downloaded to his laptop and streamed to his big screen television. Once everything was set, he settled back against his pillows and pressed play.

The team they were playing wasn't doing all that well this year, but their defense was solid. In fact, from what he could see, their defense was scoring as much as their offense. He would need to work with his receivers on protecting the ball. Turnovers could kill a team faster than anything.

An hour into the footage, his gaze drifted back to the envelope he'd brought upstairs. It seemed to be mocking him from where it lay on his nightstand. Picking it up, he saw his name handwritten on the front. It was just like all the others, and he knew what he'd find inside.

The first one had shown up two months ago at the stadium. It had been found by the front office manager and brought down to him. He'd taped it to the front of his locker. At first, he'd thought it was a fan letter, so he hadn't opened it right away. Instead, he'd taken it home. Some of his fan letters, especially ones from women, tended to be slightly more explicit, and he didn't like reading that stuff in front of the guys. In the privacy of his own home was . . . safer.

He knew from the handwriting on the front, however, that what he currently held in his hand wasn't a fan letter. Flipping it over, he took a deep breath, opened the envelope, and pulled out the contents. As with all the others, there were pictures of him and a single sheet of paper that said I'm watching you. These pictures were from last weekend when he'd gone out with some of the guys after the game. A busty blonde was sitting on his lap, making sure he could see all her assets. She hadn't really been his type—he preferred women who could at least hold their own in a conversation—but he was in the mood to party, and she was available. As he'd told the reporter, he didn't have a girlfriend. Although he didn't sleep around nearly as much as he had early on in his career, he wasn't celibate either.

He looked at the pictures again, frustrated. Whoever was stalking him was doing a bang-up job of it. He had been photographed in nearly every public place he'd gone over the last two and a half months, and he'd not been able to spot anything out of place, and it wasn't for lack of trying. Even the night the picture in his hand was taken, he'd thought he'd been diligent. The club was crowded but not any more than usual. People were moving comfortably throughout—socializing and dancing. He'd not seen any indication someone was paying him, or his teammates, any more attention than they normally provoked when they were out in public.

Throwing the letter down on his nightstand, he leaned back against the headboard of his bed and ran a hand through his hair. Tim Donovan, the team's owner, would want to know about this. He'd nearly flipped a lid when he'd found out about the last one through the grapevine and that it hadn't been the first. Tim had made Gage promise to come to him immediately the next time it happened. He'd even threated to bench Gage if he didn't, and there was no way he would let that happen.

Shutting everything off, Gage lay back on his bed and stared up at the ceiling. Who was doing this and why? It didn't make sense. He was just a football player.

Rolling over, he punched his pillow until he found a semicomfortable position. He'd need to take a detour to Tim's office first thing in the morning. There was no way he was giving Tim an excuse to keep him on the sidelines.

***

The sun was setting over the smoky mountains on Thursday when Special Agent Rebecca Carson's phone rang, disturbing the peaceful setting. Her job with the FBI often had her traveling across the country. It was rare she was able to sit back, relax on the deck of her condo, and enjoy something as simple as the sun going down behind the mountains. There had been days she'd longed for that moment of peace. Now, it was driving her crazy.

Nearly a month had passed since the agency had put her on administrative leave at the advice of one of their therapists. Sure, it had been a difficult case, and it had ended badly, but her sitting around at home wasn't helping. She wanted—no, she needed—to get back out there. Sitting around doing nothing was going to be the end of her sanity.

She pushed herself up off the lounge chair and walked into her living room to answer the call, hoping it was her boss saying she was cleared to come back to work. Knowing her luck, though, it would be her baby sister needing her help to get out of another jam. Either way, it would be a welcome distraction. "Hello?"

"Carson?"

"Yes," she said, immediately recognizing, Travis Hansen's voice on the other end of the line.

"Good. I'm glad I caught you. Something's come up, and I thought you could use something to do. I know you're probably going stir-crazy sitting at home, and I could use the help."

"Is everything all right? I can meet you tonight if you need me to."

"No, no," he said. "Tomorrow will be fine. You may want to pack a bag, though."

She knew what that meant. Whatever assignment was waiting in the wings, she'd most likely be on a plane before noon the next day. "All right. Where should I meet you?"

"Just be ready at eight. I'll pick you up."

"All right," she said, unsure but trusting her ex-partner and former mentor. Hansen had retired from the FBI, and now ran his own P.I. firm, but they'd stayed in touch. He was one of the few people in this world she would trust with her life.

"See you tomorrow, Carson. Get some rest."

After hanging up, Rebecca walked to her bedroom and began packing. Suits with matching blouses lined her closet. Her sister always gave her a hard time, saying she needed to spice things up a bit with her wardrobe, but she was an FBI agent—she didn't do flashy. Besides, she had been living in sweats and T-shirts for far too long. She pulled out a week's worth of clothing and placed them in her garment bag before zipping it up. The same routine had been gone through so many times, it didn't take her long to pack all but the toiletries she'd need that night and in the morning.

At seven fifty-eight the next morning, she was standing out in front of her building waiting on Hansen. He was punctual and pulled up in his silver sedan as her watch beeped, alerting her of the new hour. He was right on time, as always.

She walked over to the car and slipped inside. He smiled and handed her a cup of coffee before pulling back out onto the road.

"Morning, Carson."

"Hansen." She nodded in greeting. They'd been partners for a little over a year before he'd retired. Although he was perhaps the one person she was closest to in her adult life besides her sister, they still had that professional distance. It was exactly the way she liked it.

"It's good to see you. I apologize for curtailing any plans you may have had scheduled for your time off, but something's come up, and I could really use your help in Nashville."

"No problem. Anything at this point would be better than being stuck at home crawling the walls."

He chuckled. "Good, 'cause we're helping out an old friend of mine."

She looked over at him, questioning.

"His name is Timothy Donovan. He owns the professional football team in Nashville. Something has come up with one of his players, and he needs some help."

She waited for him to elaborate, but he didn't. Although she was curious, it didn't matter. As she'd told him, anything was better than sitting at home doing nothing.

Two hours and a brief argument later, they pulled into the parking lot of a nicer-than-average hotel in Nashville that would act as their base of operations. Halfway to Nashville, she'd finally decided to ask for the exact details of the assignment. Needless to say, she wasn't thrilled with his response. The problem was, either she took this assignment or she went back home again to do . . . nothing.

They checked in, under the guise of a married couple, and quickly set up shop in their assigned room. "I don't like this," she said, staring around the room at the fancy décor. She'd stayed in any number of motels since she'd become an agent four years ago, but none of them had come close to this. This was way above government budget. Of course, the government wasn't footing the bill for this one. It was compliments of Donovan, according to Hansen.

Her nose scrunched up in distaste at the frilly coverlet on the bed. "Not liking the new assignment, Carson?" her old mentor asked, smiling.

He was enjoying her discomfort way too much. "Like you'd be over there grinning if the shoe were on the other foot, Hansen."

"True." He laughed. "Thankfully, I don't look pretty on the arm of a hotshot quarterback."

Rebecca clenched her fists to keep from hurling something at him. Instead, she slipped the hotel key in her pants pocket and walked to the door. "Let's just get this over with."

Hansen kept his mouth shut on the way to the stadium, although she could see he was dying to comment. She liked Hansen. He was a good partner and had always treated her as an equal, even if she had been a rookie at the time they'd worked together. It was probably part of the reason he was getting such a kick out of this.

They followed the instructions they were given and parked in the players' lot. A security guard greeted them, and they were escorted upstairs to a long hallway of offices before he stopped at the last one on their right and motioned they should go inside ahead of him.

An older gentleman, who looked to be in his early sixties, sat behind a large wooden desk. He stood, and rounded the desk to greet them. Giving Hansen a pat on the back, and offering her a firm handshake, he introduced himself as the owner, Timothy Donovan. "I'm glad you were able to come on such short notice," he said directly to her. Then he turned to the man who'd walked them in. "Get Gage Daniels, will you? Tell him I need to see him." The man nodded, closing the door behind him.

Donovan walked back to his chair behind the desk, while she and Hansen took the seats offered to them. Putting her game face on, Rebecca answered in her usual professional tone. "I wasn't told much, Mr. Donovan. Perhaps you can fill me in."

"Of course," he said. Reaching into his desk drawer, he pulled out a large manila folder filled with envelopes. "About two months ago, Daniels, our star quarterback, began receiving these. They're all there with the exception of the first few. He just threw them away. Thought they were a joke."

She flipped through the pictures and letters. They were all of a young man, in his mid-twenties, whom she assumed was Daniels. He was doing various things, from something as simple as shopping to sitting in a bar. What she did notice, however, was that all the pictures included females. "He seems to be quite the ladies' man. Could it be a woman scorned?"

"That's always a possibility, I suppose. Gage is . . . . well, he's young, not bad to look at, and he's an athlete. The ladies like him." He shrugged.

"So, what would you like us to do exactly, Mr. Donovan?" she said, trying to keep the contempt out of her voice.

Donovan stood and walked over to the large bank of windows

behind him. He motioned them over and then pointed down to the field. "This is my team. I watch out for them." It wasn't hard to pick out Daniels from the field below. He was in full uniform with his name across his shoulder blades. It helped that the security guard was walking across the field straight toward him, too. "He doesn't know this, and I'd like to keep it that way. I don't want him rattled any more than he already is." Donovan turned to face them, his expression serious. "A security guard noticed something sticking out of Gage's car two days ago. Given the letters he's been receiving, I called a friend in the local PD."

"Explosives?" Hansen asked.

"Yes. Although I'm told it wouldn't have done much damage had it gone off, but that's beside the point. Someone's decided to put a bull's-eye on Gage's back, and I need to stop it." He paused before looking Rebecca in the eye. "Which is where *you* come in."

"Security footage?"

"Checked. There's nothing there except his vehicle. We went back a week."

As much as she didn't like the situation, putting up a fight on this one when Donovan was footing the bill would be difficult. The person behind this had clearly crossed state lines—the pictures were taken in various cities—then delivered them to Daniels, either at his home or to the stadium. A couple even looked as though they'd come through the mail. That was enough to put it on the federal radar. Add in the explosives and even she could admit she was intrigued. They were his last hope before getting the FBI officially involved, and likely the press. Something like this wouldn't stay under wraps for long.

A minute later, there was a knock at the door. "Come in." Donovan yelled.

The door opened, and there stood the man she'd be spending the majority of her time with in the near future—Gage Daniels.

Chapter 2

When Gage saw Jack, one of the stadium's security guards, lope across the field toward him, he knew something was up. The first thing that crossed his mind was that he'd received another letter, so being told Tim wanted to see him wasn't a surprise. What he wasn't expecting was to see two strangers dressed in suits sitting in Tim's office. They both stood when he entered.

The man was tall, looked to be in his late fifties, about six two, with sandy blond hair, greying temples, and eyes that told you he was tougher than he appeared. Looking him over, the first thing Gage thought was *bodyguard*. He wasn't overly muscular, but Gage knew enough from growing up with three brothers that looks could be deceiving.

His gaze fell on the woman. She looked to be around his age, twenty-six or twenty-seven. She was tall for a woman, five ten, maybe, with light brown hair that was pulled back into a high ponytail. He had to admit she had a nice figure, even though it was hidden under all that unattractive clothing she wore. Her eyes raked over him in appraisal, although from the look on her face, she didn't like what she saw. That was too bad. He was rather enjoying the view. Of course, he'd enjoy it more if she'd lose the jacket and pop a few buttons open on that blouse of hers.

Gage tried to redirect his thoughts and focus on the task at hand. "You wanted to see me, Mr. Donovan?" he asked, keeping it formal since he didn't know who these people were.

"Yes, I did. Come on in, and shut the door."

Gage did as instructed and took a step farther inside his boss's office, trying not to feel out of place. He'd left his helmet downstairs, but he was still in full gear. If he'd known it was going to be more than just a casual meeting with Tim, he'd have swung by the locker room and cleaned up a little. As it was, he was hot, sweaty, and his practice uniform was covered in grass stains from the hours he'd already spent on the field running drills.

"I want you to meet Rebecca Carson and Travis Hansen. I've known Hansen since college. He's former FBI, and he knows his stuff. I've asked for their help with your situation," Tim said.

What?

"Um. Sir. I don't think that's necessary. I mean, they're just pictures and letters. They're a little creepy, but I don't see how this is a matter for the FBI, former or otherwise. I'm sure they have better things to do." Gage's gaze drifted back over to the woman. Was she a former FBI agent, too? She looked too young to be retired, but he'd heard his brother, Paul, talking about cops who were burnt out on the job. He had to assume the same thing could happen to FBI agents.

Agent Rebecca Carson. He could definitely see it. She was just buttoned up enough to be a stuffy government agent.

If her expression was anything to go by, she agreed with his assessment. He cocked his head to the side and imagined what she'd look like with her hair down. It looked long enough to brush her shoulders, maybe even a little longer.

"That's not your decision, Daniels," Tim said, bringing him out of his thoughts. "At the very least, you have a stalker, and in my experience, stalkers don't tend to go away unless they're stopped. So this is how it's going to work. Ms. Carson is going to act as your girlfriend for the foreseeable future."

Excuse me?

"Agent," she corrected, although he was only half-paying attention.

"What?" Gage said, stepping forward. "You can't be serious."

"I'm very serious. Anytime you go out to a social event or to a club, she is to be with you. This includes any events for the team, charity or otherwise. She's trained to spot people who are acting suspicious or out of place. Plus, if this stalker decides to up the ante for any reason, she'll be there to protect you, as well."

That ruffled his feathers. "I don't need protection. I'm perfectly capable of taking care of myself."

"Again, that's not your call. Now, practice is pretty much over for the day. Why don't you go get cleaned up, and they can follow you to your house. I'm sure they'd like to take a look around, and of course, *Agent* Carson will need to get set up in one of your guest rooms."

"Wait. She's *living* with me, too?" he said, his voice getting louder.

"How else is she supposed to protect you? Besides, as your girlfriend, it makes sense." Instead of saying anything more, Gage stood there seething until he was dismissed.

His new bodyguards remained outside the locker room as he ducked inside to shower and change. At least none of the other guys had come in from practice yet, or they would have been grilling him on what was up. Not only had he been called to the owner's office, but there were two individuals in suits standing outside waiting for him. What he wouldn't have given to be back out on the field right about then.

Showered and dressed in clean street clothes, he walked out into the hallway where they were waiting. He still couldn't believe this. "Let's go." He didn't wait to see if they were following, but by the sound of feet hitting the concrete floor behind him, he knew they were.

His SUV was right where he'd left it. Throwing his duffle bag into the backseat, he slid behind the wheel and started the vehicle. As he pulled out of the players' parking lot and onto the street, he noticed a silver car following him. He sighed and concentrated on the road in front of him. How was he supposed to go out and have fun with someone like her on his arm? No one in their right mind would believe *she* was his girlfriend. He'd be lucky if anyone believed he had a girlfriend period.

A plan began forming in his head. If she was going to be his *girlfriend* for the foreseeable future, then some things were going to have to change. The first was her wardrobe. Fishing his cell from his pants pocket, he dialed his stylist. "What are you doing this evening, Charlie?"

21

***

Hansen drove, keeping pace with Daniels and trying to keep the smirk off his face.

"There is absolutely nothing amusing about this situation, Hansen."

With that, he let the laugh he'd been holding in burst out. "Oh, I beg to differ. You pretending to be Mister Star Quarterback's girlfriend is pretty funny. Do you even know who he is?"

"He's a football player. What more is there to know?"

"Oh, man," he said, continuing to laugh. "This is going to be interesting."

Daniels pulled up in front of a gate and stopped, causing their conversation to come to an end. She could see a large house beyond and assumed this was his home. The gate was smart given someone was after him. Hopefully, he had security cameras installed as well. The cameras at the stadium were helpful, but they wouldn't negate her always having to check under his vehicle before he got into it. The challenge was going to be doing so without his knowledge, since Donovan wanted to keep Daniels from knowing about the explosives. She didn't agree with keeping something like that from the football player, but for the moment, she'd let Donovan call the shots.

They followed Daniels through the gate and up the curved driveway to his garage, where he parked the Explorer beside a vintage Mustang. He got out, not acknowledging them at all, before disappearing into the house. The only concession he made to their presence was to leave the garage door open.

Hansen's chest was still rumbling with laughter when they both stepped out of their vehicle and followed him inside. "Keep it up, Hansen, and I'll make sure your wife knows you've been cheating on your diet, because we both know you have."

"You wouldn't."

She turned and gave him a big smile. "Try me." He sobered immediately, and she enjoyed her little victory before she walked through the slightly open door into the residence.

The place was even nicer on the inside. They were currently in the mudroom, and even that had granite countertops and marble floors. It was fancier than her kitchen, so she could only imagine what his kitchen was going to look like.

They followed the sound of movement down the hall to where it opened up into a large room that included the kitchen, an eating area, and what looked to be a living room. One could never tell in these big houses, though. They tended to have multiple rooms for very specific things. She didn't see a television anywhere in sight, so she imagined there had to be at least one other room for that.

Daniels ignored them, exaggerating every move as he pulled things out of the refrigerator and dumped them in a blender. His back was to them, but he had to know they were there by how immature he was acting. She decided it was time to be a professional, suck it up, and do her job, even if this was one of the least desirable things she'd done since joining the FBI. "If you'll tell me what room you'd like me in, I can bring my things inside and get settled before we talk."

"There's a guest room down the hall," he said, pointing to a hallway that ran behind the kitchen. "That's as good a place as any."

"And where do you sleep?"

"Upstairs," he said with a short, clipped tone.

"And are there any other rooms upstairs?"

He stopped and turned to face them. "Why?"

Before she could answer, her partner jumped in. "If Agent Carson is going to effectively protect you, she needs to be close. You being upstairs while she's downstairs isn't the ideal situation. If you have a bedroom upstairs, that would be preferable." Maybe he sensed she was about to lose her professional cool. This was a crap job, and Mister Football Player wasn't making things any easier. Couldn't he just work with them?

"Fine," he said, turning back to whatever he was doing. "Take any room but the last one on the left." With that, he turned on the blender effectively ending the conversation. *This is going to be fun*, she thought.

Hansen helped her carry her bags upstairs. Thankfully, they hadn't dropped them off at the hotel earlier. The last room on the left was clearly the master suite and his, so she chose the one directly across from it. The walls were a soft baby blue that matched the bedspread. It wasn't as frilly as the hotel room, but it still had that air of money about it, including an en suite bathroom that had a large shower and a soaker tub. As much as she hated to admit it, she liked it.

Since she'd only brought a week's worth of clothing with her, it didn't take her long to unpack. They were on their way downstairs within twenty minutes. As they reached the bottom of the staircase, they heard voices. Each glanced at the other before reaching for their guns and edging down the last remaining steps.

Rounding the corner, they saw a man talking with Daniels. He appeared to be about her height, wearing a dress shirt with the sleeves rolled up fashionably and neatly pressed pants. He didn't look threatening, so they both holstered their guns and stepped into the room.

Before they made it more than a few feet, the new arrival noticed their entrance and was quickly racing toward them. Correction. He was racing toward her.

"Oh! This must be her," he gushed. "I see what you mean. I can definitely help." Before she knew what was going on, he was reaching for her suit jacket, trying to remove it.

She reacted instinctively before thinking it through. Within seconds, the man was bent over the kitchen island with his arm pulled tight and high along his back.

"What in the world are you doing?" Daniels demanded.

"What was *he* doing?"

"Jeez, lady. Relax. This is Charlie, my stylist."

Glancing down at what she then realized were his designer clothes, Rebecca conceded she might have overreacted a bit. She wasn't used to people grabbing at her and trying to remove her clothes like that. She stepped back, releasing him. "Sorry," she said. "Just please don't try to remove my clothing without asking first."

"Got it. No problem," he said, glancing between her and Daniels.

Hansen recovered faster than the rest of them. "What's he doing here?" he asked, nodding at Charlie.

"My *girlfriend* is going to need some new clothing if she's going to be out in public with me. Outfits like that," he pointed at the suit she was wearing, "won't do."

"And what exactly is wrong with my clothing?"

"Honey," he said, walking up, getting way too close for her comfort. "The places I go? You'll stick out like a sore thumb in an outfit like that." Then he leaned in and whispered in her ear. "Or do you want everyone to know you're my bodyguard?"

***

Travis Hansen hadn't had this much fun in a while. He and his former partner were used to investigating kidnappings of minors, before he retired. It was serious business and wasn't a place where he found himself trying to control his laughter, which was what was happening. There were definite perks to his new line of employment. He was sure, however, that Carson wouldn't see it that way.

His ex-partner was as straitlaced as they came. She was hard working and one of the best agents he'd ever worked with. Being sidelined had to be killing her. She was the type when something knocked her down, she found a way to get up again. It was why he'd thought she'd be perfect for this job. That was the main reason why he was trying not to laugh while she stood there like a statue as Charlie circled around her over and over again, taking measurements and holding up clothing. He knew her well enough to know she hated every minute of it. He also thought this would do her a lot of good, in more ways than one.

Daniels stood leaning against the wall on the other side of the room. His arms were crossed in a relaxed pose, and if not for the smirk on his face, Travis would have thought Daniels couldn't care less about the goings on before him. There was little doubt Daniels was enjoying every minute of Carson's discomfort. The more Travis watched him, the more he had difficulty controlling his own amusement. The man was cocky and confident. He and Carson should mix like oil and water. *Should be interesting*, Travis thought.

"Here," Charlie said, handing her several outfits.

She looked down at them with distaste. "What exactly do you want me to do with them?" she asked.

"Try them on, of course," Charlie said, as if it should have been obvious.

Carson glanced up at him, then Daniels, as if seeking help. When she received none, she took the clothes from Charlie and marched into the bathroom. She had to pass Daniels on the way and looked as if she were ready to do bodily harm to the man she'd been hired to protect. Oh yes, this was going to be quite entertaining.

Chapter 3

Rebecca woke up at five thirty the next morning. It was still dark outside, and the house was quiet. She took a deep, calming breath before getting out of bed and walking into her bathroom. The harsh light above the sink did nothing to help her mood. Until last month, she'd spent more time in motel rooms than she had in her own home, but she'd never missed her condo more than she did at that moment.

The previous night had been a nightmare. After trying on outfits she'd never pick out for herself, some of which were far too revealing for her taste, Charlie had left with a promise to be back in a couple of days with her new wardrobe. She had never felt so humiliated in her life as she'd stood there like an object while he measured and positioned her to see if an item would look good with her skin tone or hair color or whatever. It was embarrassing and belittling, and she'd hated every minute of it.

To make matters worse, Gage Daniels was only adding to her discomfort. He was . . . irritatingly overconfident. After both Charlie and Hansen had left for the evening, he'd made it his mission to invade her personal space. First, he'd sat much too close to her during their uncomfortable dinner. Then, he'd followed her into her bedroom to make sure she had everything she needed. Did he really think she was that stupid?

After splashing some cold water on her face, she toweled off before returning to her bedroom for some clothes. She'd made sure to lock the door before going to bed but checked to confirm before changing. If he decided to barge in on her when she was naked, she wouldn't promise he'd come out unscathed.

Dressed in her sweats and a T-shirt, Rebecca checked the safety on her gun before strapping it to her ankle and exiting her room. Peeking through the open door to his bedroom, she verified he was sleeping soundly. With confirmation he wasn't going anywhere anytime soon, she descended the stairs, disarmed the alarm, and slipped out the back door.

Her morning jog around the perimeter of the house served two purposes. There wasn't any reason she couldn't get in her morning exercise while checking the property out. She'd meant to do it the previous night but instead had spent her evening dodging Mr. QB's advances.

As she continued her circuit, the sun's rays began to appear behind the mountains. She had to admit it was a beautiful property— extravagant, but beautiful. All the trees and bushes were manicured, so she assumed he had a gardener. There was a pool in the back, which meant pool man.

The more she thought about it, the more she realized the list of suspects was astronomical, between people who knew him personally and would have access to his schedule, and those who, with the help of social media, could track his movements enough to know his usual hangouts. Maybe they were just getting lucky.

But even as that thought crossed her mind, her instincts rejected them. Some of the pictures had been taken at places one wouldn't normally think to spot a celebrity, like the grocery store. That one shocked even her. Either way, this felt too personal. This felt like someone who knew him, not just an acquaintance.

Rounding the corner to the backyard again, movement halted her in her tracks. Crouching down, she released the snap on her ankle holster. A heavy silence filled the air and then a huge splash. She followed the noise, slowly edging toward its source.

There, in the center of the pool, was Gage Daniels. His head and bare shoulders were visible above the water as his arms moved fluidly over his head and down into the water. He was a confident swimmer and obviously in shape. The sun was still making its way up into the sky, but there was enough light for her to see the well-toned muscles tense and flex as he moved through the water. She felt something as she watched him but quickly suppressed it. The man was a pampered athlete who was used to women falling at his feet. Attractive or not, there was no way she was becoming another notch on his belt.

Once again, she made sure her ankle holster was secure before she turned to go inside. The last thing she wanted was for him to catch her watching him. She didn't need him getting the wrong idea.

***

After drying off from his morning swim, Gage strolled back into the house as he normally did with his towel wrapped loosely around his hips. He was halfway across the room before he realized he wasn't alone. The beautiful but uptight FBI agent was standing in the middle of his kitchen, staring directly at him. He slowly smiled, and decided to take the opportunity to tease her some more. If he was stuck with her for the conceivable future, then he was going to have some fun.

Crossing the room, he walked right up beside her to grab a banana. He made sure to get as close as possible without actually touching her. She tensed. "Morning, beautiful."

"It's Agent Carson."

"Nope," he said, leaning back against the counter with less than a foot between them. "You're supposed to be acting like my girlfriend, remember? I wouldn't call my girlfriend 'Agent Carson,' now would I?"

He watched her chest rise and fall under the plain button-up blouse she was wearing. The motion was altogether distracting.

"Mr. Daniels," she said through gritted teeth. "When we're out in public or around others, then yes, I am to act as your girlfriend. We are not, however, currently out in public. When we're here, in this house, or alone, there is no reason for that pretense, and I would prefer you address me in a professional manner."

He took a large bite of his banana, trying to hide his amusement. He noticed she was concentrating very hard on spreading that cream cheese on her bagel. "Sorry, beautiful. Can't do that." Pushing himself off the counter, he made sure to brush her arm with his. "I'm going to go grab a shower. You're free to join me if you want," he said, winking.

She closed her eyes, stopping all movement, but she didn't comment. He figured his job there was done, for the moment anyway, and left to go take that shower.

Two hours later, he was packed and ready to go. It was Saturday, and the team was flying out to Seattle for the game the next day. He needed to be at the stadium by eleven thirty to catch the team bus to the airport.

When Gage walked out of his room, he found Agent Carson's door shut, just as it had been the night before. Maybe he'd gone too far by following her into her room, but considering she was invading his home, he didn't feel very guilty about it. Besides, it was kind of fun pursuing someone who was a bit of a challenge. Normally he didn't have to do anything other than smile to get a woman's attention. Sometimes he didn't even have to do that, especially in Nashville. People knew who he was and that was enough. Rebecca Carson was a whole different animal.

He knocked lightly on her door and waited. It didn't take more than a few seconds for her to answer.

"Yes?"

"We need to leave for the stadium within the next thirty minutes. Are you almost ready?" He'd mentioned their flight to her over dinner last night. She'd questioned him about his schedule, trying to keep things professional, while he did everything he could to distract her. He had to give her credit—every time he'd push, she'd push back. He liked that. She was making him work for it. That was something he'd never had to do. He'd been a star player in high school, and with that, came girls. College had been much the same. The problem was, most of the women bored him to tears. Rebecca Carson was a challenge he was up for . . . and nice to look at, too.

"Yes," she said, opening the door.

She stood there wearing an outfit similar to the one he'd seen her in the previous day. "You can't wear that."

"Excuse me?"

"You can't wear that. You're supposed to be my girlfriend. My girlfriend would not wear something so . . ."

"Tasteful?"

"Boring was more what I was looking for."

"There is nothing wrong with my outfit."

"If you were going to a funeral, maybe. You've got to learn to loosen up, Rebecca." She froze when he used her first name. That was another piece of information he'd managed to weasel out of her the night before. "Lose the jacket," he said, taking a step into her room.

To her credit, she didn't move away from him. Instead, she pushed her shoulders back and stood to her full height. "You're wearing a jacket. What's wrong with mine?"

"I'm required to wear a suit when I'm traveling with the team. You, however, are going to look like the FBI agent you are if you're seen with me wearing that."

She looked at him as if she were trying to find some ulterior motive. "Fine," she said, then removed her jacket and placed it back on the hanger. When she returned to stand before him, his hands automatically went to the buttons at the top of her blouse. Before he knew it, her fingers were wrapped around his wrist in a hold bordering on painful.

"Hey! Let go of my wrist. I have to use that tomorrow."

She released him and took a step back. "What do you think you're doing?"

Gage examined his wrist. It seemed to be okay. "Are you always this touchy?"

"I don't like people touching me without my permission," she said.

"Duly noted." Without looking back, he turned and walked out of her room. If she wanted to walk around looking like she was about to enter a nunnery, then so be it. He wasn't risking his throwing arm over it.

***

Rebecca watched as he left room still examining his wrist. She hadn't hurt him, not really. Pressure points were effective in getting someone's attention, but she hadn't used enough force to do him any real harm.

Walking over to the mirror, she took a good look at herself. Did she really look like she was going to a funeral? Her hair was pulled back away from her face just as it always was, and she had on a pair of black dress pants and a cream-colored blouse. Rebecca supposed, if she were honest, she did look a little stuffy.

With a tentative hand, she reached up and liberated her hair from its binding, allowing it to flow freely around her shoulders. Then, with nervous fingers, she released the top two buttons of her blouse. It was silly, really. She wore less clothing when she worked out in the gym, but for some reason she felt less than fully dressed like this. Daniels was right. She had to look the part of a girlfriend, not an FBI agent.

As satisfied with her appearance as she was going to get, Rebecca grabbed her luggage and walked downstairs where Daniels was waiting.

"Better," he said when she emerged.

"Happy to hear you approve," she said, her voice full of sarcasm. He just continued to look at her with that cocky grin of his. "Are we ready to go?"

"Yeah," he said, reaching for her bag.

"What are you doing now?" she asked, frustrated.

He ignored her and walked toward the door. "You coming?" he asked when he'd reached the garage.

She took a deep, calming breath. *It's just part of the job.* Then, squaring her shoulders, she followed him.

The drive to the stadium was quiet. She kept watch, but no one appeared to be following them. Daniels had explained how everything worked. The team met in the players' parking lot at the stadium and was then bused to the airport. No wives or girlfriends were allowed on the bus, so she'd arranged for Hansen to meet them here and drive her to the airport.

She'd much rather be on the bus with Daniels, since it was difficult to protect him or observe his interactions with others when he wasn't in her line of sight. Making an exception for her presence, though, could tip their hand to the stalker, and that wasn't something they needed. Staying under the radar was the whole point of this girlfriend façade.

Daniels slowed down and turned into the players' parking lot. A lot of people were mingling around, mostly men, however there were a few women, wives and girlfriends, she assumed, mixed in the crowd.

He parked the car a good distance from where the crowd and the charter buses were waiting. After retrieving his duffle bag and her luggage from the backseat, he walked around to her side of the car. "Your ride's not here."

She looked around, but he was right. There was no sign of Hansen. Her phone had no messages, so she assumed he was on his away. One thing she'd learned in her first years in the bureau, Hansen was a good partner. He was where he said he was going to be when he said he was going to be there. "We're early. I'm sure he's on his way."

"Whatever, beautiful," he said, hiking the duffle bag up farther on his shoulder.

He walked away. She followed.

"What are you doing now?" he said, stopping and turning back to her.

"Coming with you, of course." She pointed to the other women in the group. "The other wives and girlfriends are waiting with the players, are they not? Wouldn't it look off if I didn't join you as well?"

He frowned.

Although she usually wanted to wipe that cocky grin of his off his face, she didn't like the way this new expression made his face look. It was out of place, unnatural.

"Fine," he said, his smile returning. This time, it held a devious quality. "Let's go introduce the guys to my new girlfriend." Before she could say another word, he grabbed her hand and pulled her forward.

It took a lot of effort on her part not to rip her hand out of his grip, but she knew that wouldn't look good. She had to play the part, whether she liked it or not, so she gritted her teeth and smiled.

When they reached the group, he introduced her to a couple of his teammates, Zach Evans and Kenny Blake. She recognized Zach from one of the pictures that had been taken of Daniels. Judging by the easy conversation she was witnessing, the three were fairly close friends. There was no sign of a wedding ring on either's finger, and no women there to see them off.

Zach and Kenny looked shocked when Daniels introduced her as his girlfriend. They both quickly introduced themselves again, welcoming her to the team. She wasn't sure she completely understood that, but her being there obviously held some significance.

They were polite, asking her the standard 'get to know you' questions. Was she from Nashville? Did she grow up around here? She noticed they didn't ask her how long she and Daniels had been together, and wondered if they'd be subjecting him to a barrage of questions once she was no longer standing beside him. That thought made her smile. It would serve him right to be put into an awkward position and try to scramble for answers.

At eleven fifteen, several men walked out of the stadium. They were all older. The one in the middle announced it was time to load the buses, and the atmosphere around her shifted. There were hugs and kisses as the players said good-bye to the women they were leaving behind.

Zach and Kenny both said a quick good-bye and then disappeared inside the bus, leaving her standing alone with Daniels. "I see your ride has arrived," he said, moving to stand in front of her.

She glanced over her shoulder and saw Hansen leaning casually against his car across the lot. He nodded when he noticed her looking. Getting down to business, she turned back around to face Daniels. "We'll follow behind the buses. I'm booked—" She stopped midsentence as he closed the distance between them.

As he came closer, she was ready to jump down his throat for invading her space, when he leaned in and whispered, "I'm going to kiss you good-bye now. Gotta keep up appearances, beautiful."

Before she could respond, his lips made contact. The kiss was brief, his mouth gone before she could even react, but it left her lips tingling.

She stared up at him in disbelief. He was still standing way too close for comfort. "Have a safe trip," he said, winking. Then he picked up his duffle that had been lying on the ground beside them and strolled over to one of the buses as if nothing unusual had happened.

Stunned, she stood longer than necessary to watch as he loaded the bus. Shaking herself out of her haze, she picked up her own luggage and walked to where Hansen was waiting. It didn't take a genius to know he'd seen the kiss. "Don't say a word, Hansen."

"Wouldn't dream of it, Carson," he said, smiling as he opened the car door and slipped inside.

Chapter 4

They attacked him the minute he sat down.

"Since when do you have a girlfriend, man?" Kenny asked.

"Yeah. I mean she's hot and all, but I thought you didn't do girlfriends," Zach added.

Gage shrugged. "It's new." What else was he supposed to say? Zach and Kenny were his best friends. The three of them went out almost every weekend together. They knew his history with women. Knew he didn't date. Not in the traditional sense at least. The other guys might not question his new relationship, but these two would. No one was supposed to know who Rebecca Carson really was, but it was going to be a challenge to make Zach and Kenny believe he'd turned over a new leaf.

"New?" Zach scoffed. "Dude, you were just with that blonde last week at the club. So either this girlfriend thing happened in the last few days or you were cheating, and you know how I feel about that. Friend or not, I'll kick your ass for her," he said, suddenly dead serious.

"I wasn't cheating." Gage hurried to assure his friend. "It . . . it happened this week."

Zach was a bit more reserved than him and Kenny. He'd left his longtime girlfriend behind in upstate New York to come play professional football in Nashville. They'd kept in contact, and as far as he'd been concerned, still dating each other exclusively. When they'd gotten a bye week between playoff games, Zach had flown back to surprise her. Only he was the one surprised. He'd found her snuggling up to another man in the local coffee shop. The fallout wasn't pretty, and Zach hadn't been able to get his head back together before the next game even though Gage and Kenny had tried everything they could to cheer their friend up. He'd ended up taking a hit that he should have seen coming and had dislocated his shoulder. It had meant the end of his playing for the rest of the season.

"Wow," Kenny said. "That is new."

The bus began moving, and Gage glanced out the window. He looked around until he found the car containing the two FBI agents. In the background, he could hear their coach had stood up to talk to the team as he usually did. It was just the standard *this is what's going to happen when we arrive at the airport, remember you are representing the entire team* speech he always gave.

Gage tuned him out and closed his eyes, thankful for the diversion. He didn't want to lie to his friends, but he couldn't tell them the truth.

The ride to the airport was relatively short. Everyone grabbed their gear and shuffled off the bus into the busy airport. Zach and Kenny were ahead of him in the group. He'd intentionally hung back on the bus and let them go ahead. Too many things were going on in his head right then. He didn't need them adding to the chaos.

He was almost at the security gates when he felt a tingle go up his spine. Glancing over his shoulder, his eyes locked onto hers. But as soon as she realized he'd caught her staring, her gaze darted away to the surrounding area.

Gage smiled, but it died on his lips as he continued to work his way through security and into the terminal with the rest of his team. Seeing her again brought that brief kiss back to the front of his mind. He'd like to say it wasn't any different from any other kiss he'd shared with a woman, but he wasn't into lying to himself. Brief as it was, the kiss had left a mark.

Being twenty-six years old, he'd kissed his fair share of women. Add to that his pseudo-celebrity status, and that number multiplied considerably. Some of those kisses over the years had made his head spin, but never had a simple peck on the lips left him reeling. He could still feel the impression of her lips against his, feel the tender softness begging for attention. It didn't make sense. Why was this kiss standing out?

Thankfully, they arrived at their gate, which forced him to concentrate on the task at hand. He needed to push Rebecca Carson out of his mind, and focus. They had a game tomorrow, and with the playoffs less than two months away, every game counted. He needed to remember what was important—the game and his team. Whatever was going on with his personal bodyguard would to have to wait until he got back home.

***

Much to Rebecca's surprise, the ticket Mr. Donovan arranged for her was in first class. The team was back in coach, and she resisted the urge to check on Daniels. They were on a plane and he was surrounded by his team. Unless all his teammates were out to get him, she was fairly certain he was safe.

She couldn't believe he'd caught her staring at him. The whole plane ride, she continued to berate herself. Watching him *was* part of her job. That wasn't what she was doing, however, and she knew it. Not in a professional sense anyway. Not like she was meant to be watching him. It was good this wasn't an official assignment. Otherwise, she might be looking at something more than a temporary administrative leave.

He was a cocky, egotistical, irritating man. Why she was wasting even a minute thinking about him in something other than a completely detached, professional capacity was beyond her. He was just part of the job, and so was putting up with him, his attitude, and . . . his kisses. More than anything else, she knew that was what was bothering her most.

The plane landed in Seattle, and being in first class, she was one of the first to exit the plane. As soon as she stepped into the terminal, she scanned the surrounding area. She was on her own in Seattle. Hansen was staying in Nashville to watch things there. It was odd not having her partner nearby, but she'd been on her own for brief assignments before.

Nothing appeared to be out of place. The airport was busy, but everything seemed normal. She walked over to the far wall, where she'd have a good view of Daniels exiting the plane, and waited.

When he emerged ten minutes later, he was once again flanked by Zach and Kenny. It reaffirmed her assessment from earlier as to their friendship. She stayed back as the team walked as a group through the airport and out the door to a waiting charter bus. Taxis were lined up along the curb as well, and she was able to hop in one and follow Daniels's bus to the hotel. Although, she would have loved to take a cursory look over the buses before he got on board, it was like the plane. The likelihood of his stalker attacking him while surrounded by his team was minimal. Either way, inspecting the buses would draw attention they didn't want. She'd have to settle for keeping his bus in her line of sight.

She paid the driver and ducked inside the hotel lobby. From where she stood, she could clearly see the team unloading. One by one, each man exited the bus and walked into the hotel. It was obviously something they were used to, as they seemed to have a system.

One of the older gentlemen she'd seen before walked up to the front desk. He was there for a good fifteen minutes, talking and signing paperwork. The team lingered around the lobby in much the same grouping they had in the players' parking lot, including Daniels. He was standing about twenty feet away from her with Zach and Kenny, although Daniels didn't look nearly as cool and confident as he had before. It made her curious as to what exactly had been said while she was out of earshot.

The older man returned to the group with a large manila envelope and proceeded to call out names. In groups of two, the guys took their keys and walked to the elevators. The process took a while. She hadn't realized just how many were on the team, although she should have. She'd seen them all in the players' parking lot back in Nashville and watched them load the three coach-sized buses.

As the group dwindled, Rebecca was able to get a better look at their surroundings. There weren't many places to hide, which she liked. No one appeared to be standing around, lingering out of place, outside of the players waiting for their room assignments. Whoever was stalking Mr. Hotshot Quarterback was either extremely good at blending in or wasn't there.

Finally, only a handful of players were left, including Daniels. Rebecca continued to watch as, one by one, everyone was given a key. He was last. "Looks like you're rooming alone on this one, Daniels," the man said.

"Yeah, I guess so." He knew she was here, and he'd not struck her as a dumb man. Whether either of them liked it or not, it looked like they would be sharing a room that night.

***

With his room key in hand, Gage walked to the elevator at the far side of the hotel lobby. He didn't have to look behind him to know his friendly FBI agent was following him. It had crossed his mind on the way here that she would either be in a connecting room or Tim would somehow manage to put her in the same room with him. Since she was supposed to be protecting him, it made logical sense. That didn't mean he had to like it any more than he liked her being in his house.

The elevator doors opened, and he stepped inside. Sure enough, she followed.

Neither spoke as they ascended. He could see her reflection in the polished silver of the elevator doors. She had on that professional mask she wore most of the time. He was going to have fun trying to break that once they went back home. For the moment, however, he had to figure out how mentally to prepare for tomorrow's game with her shadowing his every move. Usually, he would hole up in his hotel room playing video games with Zach and Kenny. As much as he loved the female population, taking the chance on one of them messing with his head the night before a game wasn't something he was willing to gamble on.

They arrived at their floor, and he wasn't surprised when she followed him to his room. He closed his eyes and sighed. The only hope he had of getting the situation changed was to call Tim, and he already knew what he'd say. *Not your call.* He was feeling that way about too many things lately.

Putting on his game face, he strolled into the room and flung himself down on the bed. With his hands behind his head, he stretched out and watched her walk in at a much slower pace. She took in their surroundings with as much concentration as he did when he was in the middle of a game standing in the pocket looking for an open receiver. Once she seemed satisfied nothing was going to jump out and attack them, she walked to the other side of the room and placed her small suitcase onto the other bed.

He frowned. How had he missed her carrying luggage? How did he not realize she'd be carrying luggage? They'd just come from the airport after all.

"Your game isn't until one o'clock local time tomorrow. Is there anywhere else you need to be before then?" she asked, her eyes on the wall across the room.

"No," he answered. "Saturday night most of the guys relax in their rooms."

"Do you?" she asked.

He felt a bit of resentment at the skepticism in her tone. "Implying?"

When she leveled her gaze on him, her eyes were hard and emotionless. "I've seen your file."

"You have, have you?" he asked, standing. She was across the room, but it didn't take long for him to close the distance between them.

"Yes," she said, and he saw a flicker of something behind those cold eyes. "I figured you'd . . . go out."

Without touching her, he leaned in. He was so close he could smell her. She smelled like peaches—soft, delicious peaches. Before he could stop himself, he glanced down. Beneath the all too conservative blouse she still wore, he caught a fleeting glimpse of cleavage.

She shifted slightly, pulling him out of his haze. "Celebrating is for after the game, beautiful. Tonight . . ." he said, tilting his head so that his lips were dangerously close to her ear. "Tonight is for relaxing."

"And how do you do that exactly?" she asked. Her voice was even, but he didn't miss the rapid rise and fall of her chest, a telltale sign that she wasn't completely unaffected by his being so near.

He stiffened, the question bringing him back to reality. "Video games," he said gruffly, stepping back and digging in his pocket for his cell phone.

What in the world had gotten into him? It was one thing messing with her while they were at home, but he needed to focus.

Kenny picked up on the third ring. "Hey, man," he said. "Zach's getting the system set up. We're in 214."

"Perfect. I'll be down in a few minutes."

"Where are you going?" she asked as soon as he ended the

phone call.

"Downstairs."

"I thought you said you didn't . . ." He watched as her mouth twisted in disgust. "Go out," she finally said through gritted teeth.

"I'm not *going out*. I'm going downstairs to play video games with Zach and Kenny."

"I'm coming with you."

"Oh no you're not. My *girlfriend* isn't supposed to be here. Even when players' wives come on a road trip, they stay in another hotel, or at least another room. I'm not going to try and explain to Zach and Kenny why you're somewhere you're not supposed to be." Gage grabbed his room key and slipped it into his pocket alongside his phone.

"How am I supposed to protect you if you're off on your own?"

"I think I'll be okay for a few hours, beautiful."

Before she could say another word, he opened the door and stepped into the hall. He didn't know about her, but he needed the space. His head was most definitely not where it needed to be when he had a game in less than twenty-four hours. Hopefully he could get lost in playing video games with Zach and Kenny as usual and be able to forget about the beautiful brunette in his room.

Chapter 5

For the next five hours, Rebecca waited like a caged animal in their room. She had no way to track him down without blowing her cover, so whether she liked it or not, she was going to have to wait him out. It was infuriating. *He* was infuriating. What was the point of her being here to protect him if he wouldn't even allow her to do her job?

Eventually she broke down and called for room service, and turned the television on to a local station. It wasn't exactly an exciting way to spend her Saturday night, but at least it kept her from watching the door all evening waiting for him to return. That would have made her feel even more useless than she already did.

The night dragged on until, at a little after ten o'clock, the door opened and Daniels sauntered into the room. She clicked off the television and sat up straighter against the headboard. Her gaze followed him as he walked into the bathroom and shut the door. The click of the lock resounded through the quiet room. She stared after him in amazement.

Roughly five minutes later, the bathroom door opened and he walked out . . . minus his shirt. She averted her gaze quickly, focusing on the blank television screen. The last thing she needed was for him to notice her staring. He certainly didn't need any encouragement from her to invade her personal space.

She braced herself for whatever he would throw at her next, waited for him to do something else that would leave her feeling on edge. To her surprise, he didn't. Instead, she heard movement and a slight creak from the mattress. When she looked, he was already in bed, the sheets covering him from the waist down. Apparently, he was ready to sleep. Relief tinged with slight regret caused her shoulders to slump when she realized there wouldn't be another confrontation with him tonight. Before she could overthink the situation, she grabbed her bag and made a beeline for the bathroom. Tomorrow would be a long day and she needed her rest as much as he did.

The next morning was beyond strange in Rebecca's opinion. Daniels was acting like a completely different person. Gone was the overconfident, in-your-face sexuality he'd shown from the time she'd met him until he'd left the room the previous night. In its place was a polite distance. He'd asked her what she'd like for breakfast, as if none of the previous tension had existed, before he called for room service. He'd even allowed her the use of the bathroom first to get ready. She wasn't sure what to make of it.

At ten o'clock, there was a knock at the door. "Are you expecting someone?" she asked.

"No."

Making sure her gun was easily accessible, she walked to the door and checked the peephole. On the other side was Tim Donovan, the team owner. She removed the chain from the door, opened it wide, and invited him in.

"I see you two figured out the sleeping arrangements," Donovan said, smirking.

"Not like you left us much of a choice," Daniels murmured.

She didn't think Donovan heard, since he walked across the room and over to the windows.

"Yes, we did," she said.

"Good, good. Well, I wanted to stop by before I headed over to the stadium, and give you this." Turning, he removed a large plastic rectangle from his suit jacket. A thin cord was attached. He handed it to her before taking a step back. "This will get you past security and up to the visiting owner's box. You'll view the game up there with me. Once Gage enters the stadium, he should be safe enough with everyone around." Then he turned his gaze to Daniels and grew serious. "No going off on your own, you hear me? If you have to leave the locker room before the game, you make sure one of your buddies is with you. I don't want you taking chances." When Daniels didn't answer right away, Donovan glared at him. "Is that clear?"

Daniels sighed. This time she could tell the older gentleman didn't miss it. "Crystal."

"Good," he said, not looking happy. "I'll leave you two to finish getting ready. Agent Carson, I'll see you at the stadium."

"Of course, sir."

She walked Donovan to the door. The man paused, turning to look at her. He wasn't that much taller than she was, but he had a presence that made it seem like he was towering over her. "Don't be afraid to crack the whip with that one. He's a good kid. I don't want to see something happen to him."

"I'll do my best, Mr. Donovan."

After closing the door, she turned back around to face Daniels and was surprised to find him sitting on the edge of the bed with his head in his hands. She wasn't sure what to do, but for whatever reason, her feet began moving. Before she reached him, he looked up, and his gaze met hers. He didn't say anything and neither did she, but she felt as if he were giving her a glimpse of something he didn't normally let people see.

Before she knew it, however, he broke their stare and stood. She felt as if a cold bucket of water had just been splashed in her face. Not wanting to analyze what she was feeling, she turned on her heel and disappeared into the bathroom for the only privacy the room allowed.

***

Gage knew he was in trouble as soon as he saw the lineman dodge Tate, his center. It all happened in quick succession. One minute he was standing strong in the pocket looking for an open receiver. The next, he was lying flat on his back trying to hold onto the ball.

It wasn't the first time he'd been sacked in his life, but it wasn't something you ever got used to as a quarterback. Whenever it happened, it usually meant one of two things—either someone on the offensive line had missed a tackle or the quarterback wasn't paying enough attention to what was going on around him. Although

Tate had missed the tackle, it was Gage's fault that he'd landed in the dirt. He was distracted, and he wasn't the only one who'd noticed.

After he was back on his feet again, Zach came over to see if he was okay. "I'm good," Gage assured him.

"You've got to get your head out of the clouds, man. Focus. We should be eating up this field."

Gage nodded, acknowledging his friend, and then jogged to join the rest of the guys in the huddle. The sack had pushed them back, and they had to pick up fifteen yards in one play or give the ball back to the other team. He didn't like the thought of that any more than the rest of his team did.

As the guys broke from their huddle and walked to the line of scrimmage, he took a deep breath and tried to push everything out of his mind except for the task in front of him. He needed to keep his head in the game or else they might as well hand the ball over to the other team and go home. As the quarterback, he was responsible for getting the ball into the hands of those who could make the plays and score the points. He couldn't do that if his mind wasn't focused on what was happening on the field. If instead, for example, he was thinking about a brown-haired FBI agent currently sitting in the owner's box watching his less-than-stellar performance. The woman was messing with his head. He didn't like it.

A hand touched his shoulder, and his head whipped around to find Kenny on his left. "Take a time-out."

Before he could think it through, Gage signaled the referee for a time-out. All the guys except for Zach and Kenny jogged to the sidelines. They didn't say anything, just stood there with him so he didn't look like the idiot he was. Too much of his life was out of his control right now, but what was happening on this field was. This was what he was good at, and he wasn't going to let anything, or anyone, take that away from him.

All too soon their forty-five second time-out was up, and they were back in formation. He cleared his mind of everything but what was in front of him on the field. With one second left on the play clock, he gave the signal and Tate snapped the ball into his hands. Everyone was in motion around him. It was organized chaos. He loved it.

Sidestepping a tackle, he found his man twenty yards downfield.

Releasing the ball, he watched it soar through the air and hit its target right in the center of his chest. Perfect. A huge grin spread across his face as he jogged with the rest of his team to the new line of scrimmage. Maybe he could give Miss FBI agent a good show after all.

In the end, they pulled out a twenty-seven to twenty-one victory. It was much closer than it should have been, but a win was a win.

The guys were all tired but in a good mood as they walked through the tunnel and into the locker room. They were having a winning season thus far, so everyone was riding the high—everyone except Gage.

He was happy they'd won, yes, but his mind still wasn't where it should be, and he didn't know how to fix it. Something had happened between him and the stuffy agent earlier that morning in the hotel room, and he didn't know how to explain it. He'd let his guard down, something he never did around anyone but his family. It was just too dangerous. Add to that this stalker of his, and it was doubly so.

Everyone stripped out of their gear and headed for the showers. No one was commenting on his lack of focus on the field, but he knew it would be a subject of conversation with his coach on Tuesday. He'd be lucky if he didn't have to run a few extra drills because of it. Pro or not, the same basic principles applied, no matter if you were playing on a little league team or earning a paycheck. If a player couldn't focus on his own, then it would be drilled into him through extra laps or some other training exercise. One way or another, the goal would be achieved.

Gage wasn't surprised to catch a glimpse of Agent Carson as he loaded the bus with the rest of the team to head to the airport. What did surprise him, however, was that she was standing with Tim. The boss didn't usually stick around after the games, but Gage figured, given the uniqueness of the situation, he was making an expectation.

Agent Carson's brow was furrowed with what looked to be worry when he caught her stare. Of course, as soon as she realized, she smoothed out her features and the professional mask was back. He couldn't help but smirk. The game was over, and for the next six days he could go back to having fun with his personal bodyguard. Maybe he could break through that shell of hers. Besides, Charlie should have her new wardrobe ready on Monday. He couldn't wait to see her in her new clothes.

***

Rebecca had never watched a football game in its entirety before. She'd never cared to. The thought of watching men tackle each other while tossing a ball around had held no appeal to her. After sitting—or standing, mostly—in a glass-enclosed booth for nearly four hours with Donovan and several others, she was beginning to change her mind.

One of the things she loved most about her job was the mental aspect. There were rules she was governed by, just as the football players had rules to follow. Sometimes the people she was sent to find were bigger, stronger, or wealthier than she was. It wasn't ultimately about what individuals had on the outside that mattered. It was the way in which they, or she, used the tools they had access to. In the end, the most important asset anyone had was his or her brain.

She found herself being pulled into the intricacies of the plays that were being made below her on the field. Everyone was shifting and moving to counter the other, like a well-choreographed dance without the music. If nothing else, she gained a new respect for the sport.

Unfortunately, Daniels hadn't explained that the team would be going directly to the airport after the game, so she hadn't brought her luggage along. Granted, it would have looked a little strange for her to arrive at the game with luggage, but she had a VIP pass and her badge. Security wouldn't have been a problem.

As it was, she had to lose sight of the bus and Daniels for the time it took Donovan to drop her at the hotel. She ran up the stairs to her room, not wanting to wait for the elevator, and threw her carry-on over her shoulder. She was grateful to find her luggage still in her room. The team must have arranged for late checkout or something. Either way, she didn't care as she rushed back downstairs. Less than five minutes had passed when she jumped into a cab and was on her way to the airport.

She caught up with the team as they were passing through security. Daniels saw her and gave her that cocky smile of his before turning his attention back to Zach and Kenny. She had a feeling that, as Daniels's girlfriend, she'd be getting to know those two a lot better.

The flight back to Nashville was uneventful. When they landed, she once again exited the plane before the team and waited off to the side for Daniels.

The team loaded the buses and were taken back to the stadium where either their vehicles or their significant others awaited them. She got out of her cab and paid the driver before walking over to where Daniels's car was waiting. Just to be sure, she walked around the vehicle, bending down at one point to look at the undercarriage to see if there were any signs of tampering. That was how he found her.

"Not that I have any objection to the view, but what exactly are you doing?"

To her embarrassment, he startled her and caused her to lose her balance. She lost her footing and fell none too gently on her behind. Of course, he laughed.

She glared.

That only made him laugh harder.

Ignoring him, she stood and brushed herself off. "Are you ready to go?" she asked, unable to hide the irritation in her voice.

"Ready when you are, beautiful." Winking, he twirled his keys as he turned and got into his SUV. With a sigh, Rebecca followed.

Chapter 6

It was just after midnight when they walked into Gage's Nashville home. Getting home late was part of the deal whenever they played away games. This time, he remembered to grab Rebecca's bag and carry it into the house. He was usually ready to crash the minute he walked in the door, but for some reason, he wasn't quite prepared to say goodnight.

Rebecca had been quiet on the ride back to his house. He'd noticed, however, that she had constantly been checking behind them in the side-view mirror just as she had the day before when they'd driven the same route. No one had been following them. He'd been checking, too. He always had, even before the stalker. Once he'd begun to make a name for himself, he never knew when a photographer would turn up trying to get a one-of-a-kind picture to sell to the tabloids.

Luckily, he didn't have to deal with that nearly as much as the Hollywood celebrities did. Not as many people cared what athletes did unless they were breaking the law. Plus, he was sure it helped that he was predictable. The only thing the press ever caught him doing was partying with Zach, Kenny, and whatever women they hooked up with that night. After a while, not even the public cared how many women he went through, as long as they were winning games.

He set their bags down at the bottom of the staircase before strolling into the kitchen. "I could eat something. You hungry?" he asked, opening the refrigerator.

She was standing about ten feet from him, gazing around the main room. He wasn't sure what she was looking for exactly. The alarm had been set while they were gone and was still on and active when they'd arrived. As far as he could tell, there was no sign anyone had been there since they had left.

Her gaze refocused on him briefly before returning to her surroundings. "Sure."

Pulling out eggs, milk, and cheese, he set them on the counter and went to get a skillet. He wasn't the best cook, but he could make the basics. His mom had made sure all of her sons could cook enough not to starve or have to live off frozen dinners.

Out of the corner of his eye, he saw Rebecca walk over to the patio door leading out to the pool. She stopped a foot from the glass and stared. The moonlight streamed in through the glass. From this angle, the delicate light framed her features, and he could see the red highlights in her hair as it rested gently on her shoulders. She'd left it loose the entire time they'd been away. It made her look softer, more feminine. She'd probably hate that. He smiled and turned his attention back to the eggs.

With a stir, he sprinkled the cheese over the eggs and went to get two plates. It felt a little strange cooking for someone other than himself. The only people who'd ever stayed here with him were his parents, and when they were in town, his mom always did the cooking or they went out. He'd never brought a woman home. His relationships, if you could call them that, weren't like that. Being in his home with a woman felt too intimate.

He turned around with two plates of scrambled eggs and found her only a few feet in front of him on the other side of the island. Somehow, she'd managed to walk back across the room without him noticing.

Setting her plate in front of her, he walked around the island and took the seat beside her. When he reached for his fork, his arm brushed against hers accidently, and he felt that tingly feeling again. Rebecca went rigid.

Suddenly, he felt the need to get them back on comfortable ground. "Eat up, beautiful. You don't want it to get cold." Not looking in her direction, he dug into his eggs. As soon as he was finished eating, he ran up the stairs to his bedroom. He needed a little separation from Rebecca Carson.

On Monday morning, Gage had been having a really nice dream about a brunette when the ring of his cell phone dragged him out of his imagined paradise. Groaning, he aggressively rubbed both hands over his face, trying to wake himself up before fumbling for the source of the annoying sound. "Hello?"

An all-too-familiar voice came through the phone. "It's eight thirty. Why are you still in bed?"

Gage's mouth opened wide as a loud yawn escaped. "I didn't get to bed until almost two, Mel. What's up?" he asked his manager.

"I've got a few things for you to look over. Do you think you can stop by my office sometime today?"

"Sure. Will this afternoon work?"

"Of course. Let's say one o'clock?"

"I'll be there with bells on."

Gage propped himself against the headboard, pressing the heels of his hands against his closed eyelids. The sun was bright this morning, and he hadn't been ready to get up. Unfortunately, he knew falling back to sleep wasn't an option. Once he was up, he was up.

Tossing the sheets aside, he slid out of bed, then padded naked into his bathroom and turned on the shower. Looking in the mirror, he noticed the dark circles under his eyes. He'd stayed up too late, sleep evading him no matter how hard he'd tried. His thoughts kept drifting across the hall and the woman who made no sense to him. He'd never met someone who was so buttoned up. Yet, sometimes, when he'd push her just a little too far, he'd see a fire in her eyes. He wanted to tap that fire.

Stepping into the shower, he moved to stand beneath the spray. The water helped lift the fog from his brain. Charlie would be stopping by at lunch with Rebecca's new clothes. They were going out tonight with Zach and Kenny, and he couldn't wait to see her in her new wardrobe. He had a feeling it was going to be difficult for him to keep his hands to himself. Lucky for him, if they were out in public, she couldn't chastise him for touching her, and he planned to find ways to do just that as often as possible.

***

Rebecca had always been a light sleeper. It probably came from growing up in a house where she had to be ready to move on a moment's notice. That wasn't something she liked to dwell on. The past was the past. She couldn't change it even if she wanted to. The upside was being able to be fully awake and alert within seconds of opening her eyes, a skill that had served her well over the years. Most of her colleagues required multiple cups of coffee to get going in the morning. She, on the other hand, was running at full speed the second her feet hit the floor.

Of course, that meant she was awake the minute she heard Daniels moving about across the hall.

Checking her phone, she saw it was after eight thirty. She stretched in the comfortable bed, feeling the pull of her muscles, before sitting up and placing her feet on the plush carpet. There was a lot to do. Not much in the way of information had been gathered over the weekend, given Daniels's schedule. They needed to sit down and come up with a list of possible suspects.

The shower turned on in the other room, and Rebecca figured it was as good a time as any to check in with her partner. Although it was doubtful he'd garnered any information over the weekend, she'd learned never to underestimate Hansen. Sometimes he was able to glean information from the most unusual sources. People talked to him. He could strike up a conversation with a perfect stranger and end up filling in a piece of the puzzle that led them to solving their case. It was uncanny.

Pressing the phone to her ear, she listened to the three rings it took for her partner to answer.

"Hansen."

"Still sleeping?" she asked.

"Carson. Hey. Yeah. Late night."

"Anything I need to know about?"

"Not really. I've been running background checks on the team. Several have had run-ins with the law, but nothing major and mostly as juveniles. It still takes time, though."

"So nothing we can use?"

"Unfortunately, no," he said, seemingly disappointed. "At least nothing solid. Anything on your end?"

"No. Nothing seemed out of place while we were gone, and I did a walkthrough of the ground level of the house before I turned in last night. No sign of someone in the house while we were away. Of course, to my knowledge that hasn't been the case in the past either. I'll take a jog around the outside again this morning."

"And how are things going with your quarterback?"

She rolled her eyes. "He's not *my* quarterback, and they're . . . fine. I'm hoping to sit down with him today and come up with a list of potentials."

"That would help," he stated. "Right now the field is too wide open."

"I agree. We need to narrow it down."

With an agreement to check in with each other the following morning, they hung up. Rebecca wanted to do that perimeter check as quickly as possible. Hopefully, she could finish and be back in her room before Daniels made it out of his. She knew she was being overly optimistic, but a girl could hope, right?

Lucky for her, everything outside seemed to be exactly as they'd left it two days before. Back inside the house, however, her luck ran out the minute she turned to go up the stairs and bumped into Daniels.

"Good morning, beautiful." A huge smile graced his face. It made him look even more handsome than he usually did, and he knew it.

"Good morning, Mr. Daniels. My apologies. I didn't hear you coming down the stairs."

"Oh, I don't mind one bit. A lovely lady like yourself crashing into me first thing in the morning isn't something that needs an apology." As he spoke, he leaned his body closer to her. She stepped back, trying to maintain an appropriate distance between them, but it didn't work. Every inch she moved, he countered by the same inch, sometimes more.

"Mr. Daniels—"

"Gage," he insisted, nearly pinning her against the wall with his body. He was too close. The scent of the soap he'd used wafted up to her nose. It smelled good. He smelled good.

She needed to get away from him. "Mr. Daniels, if you do not step back and let me pass this instant, I will physically move you." This only caused him to smile wider, if that were possible, and there was a gleam in his eye she didn't like.

Instead of stepping back, he leaned in, holding his upper body so close she could feel the heat radiating from him. His breath caused tiny goose bumps to cover the left side of her face and neck. She closed her eyes, bracing herself.

Then . . . it was gone . . . his breath, the heat, everything.

She opened her eyes, not sure what she'd find, and discovered she was alone on the stairs. Closing her eyes once again and taking a deep breath, she tried to center herself. What was this man doing to her? If it had been anyone else, she would have kneed him in the groin and had him flat against the wall in five seconds. Why hadn't she done that here? He'd cornered her. She had every reason.

Before she could analyze it further, she raced up to her room. She needed a shower. Not only would it wash the sweat of her run from her body, it would also help to bring her back to her senses.

Rebecca felt better after she showered and once again dressed in her work clothes. She was a professional here to do a job, and she would do that job and *only* that job. For some reason, Daniels seemed to push her buttons. When he was around, her brain didn't want to work right.

There was no logic behind it. He was completely the wrong kind of guy for her. The guys she went for were polished, solid. They all had college degrees and a stable career path.

Granted, she didn't do much dating. In fact, it had been over a year since she'd been on a date. Her work kept her busy, and dating wasn't something she made a priority.

A husband would be nice, someone to come home to. Hansen had that, and in some ways, she envied him. She wasn't going to settle, though. She wasn't going to end up like her mom. Like her little sister. She wasn't going to let some smooth-talking guy sweep her off her feet and destroy her life. Her career, her job . . . *that* was what mattered. One day she would find a guy who valued the same things she did and they'd get married. One day. For now, however, she was certain of one thing. Gage Daniels was *not* that guy.

Chapter 7

Gage was just finishing his breakfast when Rebecca walked back down the stairs. She was back in her dress pants and buttoned-up blouse, complete with suit jacket. Even her hair was pulled back away from her face as it had been the first time he'd seen her. He frowned. Didn't this woman ever just relax? Ten seconds later, he got his answer.

"We need to go over a few things, Mr. Daniels," she declared, taking a seat opposite him.

Sighing, he pushed his plate away, leaned back, and crossed his arms. "I'm all yours," he said with a smirk.

She ignored his remark and turned her attention to a note pad she'd laid down on the table in front of her. Holding a pen in her right hand, she asked, "Do you have any idea who might be sending these pictures to you?"

That got his attention and wiped the smile off his face. "What?" he asked, sitting up straight in his chair.

"In my experience, and statistically speaking, whoever is stalking you is someone you know. It could be someone you've only met once, or it could be a person you have regular contact with. From what I've seen, this person knows your personal schedule, at least to an extent."

"That doesn't mean I know them."

She nodded, but it was detached, like she was humoring him. "That may well be, Mr. Daniels, but we need to cover all our bases.

Shall we start?" she asked, her lips pulled tight. He wanted to reach across the table and smooth them with the pad of his thumb until they relaxed, becoming full and kissable again. At the moment, she looked too much like one of his school principals. It wasn't a pleasant picture. He sat watching her, not moving, not speaking. She raised her gaze to meet his across the table. "Mr. Daniels?"

That brought him back to the here and now. He hated when she called him that. "First, you are going to stop calling me Mr. Daniels. That's my father."

"I don't think it's appropriate—"

"I'm not real concerned what you think is appropriate or not, beautiful," he said, cutting her off. "You're in my life, my house, for the next however-many days . . . weeks . . . *months* . . . and I refuse to have you going around calling me *Mr. Daniels* the entire time. Either you start calling me by my first name, or this conversation is going to be a very short one. Your call."

She stared back at him, not shrinking from his gaze. Her back was ramrod straight, her posture perfect. He could see the wheels turning in her head as she analyzed the situation.

There was too much he had to accept, too many times he had to go along with the flow. Maybe it was silly to insist on her calling him by his first name, but it bugged him when she pulled out the *Mr. Daniels*. She was intentionally distancing herself, and he wasn't going to let her do that. He had plans for her, and her keeping him at arm's length didn't fit into those plans.

"Very well," she finally replied.

He smiled, leaning back casually in his chair again.

"Can we get started then?"

"Sure," he nodded. "Just as soon as I hear you say my name."

"Excuse me?"

"You heard me, beautiful. Ask me again, but say my name this time."

Her jaw flexed, and Gage wondered if she were gritting her teeth to keep from leaping over the table at him. That would be something he'd like to see. It would give him an excuse to get his hands on her again.

With a deep exaggerated breath, and a forced smile, she asked, "Is there anyone who comes to mind . . . Gage?"

He almost missed the slight pause before she'd said his name.

Almost. Knowing how difficult it was for her to force his name from her lips caused him a little thrill of satisfaction. She was stubborn, but so was he. One way or another, he was determined to get through that tough exterior of hers.

"Not really," he answered dismissively.

She let out a frustrated sigh. "All that and all you give me is *not really?*"

"You asked a question. I answered. I'm not sure what you're so irritated about."

"I can't help you if you don't work with me Mr. . . . . Gage," she said, correcting herself.

"I never asked for your help," he stated, leaning forward, elbows on the table.

"You like someone stalking you?" she asked incredulously.

"No," he said, "but it's just letters and pictures. I get my picture taken all the time. It's disturbing, yes, but they haven't done anything except be annoying."

Her lip disappeared behind her teeth for a second before she answered. "Although nothing has happened yet, that doesn't mean it won't. This person has invested a lot of time following you, taking pictures, sending letters. They obviously aren't getting what they want. It's only a matter of time before things escalate."

***

It took effort for Rebecca not to tell him about the explosives that were found under his SUV. She didn't agree with Donovan. Daniels had every right to know someone had tried to cause him bodily harm. Unfortunately, it wasn't her call. At least not yet. Her experience, however, told her that if a person was willing to go to that sort of trouble once, he or she would likely do it again. It was only a matter of time before this stalker of his upped the ante.

The next two hours were a test of her patience. Every time she'd try to prod him for a name, he'd dig in his heels. She had to pry every single name out of him. Over the years, she'd dealt with difficult witnesses, but it was rare the person who was being wronged was the one she had to grill for answers.

She did learn one very important thing during the process. Gage Daniels was about as loyal as they came. Most people would throw out names of anyone who had ever said a crass word to them or looked at them in a less-than-friendly manner. Daniels wasn't like that. Even when she got him to admit to a teammate being upset with him for hitting on his little sister, Daniels insisted there was nothing there, that Kelly wouldn't do that. She wrote his name down anyway.

At the end of the two hours, she had twelve names on her list, and she wasn't willing to bet on any of them being their guy. And although this man got under her skin, he didn't appear to have that problem with his teammates. From what she'd observed over the weekend, everyone was friendly or at least professional.

As the vastness of the situation sank in, her stomach churned. She was hungry. That was it. She'd been so anxious to get started on the list, she'd forgotten all about breakfast. Yes, of course. Food. That's what she needed. The unsettled feeling in the pit of her belly had nothing to do with realizing this job could last for much longer than she'd originally planned.

***

Gage all but ran to the door when the doorbell rang a little before noon. He opened it to find Charlie on the other side, arms full of bags. "Perfect timing."

"You should know by now that I'm always punctual," Charlie said cheerfully as he nearly glided into the main room. When his gaze landed on Rebecca, he frowned. "Looks like I've come just in time."

"Yes, you have. We're going out tonight, and she's going to need something to wear."

"Have no fear. Charlie's on the job."

Five minutes later, they were up in Rebecca's bedroom. Charlie was holding up outfits again, this time with everything in her size, and she was shaking her head. "I can't wear these."

Charlie was offended. "And why not? These are perfect for you. They fit your body type and will look absolutely stunning."

"You're my girlfriend," Gage reminded her. "You need to have something decent to wear."

She scowled, first at him, then the clothes. "Fine." Grabbing the outfit Charlie was currently holding, she marched into her bathroom, closing the door with a little more force than necessary. He also heard the lock click, which caused him to chuckle.

In less time than he thought possible, she reemerged from the bathroom wearing a dress that did amazing things to her body. It wasn't over-the-top flashy, nor was it revealing in the extreme. It was dark red with a square neckline that dipped just low enough to tease. He wanted to bury his face right in between her breasts.

Feeling a little uncomfortable below his waist, he let his gaze drift over the rest of her. That didn't help. The dress hugged her waist and then floated down to where it ended halfway down her thighs. Below that her legs were bare, leading to a pair of black strappy heels. Thoughts of her wrapping her legs around his waist filled his mind. Automatically, he took a step toward her.

"I can't wear this," she said, stopping him in his tracks.

He closed his eyes and took a deep breath. This was getting ridiculous. No woman had ever done this to him before. He wasn't even sure what it was she was doing exactly. Whatever it was, he was very glad for her interruption or else he may have ended up making a fool out of himself in front of Charlie.

"What's wrong with it?" Gage asked. "I think it looks good on you." That was an understatement.

"Yes, what's wrong?" Charlie chimed in. "It's perfect." Then he walked over to her and hesitantly began adjusting the top, revealing a little more of her breasts. That was the last thing Gage needed. "There," Charlie said, as if declaring victory.

Rebecca's brow furrowed, and her lip disappeared behind her teeth for just a second before reappearing again. It was the second time that day he'd noticed her doing that, and both times, it was clear she was uncomfortable. *Interesting*, he thought. He was learning her tells. That would be helpful.

Charlie had her try on a few more outfits before saying good-bye. By that point, they were running late, so Gage sent a text to Mel letting him know they would be there in twenty minutes.

His manager was big on punctuality. It wasn't something Gage excelled in outside football, but given his star status, they'd come to an agreement of sorts. Mel accepted that he would almost always be late as long as Gage agreed to acknowledge he was going to be tardy by texting him exactly how late he'd be. It was a weird sort of compromise, but it worked.

"Tell me about your manager." She prompted him once they were in the car.

"There's not much to tell. He took me on right out of college, negotiates my football contracts and any promotional stuff I do."

"Does he have any dealings in your personal life?"

He frowned. "No. Not really. I mean, he's met my parents a couple of times when they've been in town."

She nodded. "You haven't told him who I am, correct?"

"No one knows who you really are except for Tim, beautiful. I was under the impression you wanted to keep it that way."

"I do," she said quickly. "I mean, *we* do. The fewer people who know who I am, the better."

"So this is going to be the real test of you being my girlfriend."

"Yes," she said stiffly.

He smiled. "Just remember that," he said as he turned into the small parking lot that held Mel's office.

***

Mel's office wasn't what Rebecca would call extravagant, but it was nice. The furnishings were newish and modern. It was comfortable.

She stood in the lobby with Daniels while the receptionist went to get Melvin—Mel—Maxwell. When the young woman saw them walk through the door, she was up and out of her seat long before they'd crossed the small lobby. She offered them something to drink, which he refused. Seconds later, she disappeared behind a set of double doors.

The doors began to open, and she heard Daniels whisper, "Here we go," before grabbing her hand and taking a step forward.

She didn't have time to respond to his sudden gesture before an older man, maybe in his fifties or sixties, stepped from behind the door.

"Gage! You made it." The man smiled, reaching for Daniels's hand. Then his gaze fell on her. "And who do we have here?"

"Mel, I'd like for you to meet my girlfriend, Rebecca Carson. Rebecca, this is my manager, Mel."

"I didn't know you had a girlfriend. When did this happen?" he asked, clearly looking her over.

"It's new."

"Yes, well . . ." Mel said, ushering them through the double doors and into a nice-size office. "It's nice to meet you." He pointed to the two chairs across from his desk while sitting behind his own.

The man seemed to stare a little longer than was normal. Then again, maybe it was normal. Rebecca wasn't used to wearing these types of clothes.

Daniels had insisted she wear something Charlie brought over. She'd selected one of the most conservative outfits—a pair of dark blue jeans and a light blue sweater. The jeans were comfortable enough, but they were too tight. They showed off her curves.

Of course, the sweater didn't help. It ended right where the jeans began, accenting her waist. Add to that its clinging to her breasts making her want to continually pull it away from her skin, and she was highly uncomfortable. The suits she wore were fashionable for her chosen profession. They fitted her well but were tailored to show her status as a government agent rather than attract a member of the opposite sex.

Like it or not, this was part of the job, and she refused to feel out of place because of clothing. Straightening her spine, Rebecca sat up in her chair and looked the agent in the eye.

Maxwell blushed and turned his attention to Daniels. "I had a few things cross my desk this weekend that I wanted you to take a look at."

He handed over three folders, which Daniels took. She tried not to be nosy but figured it would look strange if she didn't appear the least bit interested. He was supposed to be her boyfriend after all.

Gage frowned. "Cookies?"

"What's wrong with cookies? You like them. I've seen you."

"Liking them and wanting to promote them are two different things."

"What about the other two?" his manager asked.

"Shoes? Okay. I can see that. But jeans? I don't know, Mel. That underwear shoot was too much. I'm a quarterback, not a model."

Maxwell seemed frustrated with Daniels's response. "Gage, you've got to think about your future here. This is the time for you to capitalize on opportunities, make money. You can't play football forever. You and I both know you have ten more years, tops. You can't allow . . . distractions to cloud your judgment." Rebecca didn't miss that Maxwell's gaze drifted to her.

"This isn't about distractions, Mel. You know that interview you set up for me after the underwear shoot? The woman was all over me. I just don't think modeling is the direction I want to go."

Again, Maxwell looked at her. "Okay. Fine. I'll tell them no on the jeans. What about the cookies, though? You do like cookies."

"I'll think about it."

Maxwell sighed. "Okay. I guess that's about as good as I'm going to get out of you for now."

"Anything else?" Daniels asked.

"No. I think we're good. I'll send the contract to you for the shoes when it's ready."

Daniels nodded and stood. She followed suit, and so did Maxwell.

He walked around his desk, straight for her, and held out his hand. "Again, it was very nice to meet you, Rebecca. If you're Gage's girl, then I'm sure we'll be seeing a lot of each other."

"It was nice to meet you as well, Mr. Maxwell."

"Mel."

She nodded once.

There was a soft, warm pressure at her back as Daniels's hand gently guided her toward the door. "You did well," he whispered as they walked back out into the lobby.

"Of course I did," she said. "I am a professional, after all."

She said it with complete sincerity. So when Daniels burst out laughing, she was puzzled. Then, as the reality of what she'd said set in, Rebecca blushed, wishing she could bury her head in the sand and hide. Why did she have to say something so embarrassing, and why in front of him?

Chapter 8

As soon as they arrived back at the house, Rebecca raced up the stairs. All she wanted to do was lock herself in her room and never come out. How was she going to face him again? The entire ride home, he'd continued to chuckle at her verbal slip. What surprised her, however, was that he didn't goad her. She'd expected he would, given his personality.

Once safely in her room, Rebecca pulled out her laptop. She needed a distraction, and work was always a good option. Sitting at the small desk in the corner, she logged in and pulled up her e-mail account. Ignoring everything in her inbox, she opened a new window and typed the list of names she and Daniels had put together that morning, and sent it off to Hansen.

After hitting send, she scanned the rest of her mail. Most of it was the usual spam, but there was one from her sister. There was no subject, but that wasn't unusual. She clicked on the message to open it, and the screen filled with pictures. In every one of them, her sister was laughing or smiling. She was alone in a few, but in most she was surrounded by a group of people Rebecca had never met.

Her sister, Megan, was a carefree spirit, much like their mom. She knew how to let her hair down and have fun. Responsibility took a backseat to the latest thrill. Also, just like their mom, Megan had horrible taste in men. She always fell for the deadbeats, and in the end, they broke her heart. So while Rebecca was happy for her sister, she knew it was only a matter of time before the smiles turned into tears. That was just the way things worked.

Rebecca had no idea how long she sat and stared at the e-mail. She was lost in memories of Megan. It had been over six months since she'd last seen her. Rebecca could only hope her little sister was staying safe.

Eventually, Rebecca got up and went into her bathroom to splash some water on her face. She needed to go back downstairs and face Daniels. No matter what embarrassing thing she'd said, she still had a job to do. Never in her life had she been a coward, and she wasn't going to start.

After adjusting her ponytail and her clothes, she marched to her bedroom door. Unfortunately, her grand plans to sweep down the stairs and act as if nothing had ever happened changed the moment she opened the door and found him standing on the other side, hand poised to knock.

"Well hello," he said. His gaze traveled up and down her body slowly. It almost felt as if he could see beneath her clothes. In reaction, she felt herself suddenly becoming very warm.

"Hi." Her voice didn't come out nearly as confident as she'd meant for it to, so she tried again. "I was just coming to find you."

That cocky smile was back. "You were, were you?"

"Yes," she said, ignoring any implications he may have been trying to make. "I wanted to go over your schedule for the rest of the week."

The smile remained on his face as he leaned against the doorframe. "Not much to tell. Tonight we're going out with Zach and Kenny to blow off a little steam before practice starts again tomorrow."

"We're going out tonight? Where?"

"It's a little club about twenty minutes from here."

"You go there a lot?"

"I do," he said, taking a step toward her.

She held her ground and tried to ignore how her heart rate picked up with his closer proximity. "Is this the same club where some of the pictures were taken?"

That got his attention. "Yeah," he said, shrugging. He also leaned back, putting a little more space between them again.

"Do you always go there on Monday nights?"

"Only when we have an away game on Sunday. If we're playing

at home, we usually hit the club on Sunday nights to unwind."

"I see. You know, your predictable schedule is making it easier on whoever this is."

"What can I say?" The smile was back. "I'm a boring guy."

Right, and if she believed that for one second, she was a fool. Gage Daniels was anything but boring.

They stared at each other for a long minute before she finally pulled a decent question out of her head. "When are we meeting your friends?"

Pushing off the doorjamb, he stepped back. "We need to leave in an hour. The club has decent food, so we'll eat there. Besides, with it being Monday, it will be an early night. We all have practice in the morning." He turned to walk down the hall away from her. "Oh and . . ." He paused, glancing back at her over his shoulder. "I hope you like to dance." Then he was gone, leaving her standing there staring after him.

As promised, they were out the door of his house an hour later. Instead of taking his SUV, however, they climbed into his vintage Mustang. She had to admit it was a nice car, complete with leather interior and bucket seats. Watching him, she realized how much this car suited him. He looked as if he fit behind the wheel of the Mustang more than he did his SUV.

What did that say about him? That he was wild and crazy? Reckless?

She thought back to her sister's e-mail, how happy she seemed. For the moment, at least. Daniels reminded her of Megan in a lot of ways, which made sense if she thought about it. After all, he did play a game for a living.

Even as she thought that, though, she knew that wasn't all there was to him. She'd seen him on the field and in Maxwell's office. He didn't goof off. Not all the time anyway. His plays at the game yesterday had been precise and calculated. It was quite the contrast to the guy who seemed to constantly flirt with her.

What does it matter? she thought. *He's a job. That's it. He's just annoyed that you're in his house, so he's trying to make you uncomfortable.*

Taking a deep breath, she forced herself to look out the window. She had to keep her wits about her. Whoever was stalking Daniels had taken pictures of him at the club before, so there was a good chance they would again. Maybe she'd get lucky and spot his stalker on their first night out. That would be good, right? So why did she feel a heaviness in her chest at the thought?

A few minutes later, they pulled into a parking lot adjacent to a building that looked more like an upscale bar than a club. A few people were mingling outside. None of them was overly dressed up, with most wearing jeans and cowboy boots. She was glad she hadn't changed out of the jeans and sweater she'd put on earlier.

Daniels must have noticed her staring as he walked around to the front of the car to meet her. "This is Nashville. I hope you like country." Without waiting for her answer, he wrapped his arm around her waist and guided her to the front of the club.

The interior was what she expected from the outside. The bar was front and center with tables around most of the perimeter, and there was a small dance floor carved out in one of the back corners along with a small platform. She assumed there were nights where the bar/club had live music.

It was still early in the evening, but there were already a few couples taking advantage of the space. Watching them, she felt her skin warm again at the thought of dancing with the man by her side. She had a hard enough time concentrating when he wasn't touching her.

"Hey!" The greeting caused her to turn her head toward the sound. Kenny was walking toward them, beer in hand. "We were beginning to think you two weren't going to show up."

"You should know better than that," Daniels said.

"It's good to see you again, Rebecca."

"Thanks." She smiled. She wasn't sure what she was supposed to say.

Luckily, Kenny saved her from having to come up with anything. "We got a table in the corner," he said, pointing. Seeing them all looking over, Zach waved.

"I'm going to order us some drinks, and then we'll be over," Daniels said.

Kenny didn't respond, other than to tip his beer in their direction, and then walked away.

Daniels's fingers pressed into the small of her back as he led them over to the bar. "What would you like?" he asked.

"Just water."

He looked down at her as though she'd lost her mind. "You have to have more than just water."

"I don't drink."

Again, he gave her a strange look. "Okay," he said, clearly thinking. "Have a soda then. Even that's better than water. We're supposed to be relaxing."

"I'm still working."

He sighed. "Don't you ever kick back and relax? The world isn't going to end if you let your hair down once in a while," he said, leaning in to whisper in her ear. "Who knows, you might even enjoy it."

A shiver ran down her spine at the sensation of his breath in her ear. "I have fun," she said feebly. When he didn't say anything right away, she glanced over to find him staring at her with a look in his eyes that made her stomach do flip-flops. She swallowed nervously.

"Can I get you something?" One of the bartenders interrupted them.

"We'll see about that," Daniels whispered, before facing the bartender. "A beer and . . . Coke?" he asked her. She nodded. Coke was as good as anything else. "And a Coke for the lady."

"Beer and a Coke coming up."

As the bartender went to fill their order, Daniels turned his attention to her again. His hand was still resting on her back. She wished he would remove it but knew that would only lead to a scene. As her boyfriend, it was only natural for him to touch her in that way. "Why don't you drink?"

"That's none of your business." He raised an eyebrow and waited. She pushed her shoulders back and met his gaze, not backing down.

"Fine," he said, grinning. "I'll find out sooner or later."

The bartender placed their drinks on the bar in front of them. Daniels reached for his wallet and paid.

"I can buy my own drinks, you know."

He shook his head and handed her the Coke. "Always so stubborn." He took a long drink of his beer before they headed over to the table where Zach and Kenny sat. "But just so you know, I always get what I want, one way or another."

Unfortunately, they were already at the table, and she couldn't reply. Daniels had another think coming if he thought she would break so easily.

***

"How did you two meet?" Zach asked.

Gage looked over at Rebecca. They'd discussed this. "A mutual friend introduced us."

"And obviously you hit it off," Kenny added, taking a drink.

"You could say that." Gage smiled at Rebecca. She smiled back, but it was stiff. Knowing the guys would notice if she didn't relax, he draped his arm over her shoulders and leaned into her. To his friends, it would look like a show of affection. Leaning in, he whispered in her ear. "You need to relax. They're going to notice if you don't." And then, just for good measure, he let the tip of his nose run the length of her earlobe.

In that instant, he felt a hand clamp down on his knee. It was mildly painful, but he knew she'd retaliate somehow. He could also say it was one hundred percent worth it.

Leaving his arm resting on her shoulders, he took his other hand and pried her fingers from his leg. Lifting them up over the table to his lips, he kissed the palm of her hand.

"Aw," Kenny and Zach gushed.

"Shut it." Gage admonished his friends with a smile. To turn the focus away from them, he asked, "Speaking of women. How are things looking with the new bartender, Zach?"

Zach shrugged and took a drink before leaning back in his chair. "Don't know. I haven't asked."

"What do you mean you haven't asked her out?" Kenny said. "What was all that last week when you spent over an hour at the bar putting the moves on her, huh?"

"I just lost my nerve is all. I'm not sure I could take what happened with Karen again, and you and I both know there's no guarantee I'll be in Nashville for the rest of my career. "

"Not every woman is Karen." Gage tried to assure him.

"I know that. I just don't think I'm ready yet."

"It's been four years," Kenny stated, putting it out there. If he hadn't, Gage would have. His friend needed to move on. It was time.

"Don't you think I know that?" Zach said, raising his voice before lowering it again. "I'm just not like the two of you."

"No one said you had to be, but it's just a date."

Then Kenny's gaze fell on Rebecca. "You're a woman. What do you think?"

She looked uncomfortable, but after fiddling with her straw, she answered. "I don't know the situation, but four years is a long time. If it's only a date, then I don't see a problem. It's not like you're making a lifelong commitment."

To say Gage was shocked would be an understatement. When Kenny had asked her opinion, he thought for sure she'd take Zach's side and dig in her heels. She was definitely full of surprises.

"What if she says no?"

"That's always a possibility." Rebecca nodded. "But if you would eventually like to settle down and have a family, then you have to date. How else will you ever meet the person you want to spend the rest of your life with?"

The table had gone quiet, and Gage stared at her in disbelief. Had Miss 'I Can't Let Loose For Five Minutes' just said what he thought she said? Apparently, she had, and he began to look at her a little differently.

"So you think I should ask her out, then?" Zach asked, breaking the silence.

"If you like her, which it sounds like you do, then yes."

Zach took a deep breath before downing half his beer in one swallow. "Okay." Before any of them knew what was happening, Zach was up out of his seat and walking toward the bar.

"How did you do that?" Kenny asked Rebecca.

"How did I do what?"

Gage explained. "He's been pining over her for the last two months. We've been trying to convince him to ask her out since he first laid eyes on her, with no luck. Then you come in, give your opinion, and he's out of his seat in less than five minutes."

"Maybe I just said what he needed to hear."

"Maybe."

The conversation died off as all three watched their friend take the plunge. When he returned to the table, he was smiling.

"Well?" Kenny asked.

"We're going out tomorrow night."

After that, the conversation turned to the previous day's game. Gage glanced over at Rebecca a few times, but she was busy looking around. He figured she was trying to see if she could spot his stalker, although he had no idea how she was going to accomplish that, since they had no idea who was taking the pictures.

He did like that while she was searching the club for persons of interest, the rigidness in her spine eased up a little. Even though he was still touching her, she didn't seem to mind it as much. It made him wonder if she was really as opposed to physical contact as she let on, or if it was just an automatic defensive response. He did know, though, that he wanted to find out.

Leaning in, he brushed her hair away from her face, getting her attention. He was glad she'd taken it out of that ponytail she was so fond of wearing. It looked much better down.

At the feel of his fingers against her skin, she glanced over at him. Her face was full of confusion. "I want to dance," he declared.

She frowned. "I don't dance."

"Well I do, and it would look strange if we didn't dance, since it's something I always do when I come here."

Her gaze slid to the dance floor and then back to him. "Okay. One dance."

"We'll see."

"M . . . Gage," she hissed as he stood.

Ignoring her, he stepped to her other side and held out his hand. "If you'll excuse us," he said to Kenny and Zach. "My girlfriend and I are going to dance."

His friends smiled at him before going back to their conversation. Gage held out his hand and waited for her to take it. It took longer than it should have, and anyone paying attention would think they were having a disagreement. He could tell by the look on her face she wasn't happy with the current situation, but then again, he hadn't really given her a choice. Not if she wanted to continue to play the part of his girlfriend.

When they reached the dance floor, he pulled her into his arms, making sure their bodies were pressed together. "Are you always this tense?" he asked.

"No."

He smiled. "So it's just me then. Good to know."

"What's that supposed to mean?" she asked, tilting her head up to look at him.

Instead of answering, however, he asked another question.

"When was the last time you went on a date, Rebecca?" Her brow furrowed, and her lips pressed into that tight line he hated. "And before you tell me to mind my own business, you should know I'm only asking to help us keep up appearances." That wasn't entirely true, but she didn't need to know that.

"And how do you figure that?"

"People will expect us to know about each other. It would only be natural for me to know if you've recently had another boyfriend."

Her gaze left his, looked somewhere over his shoulder for what felt like ten minutes but was probably more like one. "I haven't had a boyfriend since college," she said, but then hurried to add, "That doesn't mean I don't date occasionally, but nothing recent."

"What do you consider not recent?" he asked, spinning them around to face the opposite direction.

"It's been over a year."

His eyes widened in shock. "You haven't been with a man in over a year?"

"I haven't dated a man in over a year. What I have or have not done with the men I've dated is none of your business, nor will it ever be."

A chuckle escaped his lips before he could stop it. "Oh, beautiful, you have no idea how wrong you are." Then he bent his head and kissed her.

Chapter 9

Rebecca's body went rigid the moment she felt the contact of his lips. That didn't stop the warmth from the contact. Nor did it stop its spread from where their mouths were connected down to the tips of her toes. Her fingers dug into the skin on the back of his neck. She wasn't sure if she was trying to push him away or hold him in place. Her head screamed in protest. She needed him to stop, to let go of her. She didn't like this feeling.

But he didn't let her go. Instead, his arms wrapped tighter around her, bringing their bodies into alignment. The feel of his firm chest and thighs pressing up against her caused her brain to go haywire. *She* needed to stop this. Immediately.

She couldn't. Even as the thought crossed her mind, her body was ignoring her logic. The hands that had been gripping at his neck slid effortlessly into his hair, enjoying the softness beneath her palms.

The feel of his tongue against her lips was even more alluring than his lips themselves. Opening to him was the last thing she wanted to do, but again, her body betrayed her. Before she could register what was happening, he slid his tongue inside her mouth and began stroking, licking, teasing. Her heart was pounding in her chest as if she'd just finished a hard run, but there was no feeling of exhaustion in her muscles, only the desire to get closer to him. It was maddening.

She was vaguely aware of people dancing around them, but as

they continued kissing, even that faded into the background. The only thing she could concentrate on was the feel of his mouth, his hands, and his body. Her insides felt as if they were on fire.

Slowly, he pulled back, looking down on her. His gaze drifted first to her lips, then to her eyes. She was breathing heavily and a little disoriented. *What in the world was that?* Rebecca had experienced her share of kisses before, but none had left her feeling quite like this. What was he doing to her?

As realization dawned, anger bubbled inside her. *How dare he?*

She tried to pull away, but he tightened his hold. "Let go of me."

His cocky smile returned. "Not so fast, beautiful. People are watching, remember. It wouldn't look right for you to storm off after such a passionate kiss. Might give the impression you didn't want me to kiss you."

She stopped struggling to get out of his arms but lifted her chin in defiance. "I *didn't* want you to kiss me."

He chuckled and leaned in to whisper in her ear. His warm breath sent her pulse racing again. "Keep telling yourself that, but we both know the truth. You're attracted to me, Rebecca, whether you like it or not." His lips grazed the side of her neck before he stepped back. "Let's go order some food. I'm starving."

On their way back to the table, he picked up some menus from the bar. It was pretty standard bar fare from what Rebecca could tell. Nothing fancy, and mostly finger foods. There certainly wasn't a huge focus on nutrition. Almost everything was fried, battered, and came with some sort of sauce.

"They have good burgers."

She met Daniels's gaze. He still had that amused look in his eyes that made her want to lay him out flat on his back and . . .

Okay. Maybe that wasn't such a good idea.

Turning back to her menu, she spotted a turkey club then laid the plastic-covered paper on the table in front of her. He looked at her expectantly. When she remained silent, he prompted, "Well?"

"I'll have the turkey club."

He shrugged before turning to address the other two men at the table. "You two want anything?"

"Nah, I'm good," Kenny said.

"Well, I'm hungry," Zach chimed in. "I'll take a cheeseburger.

The usual."

Rebecca watched Daniels walk away. His broad shoulders stretched the shirt he was wearing, giving all who looked a clear view of the muscles beneath, muscles she'd gotten an unobstructed view of that first morning in his pool. She felt her body temperature rise again. This needed to stop. She didn't know what was going on with her.

Okay, that was a lie, and she wasn't in the habit of lying to herself. He was right, she *was* attracted to him. For whatever strange reason, his body spoke some sort of language that caused her body to respond. That didn't mean she had to act on it. He was all wrong for her. All wrong. She wanted a man who was well established in his chosen career, preferably a businessman. Lawyer, CPA, entrepreneur. She wasn't picky as long as he was successful. Gage Daniels played a game for a living. True, it was more complex than she'd originally thought, but it was still a game. While he was technically successful, she wasn't fool enough to think that couldn't change in an instant. One injury, and then what? No, she couldn't go there. It was just too risky.

Taking a deep breath, she confirmed the logic in her decision to keep things as professional as possible with him then looked in the direction of the bar. He was leaning against it, resting one hip against a barstool. Beside him was a pretty blonde. She felt her stomach tighten. If everything she'd just told herself was true, then why had she suddenly lost her appetite?

***

Gage stood waiting for their food. He could have gone back to the table, but he wanted to give Rebecca some time. She was attracted to him. He'd been pretty sure of it before, but after that kiss, all doubts were gone. Her response had been nothing short of explosive once she'd let go and given in to the feeling. If that was how she reacted to a kiss, he couldn't wait to see what she'd be like in his bed.

Someone approached him on his left. Glancing down, he found Angie standing there with a big smile on her face. When she realized he'd noticed her, her smile grew even bigger.

"Hey, Gage."

"Hi, Angie. How've you been?" Angie was a regular, like he was. She was petite but had enough curves to give a man something to hang on to. They'd hooked up a few times, but it had been a while. He didn't like to do too many repeat performances with women. They tended to get the wrong idea. Angie was great for a good time, but she wasn't the kind of woman he wanted to settle down with. She was the type of woman who cared more about how much he could spend on her than getting to know him. In the two years they'd known each other, their conversations hadn't gone beyond the superficial. If she really wanted to get to know him, she'd ask.

"I've been good," she said, moving closer and laying her hand casually on his arm.

He could feel the heat of her fingers, the warmth of her body as she edged closer to him. But instead of his body reacting, he felt nothing. Actually, that wasn't true. He did feel something. It just wasn't his normal response to an attractive and clearly willing woman. What was coursing through his system felt more like cold chills than the warm rush of arousal. Before he could analyze it further, he took a step away from Angie.

Her hand dropped to her side, and a frown caused her brow to wrinkle. "You're here with someone."

"Yes."

She looked over his shoulder in the direction of the table where Zach, Kenny, and Rebecca sat. "I thought maybe she was with Kenny. She doesn't look like your normal type." Her shoulders shrugged as if it were no great loss, confirming what he already knew. She was looking for action. And although she may have preferred to have him share her bed tonight, it wasn't breaking her heart that he was already spoken for this evening.

"You know, Kenny might be up for some company tonight, if you're interested."

Gage kept his tone light, joking. He doubted Kenny would object if she decided to pursue him, but he'd leave that up to the two of them.

Angie scrunched up her nose. "I don't know how I'd feel about that, you two comparing notes and all."

"You think we kiss and tell?" He couldn't help the amused smile on his face.

"You're men," she said, taking a sip of the beer he hadn't seen in her other hand. "Of course you kiss and tell. And you're football players. Locker rooms are full of that talk. I'm not stupid."

This time he laughed out loud. He couldn't help it. Sure, they occasionally talked women, but given most of the guys were married or in serious relationships, they rarely went into raunchy details. What she was talking about happened more in high school and college locker rooms where boys were trying to prove they were men. "Suit yourself."

The bartender walked over with the food. Gage picked up the three baskets and somehow managed to arrange them and the two additional drinks he'd ordered in his hands before turning toward the table. "You coming?" he asked over his shoulder.

She looked uncertain, not moving. Gage didn't wait for her to decide. For one, he had an armful of food. He might have good hands, but the heat from the burgers was seeping through the bottom of the baskets and would soon be a little too hot for comfort. Also, he suddenly felt the need to get back to Rebecca.

He took a seat and set the food down on the table. Zach picked up his burger and took a large bite before Gage had even pulled his hand away. Rebecca, on the other hand, hadn't glanced at her sandwich. Instead, she was watching Angie, who'd ended up following him across the room after all.

"Mind if I sit?" Angie asked, the question directed to Kenny.

He looked up, seemingly startled. "Yeah. Sure."

Angie pulled out the chair next to Kenny and sat down, joining the group. "Thanks."

Reaching for his own burger, Gage picked it up and took a bite as he watched Angie lean over and whisper something in Kenny's ear. Whatever it was, he smiled and nodded. Then Gage noticed Angie's hand disappearing underneath the table.

It was fairly safe to say his friend was going to get lucky. Maybe that should bother him, but it didn't. The only woman he wanted in his bed at the moment was sitting beside him. Unfortunately, she had yet to acknowledge his presence since he'd returned to the table. She hadn't touched her food either. She was too busy paying attention to what was going on at the other side of the table.

Scooting their chairs closer together, Gage wrapped his hand around her thigh. She jumped before turning to glare at him. "You're not eating your food." She looked down but didn't move. There was something in her posture. She almost looked vulnerable, something he hadn't seen from her before. "You okay?"

She sat up straight, her shoulders stiffening. She met his gaze with that cold, professional mask of hers, the vulnerability he'd seen moments before gone. Fingers wrapped around his wrist exerting even pressure. A clear sign she wanted him to remove his hand. "I'm fine. Thank you for the sandwich."

He could have defied her, left his hand on her thigh, but something about the exchange had him thinking better of it. Something had just happened, but for the life of him, he couldn't figure out what it was.

For the rest of the night, he kept an eye on her. The more relaxed Rebecca of earlier in the evening never returned. He tried to engage her in conversation a couple of times, but her answers were always direct and to the point. It was obvious she wasn't in the mood to talk. He just had no idea what had caused the shift. Nothing had changed except Angie joining the group, and he couldn't see how that would have any effect on her unless the PDA going on between the two was bothering her. Even that didn't make sense, however, since they hadn't started getting hot and heavy about it until well after her change in attitude. No. He was completely at a loss as to her change.

At ten o'clock, Gage and Rebecca said good-bye to the others and walked through the remaining crowd to the entrance. Most of the people at the club had already left for the evening, although since the place didn't close down until two in the morning, there were still quite a few lingering. Rebecca scanned the room as they walked. He hadn't seen anything tonight, but maybe her trained eyes had.

The cool night air went right through him when they stepped outside. It was mid-November, and even in Nashville that meant cool nights. On pure instinct, he wrapped his arm around Rebecca, pulling her against him. Despite her inflexible posture, she felt good against him.

Some cars passed as they walked to the parking lot, but other than that, they were alone. He wanted to ask her what had happened. Taking a breath to steady himself, he walked her to the passenger side of the car and unlocked it.

Opening the car door, he sighed then turned to face her. Instead of coming face-to-face with her, however, he was met with the sight of her bending over to retrieve the small purse she'd brought with her.

"Did I miss something?"

She twisted her head around to look up at him before standing. "Miss something?"

"Yeah," he said, crossing his arms over his chest. "What was with the—"

The sound of something hitting the top of his car got his attention. Before he could process what was happening, he was on the ground, Rebecca's body pressing down on top of his. He heard the sound again. This time whatever it was sounded like it hit the side of the brick building.

He tried to raise his head, but Rebecca pushed him back down. She was stronger than she looked. "Stay down."

"What?"

Then he noticed that although she had one hand on his chest, holding him down, her other hand was holding something. He looked closer and could barely make out the shape of a gun in the dim light of the street lamps. It was then the pieces, the sounds, fell into place. Someone was shooting at them.

Chapter 10

The air around them was cool, but Rebecca didn't feel anything beyond the solid form of Gage beneath her and the adrenaline rushing through her body. She knew they were under fire the moment she heard the first bullet hit his car. Instinct had her diving for cover and pulling him right along with her. They waited, lying as flat as possible on the ground beside his car, waiting.

If she'd not been undercover protecting the man beneath her, she would have let off a shot or two of her own, or at the very least, worked her way around the vehicle to get a better look at the situation. However, the only thing she could do was hold her position and be prepared should someone approach them. Her gun was in hand, ready, should she need it.

Two more bullets hit somewhere behind them before the shooting stopped. The silence that followed was eerie. No cars passed on the street, no club patrons exited to see what all the noise was. It was just the two of them, pressed together against the cold asphalt of the parking lot.

When nothing else happened after a few minutes, she pushed herself up into a sitting position, her back against the car. Gage began to sit up, too. "Stay down," she ordered again.

He didn't listen. Instead, he sat up as well, taking a similar position beside her. "Was that what I think it was?"

She glanced over at him. "Yes."

His reaction wasn't what she was expecting. Most people who'd just had confirmation they'd been shot at would either go into a state of shock, panic, or both. Gage did neither. Instead, he frowned, his brow furrowed, as he looked her up and down. "Are you all right?" he asked, reaching for her arm.

"Shouldn't I be asking you that question?"

"Maybe," he said, the cocky grin returning. "But I know *I'm* fine."

Rebecca started to pull away but stopped herself. Although he was smiling, his eyes were serious and still watching her cautiously. She met his gaze and held it. "I'm good."

He nodded and released his hold on her arm. "What now?"

"Normally, I'd call the local police, have them secure the area. I don't think that's a good idea, however, given the situation."

"I agree," he said. "Cops mean reporters. It would be all over the evening news tonight."

Nodding, she pulled her phone out of her pocket and dialed her partner. She saw the question in Gage's eyes, but before she could respond, Hansen answered.

After explaining the situation to him and giving him directions to their location, she leaned back against the cool metal. "Hansen will be here soon. The hotel isn't far from here."

Gage nodded. "What do we do now?"

"We wait."

"Waiting has never been something I excel at," Gage said, smirking.

She could tell he was trying to lighten the mood, so she gave a small smile in return. Her heart wasn't in it, though.

As she continued to hold tightly to her firearm, she kept watch on their surroundings. Someone had taken a shot at them. Several shots, actually. This was much more serious than the specs she'd seen on the small amateur explosives that had been attached to his vehicle. Given their size and location, the explosives would have caused a minor injury at best. Bullets, however, could easily kill, even if unintentional.

Neither one of them said much as they waited for Hansen to arrive. Gage couldn't seem to keep his legs still. He was constantly bouncing them in time to a rhythm only he could hear. At first, she'd thought it was impatience on his part, and maybe some of it was, but she also noticed the tension in his jaw. What happened had affected him, even though he was trying to play it off. Before she could stop herself, she reached out and laid a hand on his forearm.

A car door slamming caused Rebecca to raise her gun from where she'd been resting it at her hip, and she scrambled to her feet. Glancing through the Mustang's windows, she breathed a sigh of relief as she saw Hansen walking toward them. He wasn't focused on either of them or the car. He took in the surrounding area, looking, searching for anything suspicious or out of place.

She knew as well as Hansen did that the chances of finding much tonight in the dark were minimal, at least not without drawing unwanted attention. No, they would have to come back in the morning. Correction, *he* would have to come back in the morning. She was still undercover. Poking around in broad daylight could compromise that. Given the events of the evening, even she couldn't deny that Gage Daniels needed protection. Someone was out to get him. The question was why?

***

Gage tried to stay out of the way as Rebecca and her partner did their thing. He felt a little like a fish out of water standing there doing nothing. Someone had shot at them. Actually taken a gun, aimed, and pulled the trigger—at them.

His gaze roamed over Rebecca as she walked around the car and surrounding area. She appeared to be all right, although he would feel much better if they could leave and go home, so he could make sure. He wanted to feel her under his hands again, to confirm that she was truly still there in front of him.

About five minutes later, she said good-bye to her partner and returned to stand in front of him. "Are you okay to drive or should I?"

It took him a second longer than it should have to answer. "Yeah, I'm good."

She nodded, and before he could react, she opened the passenger side door to his Mustang and slid inside.

Blowing out a lungful of air, he walked around the car and got behind the wheel. The night hadn't exactly gone as planned. Any progress he'd made tonight to chip away at those walls of hers had completely been undone. All he wanted to do at that point was get them home. At least there he knew they were both safe.

He went about his normal routine the next morning, trying to put what happened the night before behind him. It wasn't easy. The seriousness of the event replayed on a continuous loop in his mind. Although it was hard for him to believe his stalker was responsible for what happened, he knew it had to be. No one else had threatened him . . . well, not really. He occasionally received heated fan mail after a bad game, but it was a one-time deal and then it was over. They'd win, and the same fans loved him again. Fans were passionate. It came with the territory.

Rebecca hadn't said much on the ride home other than to ask him again if he had any injuries. The few bumps he'd received from being forced to the ground weren't anything to complain about or even acknowledge. He'd had the same and worse over the years playing football and wrestling with his brothers.

When they'd gotten home, she'd quickly checked the house to make sure it was secure then retired to her room, mumbling something about needing to check e-mail. He'd watched her rush up the stairs and firmly shut the door to her room. She hadn't given him any opportunity to approach her.

As a result, he'd not slept well. It was well after midnight before he'd dozed off, and even then, he'd tossed and turned restlessly. Given her job, he doubted this was the first time she'd been shot at, but it was a first for him. Even if she was okay with what had happened on a psychological level, he wasn't. The experience had shaken him.

He tried to work off some of the feelings the previous night had left behind during his morning swim. The water felt good surrounding him, but it couldn't wash away whatever it was that lingered. Pushing himself up out of the pool, he reached for the towel he'd left nearby and quickly dried himself off before securing it around his waist.

When he walked through the patio doors and into the kitchen, he expected to find her making breakfast for herself, but the space was empty. Not lingering, he grabbed a banana and ran up the stairs, taking them two at a time.

Before he walked into his room to take his shower, he stopped outside her bedroom and checked her door. Locked.

Taking a deep breath, he forced his feet to move. He needed a shower. Then he had practice. Whether he liked it or not, he didn't have time to get into it with her. Whatever it was that had her running and hiding in her room was going to have to wait.

Practice was a nightmare. He couldn't maintain focus and landed in the dirt more times than he could count. If that wasn't bad enough, his timing was off and he kept throwing the ball short of his receiver. Finally, the coach pulled him out and had him run laps. It was probably for the best. He needed time to get his head around what was going on before the weekend. They were playing one of their division rivals at home. Losing because he couldn't concentrate was not an acceptable option.

As he ran, some things became clearer. What bothered him most wasn't the shooting, but more the feeling of helplessness. He hadn't been able to do anything to help. Instead, he was put in the position of sitting back—or lying there, as it were—and watching Rebecca take charge of the situation. Maybe that made him a Neanderthal, but it was how he felt, nonetheless. Then being shut out after they arrived home had just compounded the problem. It hurt that she didn't seem to need him.

Shaking that thought off, he checked his watch. With only an hour left of practice, he figured he'd spend the rest of his time in the weight room. At least there he could let his mind do whatever it was going to do without having to worry about any major injuries. After talking to his coach, he headed inside. He wouldn't be able to do any heavy lifting without a spotter, but anything that didn't require all that much thought was welcome at this point. He needed to stop thinking.

***

Travis Hansen sat with his partner in a small coffee shop across from the football stadium drinking a cup of halfway decent coffee. The pastries were calling out his name, but he was trying to resist. The salad he'd eaten an hour ago hadn't done anything to curb his craving for something sweet.

Turning his gaze away from the tempting treats, he watched his partner as she looked over the pictures he'd taken. He'd spent most of the morning outside the bar looking for evidence. It was a long process, especially since he was trying hard not to draw too much attention to himself or what he was doing.

The parking lot was littered with all sorts of small pieces of metal. Most of it looked to be buttons, zippers, and earrings. The majority of the trash seemed to revolve around a more secluded part of the lot near the back. It was obvious that area saw a lot of action. He was surprised he hadn't found any less-sanitary items.

Carson had told him there'd been six shots. Two had hit the vehicle and ricocheted. Those had been the easiest shells to find since they were lying loosely on the ground. The remaining four had taken a bit longer to locate. He took a sip of his coffee. "One was lodged in the dumpster at the back of the lot. The other three were buried in the brick."

"Any noticeable pattern?" she asked, sifting through the photographs again.

He shook his head. "If anything, there was a complete lack of a pattern."

"So an amateur?"

"Either that or they want us to think they are. It's a good thing there wasn't any pedestrian traffic on the streets last night or they could have easily caught a stray bullet."

"Anything else?"

Travis noticed she wasn't relinquishing the pictures. She kept flipping through them as if she were looking for something. "The shots came from across the street. Not much there, but I did find a partial footprint. We might get lucky, but I wouldn't hold my breath."

She nodded but remained silent. He watched as she brushed her hair back behind her ears, hair that he'd never seen down before the previous Friday at Daniels's house. She was also wearing jeans and a long-sleeved shirt that left little to the imagination. His partner looked almost completely different. Aside from her outward appearance, there was a nervousness that he'd only ever seen from her once before.

They'd only been partners for a short time when her sister had shown up on her doorstep crying one night. Travis didn't know much about what happened—his partner wasn't in to sharing personal information—but for the two weeks her sister had been around, Carson acted like she was walking on eggshells. Her sister wasn't here, though, so he was curious as to what was going on with her. He knew better than to ask, however. Instead, he sat and sipped at his coffee until she'd gathered her thoughts.

When she finally did speak, it wasn't about the shooting at all. "Were you able to finish the background checks on the team?"

"Yes. I'll e-mail you the few I think we should keep an eye on, but I don't see a motive."

Carson reached into her pants pocket and took out a folded sheet of paper. "There were some people at the club last night we should check out."

He unfolded the piece of paper and looked it over. There were very few names on the list, mostly descriptions. "No names?"

She shrugged, which was not like her at all. "I wrote down the few names I overheard, but most are employees at the bar. Should be easy enough to track down."

That was true. If the bar filed payroll taxes, he should be able to pull names from there and match them with their job descriptions. If worse comes to worst, he could get pictures from the DMV, and Carson could identify them from there. "Daniels doesn't have names?"

She straightened in her seat but didn't meet his gaze. "I didn't ask him."

He frowned. "Something happen?"

"No," she said a little too quickly. "I just . . . I didn't get a chance to ask him before his practice."

She took a sip of her coffee and continued to look anywhere but at him. Something had happened, whether she wanted to admit it or not. Was Gage Daniels starting to crack that hard shell of hers?

Chapter 11

Rebecca jogged across the street toward the players' lot where Gage's SUV was parked. His practice would be wrapping up soon, and she wanted to be in the vehicle waiting for him.

Her meeting with Hansen had gone almost exactly as she'd expected. The chances of him finding something earth-shattering had been minimal. At least he'd been able to recover all of the bullets. Once they had a suspect, it would make prosecuting easier if they got a ballistics match. Of course, they'd have to get their hands on the weapon first. Who knew, maybe they'd get lucky and there'd be a usable fingerprint on one of the bullets. It was a long shot, but she wasn't above asking for miracles.

When she reached the SUV, she dropped down to the ground to check underneath. Once she was sure there wasn't anything there that shouldn't be, she hurried into the vehicle and out of the cooling temperatures. A rush of wind followed her inside as she closed the door behind her. Unfortunately, it wasn't enough to dispel the lingering scent of its owner.

The night before, she'd made sure the house was sealed up tight before taking refuge in her bedroom until she was sure he was asleep. She knew it was the coward's way out, but with her emotions so out of control, it had been the only thing she knew to do. Before going to bed, however, she'd felt compelled to check on him, and ended up standing just outside his bedroom door until almost two.

The morning wasn't any better. Even after getting to bed late, she'd woken up extra early. She went for her morning run and was showered and dressed before he emerged for his morning swim, all in an effort to continue to avoid him. Continuing her cowardly behavior, she snuck down to the kitchen while he was outside and quickly put something together for her breakfast. She could easily see the pool area from there and was able to keep tabs on his progress in the pool. As soon as he pulled himself up out of the water, revealing what had only been hinted at the last time she'd seem him with a towel around what appeared to be bare hips, she'd gathered up what was left of her food and hightailed it back up the stairs to her room.

In her own defense, she'd paused at the top and listened, making sure he'd made it inside. Once she'd heard the patio door close, however, she went to her room and locked the door. It was unprofessional, she knew that. She should have been down there with him. They should have been discussing what happened, trying to figure out who was behind it, and why. But something was wrong with her, and she needed to figure out what it was. Going to bed hadn't been any help. All she'd done was toss and turn, getting little actual sleep.

She leaned her head against the vehicle's headrest, closing her eyes. Seeing Gage with that woman at the bar had thrown her. She'd seen the pictures that first day, knew he got around. Of course he did. He was good-looking and a popular athlete. When she'd seen the evidence of it right in front of her face, she'd felt a surge of anger toward the other woman, which was crazy. She had no claim on him. No real one, anyway.

That thought made her even more uncomfortable. The man was part of her job. She'd protect him, as she was supposed to, and then go back to Knoxville, back to her apartment, and live her life just as she had before. Nothing would change. It would be for the best.

Reaching into her bag, she took out her e-reader. She still had at least twenty minutes before Gage would be finished, and she needed something to distract her. The last thing she wanted to do was spend the time analyzing all the strange emotions he brought out in her. But even as she began reading her newest crime novel, Rebecca knew she couldn't keep avoiding him. One way or another, she was going to have to figure out a way to work with Gage. Somehow.

It wasn't until a half hour later that she noticed guys slowly beginning to trickle out to the parking lot. Gage emerged about five minutes later with Zach, Kenny, and two other guys she didn't know. He was freshly showered, his dark brown hair slicked back, and wearing a pair of jeans, a grey T-shirt, and a black leather jacket. His gait was confident. He stood out from the others without even trying. She felt her body temperature rise with every step he took toward her. It made no sense!

Once they reached the rows of vehicles, he said good-bye to the others and closed the remaining distance between them. Rebecca didn't turn away, but she kept her gaze at chest level, refusing to look at his face. She didn't need to see that cocky grin of his letting her know once again that he could read her like a book, that he knew she was feeling that indescribable pull toward him.

Opening the back door, he threw his duffle bag down on the seat before getting behind the wheel. She turned in her seat to face straight ahead.

"Hi," he said.

Keep it professional. "How was your practice? Anything out of the ordinary happen?"

There was a long pause. "No."

An uncomfortable silence filled the space. She needed to fix this between them. They had to work together for the near future. "Good," she muttered, pushing past the lump in her throat. "I met with Hansen. He was able to recover the bullets from last night and a partial footprint. He's sending everything to the lab."

"So what happens now?" he said, starting the vehicle.

"We wait." It wasn't the best news to deliver, but it was honest. He nodded, and pulled out onto the street. They drove for a few miles before he took an unplanned detour. "Where are you going?"

"I'm taking you out to dinner."

There was no question or request in his tone. He was telling her, not asking her. "There's food at your house."

"And at my house, I have no guarantee that you won't run and hide again."

Rebecca turned in her seat to look out the window and hide her blush. She should have known he wouldn't let her continue to avoid him. Still, the fact that he was forcing her into a situation where there was no easy escape made the hairs on the back of her neck stand up and her stomach queasy.

"I don't know what you're talking about." Even as the words left her lips, she wished she could take them back. Lying wasn't like her. This—whatever this was with him—was making her act not like herself.

He chuckled. "Sure you don't."

Before she could figure out something to say that would make him change directions and turn the SUV around, they pulled up to the restaurant.

***

He'd known what Rebecca's response to their going out to eat would be. That was exactly why he'd not mentioned it before they'd left the stadium. The last thing he needed was for her to have time to weasel her way out of it. Or try, at least.

The restaurant he'd chosen was casual, but nice enough that he'd be able to get them a semiprivate booth in the back. They needed to talk, and the last thing he wanted was to be hounded by fans wanting pictures and autographs. Home would have been a preferable option to have a conversation like this, but he couldn't trust her not to run. He may not be a therapist, but he knew enough about body language to know she was running scared.

When he parked in front of the restaurant, he peered at her out of the corner of his eye. She was looking out the window at the restaurant and biting her bottom lip again. Her hands were clenched into fists as they lay on either side of her legs. A part of him loved that he had her off balance. The *why* of it had him confused. At the bar, she'd met him push for push, until he'd returned to the table with their dinner.

Getting out of the vehicle, he walked to the parking meter and deposited enough money to last them for the next two hours. Then he went to the passenger side and opened Rebecca's door for her. She remained seated, staring up at him for several moments before ignoring the hand he held out for her and exiting on her own.

Once she was clear, Gage closed the door behind her, took her hand in his, and began walking toward the restaurant entrance before she could protest. It was a good thing, too. By the time they'd reached the hostess stand, her neatly trimmed nails were digging into his skin, displaying her displeasure.

He was glad to see some of her fight back. It was certainly better than that 'broken little girl' look he'd seen since the previous night. His only response to her show of aggression was to give her hand a firm squeeze and wink at her after expressing their needs to the hostess.

As they followed the restaurant employee to their booth, Rebecca's hand held firm to his. She tried shifting it a few times, but he wouldn't let her. Given what she'd done in the past, he was willing to bet she was trying to do that pressure point thing to his wrist again. No. He liked her hand just where it was for the time being.

Reaching their table, he thanked the young lady and reluctantly released Rebecca's hand. "After you," he said, smiling.

She scowled but slid into the booth.

He sat down and moved to sit next to her. She scooted further, putting more space between them, space he quickly removed by following her. "Not going to get away from me tonight, beautiful."

With her game face on, she met his stare. "I don't know what it is you think you know, but I'm not trying to do anything other than my job," she hissed low enough not to be overheard.

Unfortunately, the server came to take their drink orders, and he couldn't answer her right away. Once the man was gone, Gage angled his body to face her. "What happened last night?"

"I'm not sure what you're referring to, Mr.—Gage. A lot of things happened last night."

He reached up to brush a loose hair from her face. She leaned away, but he persisted. "Is it that you don't like being attracted to me? Is that the problem?"

"I'm not—"

"Have you decided what you'd like to order?" the server asked, interrupting them.

Gage didn't turn his gaze away from Rebecca. "We'll both have a burger and fries."

"Did you want everything on those?" he asked, completely oblivious to the tense atmosphere surrounding his two customers.

"On the side, please."

"Yes, sir. I'll put your order right in."

As soon as he was gone, Gage picked up where they'd left off. "You can deny it all you want, Rebecca, but we both know the truth," he said, his fingers trailing down the side of her neck, shoulder, and arm. When his hand met hers, he clasped it between both of his. "It's nothing to be ashamed of, you know."

She didn't say anything for a long time. Given the look on her face, he wasn't even sure if she'd answer. Finally, however, he saw her push her shoulders back in the way she always did, as if preparing for battle. "Yes. I *am* attracted to you. You're a good-looking man. That doesn't change the fact that I'm here in a professional capacity, not a personal one. It wouldn't be wise to cross boundaries, nor do I have any desire to do so." Her eyes blazed with determination. She wanted to believe what she was saying, but he'd felt how she responded to his kiss.

Edging closer, he brought up his right hand to cup the back of her neck, tilting her head slightly. The rush of energy he always felt near her was as intense as it had been at the bar. He moved his fingers gently along the back of her neck as he leaned in. "You may wish you didn't have any desire, beautiful, but you do. It's in your eyes. It's in the way your breathing accelerates when I touch you. Nothing is stopping you but you."

Any other words from both of them were cut off as his lips made contact with hers. Unlike before, there was no resistance, not even at the beginning. She wanted this as much as he did.

Before he knew what was happening, he was completely lost in their kiss. Her lips were soft and warm . . . welcoming. His hand at the base of her neck moved to angle her head in an effort to deepen the kiss. Unfortunately, his attempt to leave her breathless was derailed by their server returning with their meals.

Straightening in his seat, he thanked the server and glanced over at Rebecca. Her gaze was locked on her plate, her chest moving up and down at a rapid pace. He could tell she was trying to calm down. She looked vulnerable again, and for whatever reason, he felt the need to provide comfort.

"Hey," he said to get her attention. When she looked up, he reached out and touched the side of her face. "There's nothing wrong with desire. It's perfectly natural. And in case you haven't noticed, I'm attracted to you, as well."

Unfortunately, she didn't answer. Her only reaction was a blank stare before turning her attention back to her meal.

Chapter 12

It wasn't until the following morning, while checking in with her partner, that it hit her Gage had ordered her dinner for her. As soon as it did, she wanted to run out of her room and make it perfectly clear that she didn't appreciate his chauvinistic display of caveman behavior. She was perfectly capable of ordering her own food and making any other decisions in her life that needed making.

After hanging up the phone, she stood and marched to the door to do just that. By the time she reached the bottom of the stairs, she was poised to attack, ready to put him in his place and make him wish he'd never met her. He wasn't in the kitchen or anywhere else she could see, so she stalked to the basement stairs ready to do battle. The lights were out, and she started to lose steam when she couldn't locate him.

It took her another five minutes of searching before she caught a glimpse of red outside on the back patio and followed it. There, Gage sat on a lounge chair with his head bowed, shoulders slumped. Something in his posture sent a prickle up her spine.

He glanced up when she opened the door and stepped out into the cool November air. His eyes were haunted. "What's happened?"

He picked up an envelope she hadn't seen lying on the ground next to him, and then he held it out to her. It was the same kind of envelope the other pictures had arrived in, the same barely legible handwriting on the front. Before she looked inside, she already had a pretty good idea of what she'd find.

She motioned for him to lay it down on the small cocktail table beside him. "I'll be right back." Before he could say another word, she went back into the house and up to her room. She hadn't brought a lot with her, but she rarely went anywhere without a pair of latex gloves.

When she returned to the patio, Gage was sitting exactly where she'd left him. "How was it delivered?" she asked, pulling the gloves tight over her small hands.

"The mailman found it at the gate." He had a defeated expression on his face, one she'd not seen from him before.

"So he touched it."

Gage frowned. "Of course he touched it."

"Did he touch the others, too?" she asked, pausing before she picked up the envelope to examine it more closely.

"Yeah, I guess."

When she first picked up the envelope, she noticed it was a little thicker than the others had been. "We're going to want his fingerprints. I'm sure they're already on file, but it will be easier getting them directly from him, if he's willing. It'll take a while to get anything back from the lab, but we might as well have his ready to be eliminated." She gently opened the envelope and removed the small stack of pictures.

As she flipped through the photographs, she was filled with too many emotions to name. Every single one of them had been taken on Monday night at the bar. Someone had been there taking pictures of them, and she'd missed them. How could she not have noticed?

The pictures were taken from all different angles throughout the night. Some were of them sitting at the table with Zach and Kenny. There were even some with Angie. Seeing her again brought another surge of anger. Not wanting to try and analyze her feelings over the woman again at that exact moment, Rebecca focused on the details. Some of the pictures were blurry, while others were crystal clear. Most of the pictures looked to have been taken by a camera with the ability to zoom in. That would've taken time to focus the picture. She would have seen that.

She closed her eyes and tried to recall seeing anyone who could have taken all these pictures. Anyone who would have stood out. There were people there with cameras taking pictures, but other than the occasional snapshot of the group by various individuals, no one had set off alarm bells. The whole situation was frustrating. She felt as if she'd failed to do her job, and maybe she had. She'd been so wrapped up in Gage that she'd missed something. Obviously.

Kicking herself, she placed the pictures back inside the envelope. "I need to get these to Hansen. I'll have him meet me at the café again once you're safely inside the stadium. You need to leave for practice soon, don't you?" she asked, glancing at her watch.

He appeared to be in some kind of haze. At her mention of practice, his face cleared a little. Looking down at the watch on his wrist, he uttered a curse before running inside. Before she knew it, he was bounding back down the stairs, duffle bag in hand. "You ready to go?"

"Sure," Rebecca said uncertainly.

She watched him, waiting for a sign of . . . well, she wasn't sure exactly. He'd gone from extremely distant to a man on a mission.

Grabbing their coats, they were out the door and into his SUV on their way to the stadium in a matter of seconds. Not once on the way there did Gage flirt with her or make any inappropriate comments. For some reason, it bothered her, although she didn't understand why. Wasn't this what she'd been wanting from him all along?

When they arrived at the players' parking lot, he turned off the engine but didn't get out. "You'll be careful today?"

Rebecca's eyes widened. "I'm always careful."

"I know. I just . . . just be careful."

Before she could say anything more, he was gone.

She watched him jog into the stadium and disappear before getting out of the vehicle and walking across the street to the little café. It was perfect. They had decent food and coffee. Plus, they were directly across the street from the players' lot. It couldn't have been more ideal.

After ordering herself a large coffee with extra cream and a Danish pastry, she slid into one of the front booths. She took a bite of her pastry before pulling out her phone and dialing Hansen. They hadn't scheduled a meeting, but this was important. She'd known Gage's stalker had to have been there on Monday night given the incident afterward, but no one had tripped her radar inside the bar. They needed to come up with some leads and soon, before whoever it was took another shot at him—or worse.

***

Practice Wednesday didn't turn out to be as horrible as Gage had expected. Granted, he was made to run laps for his tardiness, but once he got out on the field, all his frustrations turned into focused energy. His receivers complained their chests and hands were hurting from the force of his throws. Never before had he cared that whoever this was had photographed him with women. Seeing Rebecca in the pictures, however, sent his blood boiling and left him feeling completely helpless. He wasn't used to that, and he didn't like it.

When they arrived back home, Hansen was there waiting for them. It was a long night. They sat around Gage's dining room table eating pizza and going over every photograph. Hansen wanted to know where each one had been found, who had access to each location, and how many people had touched the envelopes. The interrogation—that's what it felt like anyway—went on until almost midnight. After the restless night he'd had before, he fell into his bed and was asleep within minutes.

Hansen waylaid the mailman the following day, getting his fingerprints and asking if he'd seen anything. The poor guy looked out of his element and a little scared being questioned. No doubt he'd thought having a route in such an upscale neighborhood would never put him in that position.

On Thursday night it was more of the same. They went over everything again. It was honestly giving him a headache. He didn't understand what they hoped to gain by all the repetition. It was the same information no matter how many times they looked at it.

When he climbed into his vehicle on Friday night after practice, he took one look at Rebecca and knew what was coming. "No. Tonight is about relaxing. If you two want to put your heads together again and rehash everything, feel free. I'm not being part of it."

Her eyes were serious. "We have to figure out who is behind this."

"I understand that," he said, reaching for her. She pulled her hands out of his reach, but he persisted until his right hand held tight to her left. "But you can watch a play over and over again. After you've dissected it from every angle, you're not going to get any new information out of it, no matter how many times you watch." She started to open her mouth again, but he cut her off and continued. "Look, I want to catch this person just as much as you do. More probably," he said, gritting his teeth. The picture of them dancing flashed through his mind. "But I need to relax and forget about it for a while."

Reaching over with his free hand, he cupped the back of her neck. He felt her muscles stiffen under his hands but ignored it. She'd been using this and Hansen as an excuse to keep distance between them the last two days. He was tired of it. He needed to feel her lips against his again. Without any hesitation on his part, he rose up out of his seat to clear the console separating them, pulled her head toward him, and kissed her.

She resisted at first, clinging to whatever it was that was holding her back. Releasing her hand, he slid his arm around her waist, bringing their upper bodies closer. "Stop thinking," he murmured, his lips never completely relinquishing her mouth.

It took longer than what he would have liked, but she finally gave in. He'd watched her put a lock on her emotions since Wednesday morning. At first, he'd thought it was because of the pictures. He was beginning to think, however, the pictures had just given her a convenient excuse.

His tongue dipped into her mouth, exploring and caressing. She released a sigh and kissed him back. It felt so natural, so right. There was heat and passion in every touch. He never wanted to stop.

The hand he had secured around her waist inched underneath her sweater, feeling the soft skin beneath. His desire to take this much further than was appropriate in the middle of a parking lot pulsed through every cell of his body. It had been years since he'd had sex in the backseat of a car. Beds, tables, floors . . . they all allowed a lot more movement and leverage than a car. His body didn't appear to care about the logistics. He wanted her. Immediately. In any way, he could get her.

His left hand left her neck and joined its counterpart around her waist. Lifting her effortlessly out of her seat and over the center console, he positioned her on his lap, her legs straddling him. "What—?"

He leaned the seat back as far as it would go to give them some more room. "Shh," he whispered against her lips before placing both hands to surround her face and bringing her down with him on the reclined seat. "Don't think. Feel."

The next several minutes were a blur as they both became caught up in the moment. Her hands gripped his shoulders as the kiss became hotter and hotter. He released his hold on her face, once he was fairly sure she wasn't going to pull away, and returned to exploring the soft skin of her lower back. This time, he surged upward until he found the back of her bra. The contraption was begging him to release it, to free her breasts so he could plunge into uncharted territory.

Just as he was about to make that happen, she pulled back. Her eyes were glazed over, her breathing ragged. He reached up and brushed the hair away from her face, resting his hand at the base of her neck. "Why did you stop?"

She shook her head. "I can't."

"Why not, Rebecca? You want this. I know you do."

"It's wrong. I can't . . ."

She attempted to get off him, but he held her tight. "Why is it wrong? We're both adults. There's nothing that says we can't."

Her eyes closed, and for a second, he thought she was going to cry before she regained her composure. "There's no future in this. Why pursue something that has no hope of ever lasting?"

He smiled. "Fun. Enjoyment. Mutual gratification. I can go on."

She shook her head again and slid off him. This time he didn't stop her even though he wanted to. He didn't understand. She wanted it. Him. Why was she pushing him away?

Before he could ask, her cell phone rang. It was Tim wanting to know if they could come up to his office before they left. She didn't even ask him before agreeing, so any further discussion on the subject would have to wait.

The meeting was brief. Tim only wanted to know how things were going. He wasn't happy to find out they'd been shot at, but there wasn't much he could do about it either way. Rebecca assured him they were working diligently to find out who was behind this, but unfortunately, they hadn't come up with much.

When they arrived home just before six, something seemed to be in the air, and Gage was reluctant to bring up the subject of *them* again. Instead, he stayed close by, working with her to make a simple dinner. It seemed her cooking skills matched his. Neither of them would be creating any lavish meals anytime soon. They ate in near silence, and he offered to clean up after, leaving her to go upstairs to her room and do whatever it was she did in there.

Instead of taking him up on his offer and rushing up to her room to hide, she lingered. He was halfway through washing the dishes before he couldn't take it anymore. "Something on your mind?"

She glanced up at him before walking to the other side of the kitchen island, placing it between them like a shield. By the way she was acting, he was fairly certain he wasn't going to like whatever it was she had to say.

"I need to tell you something."

"Go ahead," he prompted when she didn't continue.

Rebecca looked down at the granite countertop in front of her and reached out to grip the edge, her knuckles turning white. "The reason Donovan called us in wasn't because of your letters. Well it was, but . . . "

"But what?"

She raised her head and looked him dead in the eye, sending chills through his entire body. "Stadium security found explosives under your SUV. It was an amateur job, wouldn't have caused a lot of damage, but it was enough." She paused. "I thought after the shooting, you should know."

Before he could gather his wits about him after the bombshell she'd just dropped, however, she walked silently up the stairs and disappeared. He was left alone in the kitchen, stunned.

They tiptoed around each other for most of the weekend. Rebecca didn't say any more about the bomb that had been found under his vehicle, and neither did he. It was almost as if the entire conversation had never happened.

Sunday's football game was brutal, as he knew it would be. Division play always had an extra intensity to it above other regular season games. He was pretty beat-up and was limping a little by the time he made it out of the stadium.

When she saw him, she rushed to his side and took his bag, even after he insisted he could handle it himself. She wouldn't hear of it, though. They even had a little argument over who was going to drive. He had to admit, he loved seeing that side of her, all protective of him. It was completely opposite to the distance she exhibited toward him most of the time, or even the heated passion when she let her guard down. This was something new.

He spent the evening in his hot tub soaking his aching muscles. The team doctor had checked him out before he'd left. Nothing was broken. There were just a lot of bruises and overused muscles. He'd be fine. It helped that they had the next week off. Thursday was Thanksgiving, and for the first time in his professional career, the holiday fell on a bye week for them. He was going to be able to go home and celebrate the holiday with his family. Most Thanksgivings for him were spent heating up a preordered turkey dinner from the local market. This year it would be different. He'd have his family.

As he thought of his family, his thoughts drifted to Rebecca. Unless something major happened in the next few days, she'd be going with him. He had no idea how his family would react to her. Would she want them to know the truth—that she was there to protect him—or would she want to keep up the ruse?

He wasn't sure how he felt about either scenario. If he presented his family with the truth, they would lose it. His mom would be frantic with worry. His brother Paul would grill Rebecca for all the details. He was sure Paul would insist on being involved, and that was the last thing he wanted. Thanksgiving would be ruined.

If he introduced her as his girlfriend, his parents were going to start hearing wedding bells. He didn't date, not in the traditional sense, and if he was bringing a girlfriend home, it had to be serious. When Rebecca's gig was up, she'd head back to Knoxville, leaving him and breaking his family's heart. It was a no-win situation.

Stepping out of the hot tub, he reached for the towel he'd laid on a nearby bench then quickly dried off. It was getting late, the sun was already dipping down behind the mountains, and the wind was whipping up. It was too early for snow, but he wouldn't be surprised if there was some frost on the ground by morning.

Wrapping the towel around his hips, he hurried into the warm house. His muscles weren't aching as much as they had been earlier. All he wanted to do was shower and head over to the club to meet the guys. He could really use a beer.

He jogged up the stairs toward his room, and then he paused at the end of the hall. Rebecca's door was ajar, which was unusual. She typically made sure it was locked up tight whenever she was inside. He walked closer and heard her talking. Figuring she was talking shop with Hansen again, he turned to go. Her next words, however, had him stopping in his tracks.

"I don't know when I'm going to be home." She paused, and when she spoke again, he could hear a hint of desperation in her tone. "No. Of course you can stay at my house. I . . . I doubt I'll be there for Thanksgiving. I understand. I'm sorry. No. I'm . . . working. Nashville."

He pushed the door aside and walked into her room. She was sitting on the edge of her bed, her phone pressed firmly against her ear. As if sensing him, she turned sharply, her gaze meeting his. That vulnerable look was back, and he didn't hesitate to go to her.

"What's wrong?" he mouthed. She shook her head. "Tell me."

She looked unsure, but eventually asked the caller to hold on for a minute. Not looking at him, she said, "It's nothing you need to worry about. I'm sorry to have bothered—"

He took hold of her chin and made her look at him. "Don't even think about finishing that sentence, beautiful."

"It's my sister. She . . . something's happened, and she needs a place to stay."

"So have her come here." It seemed like an easy solution. Rebecca's sister clearly needed her. He could understand that. Even with him living in Nashville and not seeing his family often, they were still close. His mom had made sure of that.

"I couldn't—"

Before she could react, Gage took the phone from her. "Hello?"

A timid voice on the other end answered through what sounded like tears. "Hi."

"Rebecca's staying with me in Nashville at the moment. Can you come here instead?"

She sniffed. "Yeah, I guess."

"Just let us know when your flight arrives, and we'll pick you up."

"Um . . . I'll be taking the bus."

"Okay, then, let us know when your bus arrives."

"Um . . . okay." She was quiet for several seconds. "Can I talk to Becca again?"

He glanced up to find Rebecca staring at him with wary eyes. "Sure. Hold on," he said into the phone.

Laying the phone down on the bed for a minute, he reached for

Rebecca's hand. For once, she didn't try to flee.

"You don't have to do this, you know," she said. "She can stay in my apartment."

"There's no need. I have plenty of space here. Besides, Thanksgiving is only a few days away."

She looked away. "I know."

"We should talk about that," they both said in unison.

The slip lightened the mood a little, as they both chuckled. "We don't have a game this week, so I'm going home for the holiday."

"You can't go alone," she said, quick to remind him.

"Yeah." He smirked. "I didn't think you'd release me for the weekend."

"So what do you want to do?"

He reached up to brush his fingers along her cheek. "The only thing we can do." She raised her eyebrows in question. "Bring my girlfriend." Before she could comment, he leaned in and placed a firm kiss to her lips, then stood before heading toward the doorway. He paused, twisting back to face her. "Let me know when your sister's bus arrives, and we'll go pick her up." When he reached the door, he stopped again. "By the way, what's her name?"

"Megan," she said, her voice cracking slightly. "Her name is Megan."

Chapter 13

Rebecca hadn't said much after her phone call with her sister. The only conversation they'd had for the rest of the evening was when she, once again, insisted that he didn't have to take her sister into his house. She was wrong about that. For some reason, it really had felt like he did. He wasn't sure of the why, but he'd learned to follow his gut over the years, so that's what he was going with.

At five thirty in the morning, Gage found himself standing inside the bus station with Rebecca waiting for her sister Megan to arrive. There were more people in the bus station than he'd thought there'd be at so early in the morning. Some of them were waiting on buses themselves. Others, like him and Rebecca, were waiting on arrivals. Everyone seemed to be in their own world. No one was interacting with anyone else, content in their own little bubbles.

Rebecca stood at his side, arms crossed over her chest, staring out the large window. Her fingers were dug into her arms so hard he was sure there would have been marks had she not been wearing a jacket and sweater.

He'd kept some distance between them since they'd walked into the bus station, but he'd had enough. Even if she got angry with him, it would be better than quiet aloofness. Her anger he could deal with.

Taking a step to the side, he closed the gap between them and wrapped his arm around her waist. She stiffened, just as he'd suspected, but she surprised him when a moment later she released a deep breath and relaxed, leaning into him slightly. He pulled her closer and kissed her temple. He wanted to ask her what was wrong, what she was so nervous about. He didn't, though. Not only did he think she wouldn't answer him, but he also didn't want to break the mood. At the moment, she was allowing him to comfort her. The last thing he wanted was to give her a reason to remember that wasn't in her *professional* plan.

It was almost six before the bus transporting Megan pulled in. As the air brakes released, Rebecca took a step forward, out of his embrace. He stayed back, watching.

One by one, people disembarked and filed into the station. As passengers reunited with their friends and families, the noise level increased tenfold. Some people were crying. Others were jumping up and down, hugging each other. Then there were those who didn't appear to have anyone waiting, who either drifted to a corner to await the next leg of their journey or walked almost silently out the door.

He watched each person find their place with no reaction from Rebecca to indicate her sister was among them. A full ten minutes after the flood of passengers into the building began, a woman with short, dark hair crept inside. She was shorter than her sister by maybe three inches, but the resemblance was there.

Rebecca noticed her first. "Megan?"

The young woman's head whipped around, and her gaze locked on her sister's form ten yards away. There was an immediate change in Megan's facial expression. Before where it had been cautious and guarded, it now held relief mixed with pain. She hiked the bag she was carrying high up on her shoulder and rushed across the short distance to where Rebecca waited with open arms.

Gage stayed back, allowing the sisters their greeting. He had no idea what Rebecca had told Megan about him. They'd get to that soon enough. For the moment, they both seemed oblivious to his presence. Megan was currently clinging to her sister as if her life depended on it. And Rebecca, who had minutes before looked like a worrying mother hen, soothed and comforted her.

It was somewhat strange to witness from an outsider's point of view, but every family dynamic was different. Maybe it had something to do with the age difference. Megan appeared to be in her early twenties. He would guess there were at least five years between them, if not more. He knew how protective Paul had been of his younger brothers growing up. Maybe this was the equivalent between sisters. He didn't know.

Rebecca pulled back first, bracketing her sister's face with her hands, brushing tears away. "Are you hurt?" she asked.

Megan shook her head.

Although the look on Rebecca's face showed doubt, she didn't pursue it any further. Instead, she glanced up at him with raw emotion in her eyes. Seconds later, however, she blinked, and it was gone. He wasn't sure what to make of it. Either way, it wasn't the time to push to find out.

Stepping forward, he offered his hand. "You must be Megan. I'm Gage."

She stiffened and reached out to take his hand. "Hi."

He didn't get any more than that, but considering the sun was just coming up over the horizon and she'd been on a bus for the last who-knew-how-many hours, he didn't blame her for the short response. "Do you have any luggage you need to get before we head out?"

"No." Her voice was much more timid than her sister's. "I have everything right here."

Gage frowned. All she had was in a single backpack? That didn't sound right. He thought about offering to carry it for her, probably should have, but something in her posture and the way she gripped the padded strap made him change his mind.

He was going to suggest they leave, but before he could get the words out, Rebecca said, "Come on. Let's get you back to the house. I'll make you some hot chocolate, and you can get some sleep."

"I could really use a beer."

Rebecca brushed the hair out of Megan's eyes. "Not until you've had some rest and some food. Who knows how long it's been since you've eaten, and I'm not giving you alcohol on an empty stomach."

Megan sighed but didn't argue. The sisters walked out of the bus station, leaving him to follow and wondering what he'd just witnessed.

***

Rebecca closed the door to the room Gage had given Megan.

She and her sister had talked until Megan's eyes had begun to close from sheer exhaustion. At least she was fairly certain her sister wasn't hurt. Not physically, anyway.

True to form, Megan had picked the wrong guy and he'd broken her heart. Rebecca would press for more details later when her sister was fully rested, but it had come down to her walking in on her boyfriend snorting what she assumed was coke. That was one thing she would give her sister credit for—she drew the line at illegal drugs. Megan could drink and party with the best of them, but she didn't mess around with drugs no matter what they were.

Leaning against the wall for a minute to regain her composure, Rebecca had no idea why Gage had been so generous. He didn't owe her or her sister anything. In fact, she should have refused his offer, should have asked Hansen to cover Gage for a day while she got her sister settled at her apartment. The offer had been too tempting, however. She only hoped she didn't regret taking him up on it.

With Megan finally asleep in her bed, Rebecca walked down the short hallway and into the kitchen. The room her sister was staying in was the only one with a bed on the main floor. There were empty bedrooms upstairs, one right beside hers, but Gage had said Megan might feel more comfortable having her own space. Much to Rebecca's dismay, Megan had agreed.

The kitchen was empty, but the lights were on, so she knew Gage was nearby. Like everything else regarding him, she wasn't sure how she felt about that. Deciding her brain had thought enough for the moment, she took out the orange juice from the refrigerator and poured herself a glass.

"Hey." His voice sounded loud in the quiet room.

She turned around and leaned back against the counter, taking a sip of her juice. "Hey."

"She asleep?"

"Yeah."

He nodded, not saying anything right away, but she could tell by his stance that wouldn't last long. Gage didn't disappoint, but what he said surprised her. "You should get some sleep."

"I'm fine. I need to check in with Hansen anyway." It was after eight. The sun was already up, promising a warm November day. He was going to call her soon to see if something was wrong if she didn't call him first.

"So call Hansen and then go take a nap. Neither one of us got a lot of sleep last night." She shook her head again. "The alarm is on and I'll stay in the house. You don't have to worry about me or doing your job. It'll be fine."

"I don't . . . " Her words died in her throat as he stalked toward her.

"That wasn't a suggestion, beautiful. You can't protect me if you're dead on your feet, and something tells me your sister is going to need you, too." He ran the tips of his fingers down her arm, leaving a tingling trail of sensitive nerves in their wake. She was very aware of him—his body, his heat, his breath against her face. Her eyes closed involuntarily, too tired to resist the pleasant sensations his nearness brought to the surface.

She felt the brush of his lips against hers a moment before they connected. The kiss was soft. Softer than anything they'd shared before. It made her want to sink into him and forget about everything else.

Before she knew it, he had removed the glass from her hand and was putting her arms around his neck. She didn't resist him. Didn't want to. Somewhere in the back of her mind, she registered that she should push him away, but she ignored it. Right there, right at that moment, all she wanted was to keep feeling his mouth kissing her, feeling the silkiness of his hair beneath her fingers, and enjoying how good his hands felt pressing into her back.

All too soon, Gage broke the kiss and rested his forehead against hers. Their gazes met, and the desire lurking behind his brown eyes made her forget about everything else but him.

"As much as it pains me to say it, you need to call your partner." He handed over her cell phone. It had been attached to her belt, and he'd somehow managed to get it off her without her noticing.

That happens way too much with him.

Strangely, his reminder of her job, her duty, wasn't the wake-up call she knew it should have been. She took the offered phone and made the call. Gage didn't budge. He stayed right there with her, their lower bodies nearly fused together.

His hands never stopped caressing her the whole time she was on the phone with Hansen. It was utterly and completely distracting. At one point, she lost her train of thought, and she saw his lips tilt up in a smile. She wanted to be annoyed with him, push him away, but for some reason she didn't.

The phone call lasted a lot longer than she wanted. By the time she hung up, her eyes were drooping and her limbs felt as if they'd been weighted down. The only thing holding her up was Gage.

"Finished?" he asked when she pressed the button on her phone and slipped it into her jeans pocket. It would have taken too much coordination to clip it back on her belt.

"Yes," she whispered, her eyes drifting closed. She felt him shift his weight, and then she was no longer standing. Her eyes popped open, and her fingers gripped his shoulders. "What—"

"You need to sleep." When she opened her mouth to protest, he cut her off with a hard kiss. By the time he lifted his head again, she was no longer thinking of how to get out of his arms.

Giving in, and relishing the way being in his arms made her feel, Rebecca rested her head on his shoulder and closed her eyes. Just this once, she'd forget all the things she should do, and enjoy this moment. She knew there was no future with Gage, but for whatever reason, fate had thrown them together and made him nearly impossible to resist.

His body moved beneath her as he walked up the stairs and down the hall. He lowered her to the bed, but she didn't open her eyes. The mattress sunk in response to his weight.

As he released her arms from around his neck, the cool air hit her skin and she frowned. She felt his fingers ghost into her pocket. Absentmindedly, she realized he must have been removing her phone for her. That brought a small smile to her lips. Then he was gone, and the cool air of the room wrapped around her body once again. The sun was shining through the curtains of the large windows, but it was no comparison to the warmth she'd felt nestled up against Gage's body. She felt the scowl beginning to return. Before she could think it through any further, however, the bed dipped and arms encircled her. She rolled over instinctively and buried her face in his heat. Seconds later, she was asleep.

Chapter 14

The first thing that registered in Rebecca's mind as consciousness returned was that she was not alone. A very warm body pressed against her back. A very warm, very large male body, with his arm slung over her hip. There was no way it was her sister snuggled up behind her.

Her heart rate immediately spiked in panic, and she quickly took in her surroundings. She wasn't in her room. The walls were a warm tan color, not the blue of the guest room where she'd been staying. They were also darker than the cream in the room her sister was using. No, she was quite certain she was in Gage's room. Lying in his bed. With him. The only consolation was that she was still completely clothed. She could feel her gun and ankle holster pressing into her leg.

She racked her brain trying to recall how she'd ended up in his bed. After they'd picked up her sister from the bus station, she'd been exhausted. Her defenses against Gage's pull weakened. Closing her eyes, she groaned as she remembered him carrying her up the stairs and putting her into bed. She'd thought it had been her bed, not his. What was wrong with her?

Before that train of thought went any further, she gently lifted the arm holding her and extracted herself from his grasp. Out of the bed, she spotted her phone lying on the nightstand and her shoes at the end of the bed. Grabbing them, she tiptoed as quietly as possible across the hall to her bedroom.

After making sure the door was shut and locked, she let her body sink to the floor, her head falling into her palms. The weight of everything finally hit her, and she let all the emotions she'd been holding in crawl to the surface. Her baby sister was downstairs needing her to be the strong, confident rock she always was. Megan was counting on her. The problem was, Rebecca felt anything but confident. The man in the next room was playing havoc with her emotions, her body. She had no idea how to act around him, how to do her job. Now she was going to have to find it in her somehow to deal with her sister's crisis, too. She just didn't know how.

She had no idea how long she stayed there, sitting on the floor, but eventually she got herself under control. Pushing herself up off the floor, she stood then walked into her bathroom and turned on the shower. Steam filled the room as she stripped off her layers of clothing one by one. Standing naked in front of the mirror, she looked at her reflection. Unfortunately, her reflection held no more answers than it usually did.

Brushing the hair away from her face, she turned her back on her reflection and stepped into the shower spray. Tears threatened as the water cascaded over her, but she refused to let them fall. She was better than this. Stronger. No matter what life threw at her, she could deal with it. She always did. Little by little, she washed away everything, including the memory of how it had felt to wake up in Gage's arms.

The shower did help. She didn't feel quite as raw as when she'd walked into her room almost an hour before. That was good. With her sister there, she wasn't going to be able to hide out in her room as she'd been doing. She was going to have to go out there and face her sister . . . and Gage. As she thought his name, that feeling of unease began to creep up again.

Squashing the feeling quickly before it had time to take hold, she hurried across the room to her closet. Her hand hovered over one of the many pairs of jeans Charlie had brought over for her, the ones she'd been wearing without thought for the last week and a half, but she stopped herself. She needed distance, something that would make her feel as if she were in charge of her life again. Without second-guessing herself, she pushed the designer jeans and sweaters aside and reached for the navy blue pantsuit she'd brought with her from home.

The fabric felt good against her skin, almost like a security blanket. As much as she hated to admit it, she needed as much normalcy as she could get. Maybe that made her weak, but it was what she needed.

Looking in the mirror, she gave herself a once-over. She'd left her hair down, and debated putting it up in a ponytail or a bun, the way she used to wear it. Gathering her hair, she pulled it up behind her head and held it for all of five seconds before releasing it to fall back down to brush against the lapels of her suit jacket.

She contemplated for another five minutes before she finally decided to leave her hair as it was. No man was worth all this drama—she'd learned that a long time ago. Grabbing her gun and holster, she strapped her weapon to her ankle and headed toward the door.

The hallway was empty when she emerged from her room. Gage's bedroom door was open, but she hadn't closed it when she made her escape earlier. She was tempted to sneak a look inside to see if he was sleeping, but she was almost afraid of what she'd find. What if he was still in there and woke up the moment she peeked in to check on him? She wasn't ready for a confrontation like that . . . especially not in his bedroom.

Tentatively, she walked down the stairs onto the main level. No one was visible, so she decided to go straight to her sister's room first. Before she reached the end of the hall, however, she heard voices coming from downstairs. A few moments later, she heard it again—two distinct voices—one male, one female. Changing direction, she walked back to the staircase.

She paused before she reached the bottom of the stairs. Whether she liked it or not, she needed a few extra seconds before coming face-to-face with Gage again. She had no idea how he'd react. Her defenses had been down, and he'd taken advantage. One side of her was angry that he'd crossed into territory he knew she had no intention of crossing, when she was at her most vulnerable. The other reminded her of the mixed signals she'd been giving him for the last two weeks, one moment pushing him away, the next welcoming his kisses. It had to stop. Tugging on the bottom of her jacket, she thrust her shoulders back and took the final steps.

Gage came into view first, his broad shoulders hunched over slightly and shaking with laughter. His face was in profile, a broad smile lighting up his handsome features. Of its own volition, her body reacted. She felt a tightening in the pit of her stomach, a tingling in her fingers.

Fortunately, her sister took that moment to notice her standing on the other side of the room. "Hey!" Megan hopped down from the stool she'd been sitting on, laid down the cards Rebecca had missed in both their hands, and walked toward her sister.

Rebecca planted what she hoped was a sincere smile on her face as she greeted Megan. "Feeling better?"

"A little," Megan said, sobering.

Reaching out with her right hand, Rebecca brushed the hair out of her sister's eyes. Megan needed her bangs trimmed, it seemed. Normally, her sister kept up her appearance, liking her short, no-fuss hairstyle. When it came to relationships, however, her sister got distracted. She'd put everything into making it work, even if the guy on the receiving end wasn't so generous.

Rebecca felt a wave of sadness wash over her. She wanted to help her sister. She just didn't know how.

"Do you want to join us?" Gage's voice pulled her out of the fog. Her gaze rose to meet his for a split-second before going back to Megan. Rebecca couldn't look at him. Not yet. If she looked at him, she was afraid she'd crumble.

"Yeah," Megan said, chiming in, the smile beginning to return. "We're playing cards. I wanted to play poker, but Gage didn't think you'd approve." As Megan spoke, she pulled her sister toward the table where they'd been sitting.

The urge to glance over at him was there, but she resisted, keeping her focus solely on her sister. "Why would I object to you playing poker?" Rebecca asked, confused. Yes, she was protective of her sister, but—

"Strip poker. I said I doubted your sister would approve of us playing *strip* poker."

Megan pouted playfully. "That's the only fun way to play poker. The regular way is just plain boring."

Ignoring her sister's comment, she addressed the drink Megan had obviously been nursing. "Have you eaten anything?"

"Yep. Gage made me a sandwich," Megan said, taking a sip of her beer.

"Do you want to play with us?" Gage asked again.

Rebecca glanced down at the table. "UNO?"

He smiled, and Rebecca felt her stomach do a little flip. "I figured that was safest."

"You want us to deal you in, Becca?"

"No. I need to go back upstairs for a little while," she said, already moving back toward the stairs. "I'll be back down later. If you're still playing, I'll join you then." She gave her sister a weak smile and then raced upstairs. This was going to be much harder than she thought.

***

Gage watched as Rebecca disappeared up the stairs. He didn't like seeing her back in her stuffy old suits, but he couldn't say he was surprised. She'd been more open to his affections that morning than she'd ever been. He should have known she'd try to compensate. The fact that she'd left her hair down, made him smile. Whether she realized it or not, he'd broken through some of those sky-high walls of hers. Maybe broken through was a little much. Maybe chipped away was more accurate.

"What's going on between you and my sister?" Megan asked, pulling him away from his thoughts.

"I'm grabbing a water. Want some?"

"No. I'm fine. And stop trying to avoid the question," Megan said. The look on her face at that moment reminded him of Rebecca.

He chuckled and squeezed behind the bar for a glass. "I'm not avoiding, but maybe you should ask your sister that question."

"Maybe I will."

"Good," he said, sitting back down at the table. "We gonna finish playing this hand or what?"

"Yeah."

Throughout the rest of the hand, she continued to watch him speculatively, like if she could look hard enough, she might find the answers she wanted.

Megan was the exact opposite of her sister in many ways. She was a lot more outgoing, dressed more like a teenager than a twenty-three-year-old woman, and she was extremely comfortable with her sexuality. Like her sister, however, she also appeared able to beat a subject to death if it would get her what she was after.

Deciding maybe a change of subject was best, he played his next card and asked, "Your sister seems really worried about you."

"Yeah," Megan said, picking at invisible lint on her fitted T-shirt. "Then again, Becca always worries about me."

Even though Gage didn't want to get into the drama, he was interested in learning more about what made Rebecca tick. "And why's that?" he asked, trying to keep it casual.

"Because men suck."

He laughed.

"Sorry," she said, not appearing to be that remorseful.

"It's okay," he said, leaning back in his chair. "So you've had a lot of trouble with men, then?"

Megan took another long pull on her beer, emptying it. "You got another?"

"Yeah, behind the bar in the fridge." He motioned over his shoulder.

She slid off her chair, causing the skirt she was wearing to ride up to indecent places. Other than acknowledging the event, his body didn't react. Megan was an attractive woman, and she'd already made it clear that she'd have no problems having *a little fun* if he was willing. He wasn't. For reasons he didn't quite understand, Rebecca was the only one his body seemed to be interested in, and she was too busy trying to rebuild those walls of hers.

"I always pick the wrong guys." Megan's voice floated up from behind the bar. She reappeared a minute later with another beer in her hand. "I trust them too easily, and they break my heart every time," she said, retaking her seat at the table. "Sometimes I wish I could be more like my sister, but then again, I don't think I could be a monk."

Unfortunately for Gage, he'd chosen that same moment to take a drink of his water and nearly choked. "Your sister's not a monk."

"And how would you know?" Megan asked. Her eyes were wide, innocent. He knew she was anything but.

"Not a chance," Gage said, getting up. "I've got some calls to make. Make yourself at home."

Megan laughed, and he joined in, shaking his head. The next few days should be fun.

On the way to his room, Gage noticed Rebecca's door was open, her room empty. He hadn't seen her on the main level, so he assumed she was outside doing whatever it was she did out there every day. That, and avoiding him, of course.

Shaking off those thoughts for the moment, he shut his door, picked up the phone, and dialed. It rang several times before someone answered.

"Hello?"

"Hey, Ma. How are you?"

"Busy as always. Your father is outside trying to help Trent with some sort of pruning he insists has to be done before winter. I don't know. You know me. I've never been the one with the green thumb. That's all your father and brother."

"I'm sure Trent can handle anything Dad comes up with," he said, smiling. He missed his family more than he'd care to admit most of the time. Trent, who was four years older than him, lived just outside Cincinnati where their parents lived. Out of the four brothers, Trent was the one who typically helped around their parents' house the most, since he lived closest. Gage, being the farthest away, was home the least. He didn't let it get to him often, but there were times such as these when he wished he could be closer to his mom and dad.

"Is everything okay, Gage? You're still coming for Thanksgiving, aren't you?" He could hear the worry in her voice.

"Yeah. I'm still coming, don't worry."

He heard her release a breath she'd been holding. "Good. I'm so looking forward to having all my boys here this year. Elizabeth will be joining us, too. I can't wait until the wedding. She's perfect for Chris."

"Wedding?"

"Your brother didn't tell you?"

"No." He frowned. Even though he hadn't talked to his brother on the phone for about a month, he would have thought that would be something important enough to warrant a phone call.

"Oh." She paused. "Maybe he was waiting to tell you in person since he knows you're coming home for the holiday."

"Maybe." Gage tried not to let it bother him too much. His mom was probably right. Chris was most likely waiting until he could make the announcement in person. It made sense.

"Ma, the reason I called . . . "

"Yes?" she prompted when he didn't continue right away.

"I'm going to be bringing a girl with me. *Two* girls, actually."

She was silent for several long heartbeats. "Gage Lucas Daniels, I don't usually say anything about how you live your life, but I will not have you bringing any of those women you . . . you do what you do with into my house for family time, do you hear me?"

He lowered his head, shame hitting him full force. His mom never said anything about all the women he went through on a regular basis, but he'd known on some level she was disappointed in him because of it. "It's not like that. Rebecca . . . she's my . . . girlfriend, and her sister showed up last night. It's a long story. I don't really know it all, but it looks like she's going to be sticking around for at least a little while. I was hoping to bring Rebecca with me, and I didn't think it would be a good idea to leave her sister here alone." There. He'd said it.

His mother was quiet for a long time, and he began to get nervous. He had no idea what he'd do if she said no.

"You have a girlfriend?"

"Yes." He felt bad lying to his mom, but it couldn't be helped.

"Is it serious?" Gage could hear the excitement in her voice.

"It's still pretty new, but . . . I like her." To most people that would have sounded lame, but his mother knew him better than most.

"I can't wait to meet her, Gage. I'm happy for you."

"Don't get your hopes up, Ma, okay? I mean, we've only been dating a short time and—"

"I don't care. You haven't brought a girl home since high school. Of course she's welcome. And her sister. All the bedrooms will be full, but I'm sure we can figure out something. The couch folds out. I was thinking maybe you and Trent, but—"

"You don't need to do that. I can get us hotel rooms."

"Nonsense. You'll all stay here and that's that. I won't hear of anything else."

He chuckled. "Okay, Ma. Whatever you say."

A few minutes later, he hung up with his mom and placed the receiver back on the nightstand. Thanksgiving should be interesting. For the first time in years, the Daniels clan would all be back under one roof.

Chapter 15

Rebecca was on her way to her sister's room when Gage ambushed her. She'd just come from another patrol of the outside. Normally, she only went out once a day, but she found being outside in the cooling temperatures a better alternative to being in the house trying to avoid him. All her efforts were moot, however, when she turned the corner, and there he was.

"Hi, beautiful." He smiled, causing her insides to do somersaults again.

She put on her game face. "Hello, Mr.—"

He moved fast, wrapping his right arm around her waist, pulling her front flush against his chest. "Oh no you don't. You're not starting with the whole *Mr. Daniels* thing again."

Palms flat against his torso, she tried to push herself off him or at least gain some distance. She didn't get far, and he followed her step for step until her back was against the wall. "I need to go check on my sister." Rebecca hated how weak she sounded, how much power this man had over her. She steadied herself and tried again. "I need to make sure she's okay."

"Megan's fine," he said, crowding her more. He held her firmly in place with his arm while he took his other hand and ran his fingers down the side of her cheek, her neck. She closed her eyes, trying to resist. She *needed* to resist, get back onto stable ground with him.

"Everything's set for this weekend. I talked to my mom and let her know you and your sister were coming with me," he said, his lips brushing against her cheek.

"What . . . what did you tell her . . . them . . . your family?" It was difficult to concentrate when he was this close.

She felt his lips curve into a smile against the side of her face. "I told her I was bringing my girlfriend and her sister. She's very excited to meet you."

"Gage—"

He chuckled and leaned back. "See. That wasn't so hard was it?"

It took her a moment to grasp what he was saying. When she finally did, it reaffirmed what she knew she had to do. She took a deep breath, her chest brushing against his, distracting her from her purpose. "I think . . . I think we need to go over some guidelines . . . for the weekend."

Ignoring her, he asked, "What did you tell your sister about why you're here with me?"

He shifted his position a little to give her some breathing room. Not much, but she'd take what she could get. "She knows I'm here on assignment. I didn't go into detail. She didn't ask." When he didn't say anything more, she took her opening and slid out from between him and the wall.

Once she was a few feet away, she chanced a look back at him. He was standing there with a huge smirk on his face. His cocky grin told her he'd been waiting for her to do just that.

He stood his ground, hands casually in his back pockets, and said, "This weekend . . ."

"Yes?" she asked when he didn't continue.

He chuckled and walked away, leaving her standing in the middle of the hall feeling like a fool. She should have known better than to try to establish rules of conduct with a man like Gage. He'd made it perfectly clear on any number of occasions that he wasn't interested in her rules, especially ones that would create professional distance between them.

Sighing, she walked the remaining steps to her sister's room and knocked, hoping she was loud enough to be heard over the music coming from inside.

Quicker than she thought possible, the volume of the music was lowered, and the door opened. Megan stood in the doorway looking very different than how she had just over an hour ago playing cards downstairs. The woman before her had red, bloodshot eyes from crying, along with a few fresh trails of tears on her cheeks. She also had a smudge of chocolate running from the corner of her mouth where she'd probably stuffed a huge piece in. Megan always went for chocolate when she was feeling down.

Seeing her sister so disheveled, Rebecca opened her arms. Megan fell into them silently, the tears resuming. They stood there for several long minutes before Rebecca maneuvered them back into the room and over to the bed. She brushed the twenty or so mini candy wrappers out of the way and sat them both down.

"You want to talk about it?"

"Not really," Megan mumbled into Rebecca's shoulder.

"Okay." Rebecca continued to hold her sister, trying to comfort her as best she could. She hated seeing her like this.

They were quiet for a long time before Megan began talking, as Rebecca knew she would. "They always seem so great and then . . . am I so horrible? Why can't they love me the way I love them?"

"You're not horrible, Megan. You have a big heart, that's all. One day you'll find someone. The right someone," she clarified.

"You haven't."

Rebecca knew her sister hadn't said it to be cruel, but she cringed anyway.

"Sorry," Megan mumbled.

"No, it's okay. You're right. I haven't."

Megan sat up, wiping the moisture from her cheeks with the backs of her hands. "What about Gage? I like him, and I think he likes you."

Rebecca shook her head. "I told you. He's an assignment."

"Uh-huh. What I saw in the hallway didn't look like he was only an assignment."

She blanched. "It's not . . ." What was she supposed to say? "I'm here to do a job."

"You can't do your job and get some action at the same time?"

Rebecca's eyes widened in shock at her sister's blunt comment.

Megan laughed, her melancholy momentarily forgotten. "Look, I know I'm not always the best judge of character when it comes to guys, but he really seems to like you. What's the harm in having a little fun?"

"It's not professional?"

Her sister waved her protest away. "Becca, I love you, but you're too serious. You need to learn to live a little. Enjoy life. I saw the way you reacted to him. It's not going to hurt anything to have a little fun, and I think tapping that . . . you could have a whole lot of fun."

She wrinkled her nose. "That was crude."

"But true." Megan shrugged and reached for a piece of chocolate, handing it over to her sister. "You like him, right?"

Rebecca sighed. She was through lying. "Yeah. I do."

Megan smiled.

"I know I make some stupid mistakes when it comes to guys, but you know what?" She paused, putting another mini candy bar in her mouth and chewing. "I don't want to have any regrets. Even if I make mistakes along the way, at least I know I tried. I know our parents were screwed up, Becca, but don't let their mistakes keep you from living."

Rebecca looked at her sister, and for the first time she didn't see the teenager she'd all but raised. "When did you grow up and get so smart?"

"Eh," Megan said, bumping her sister's shoulder playfully. "I think it happened somewhere between Texas and Chicago. Mostly, though, I learned it from my big sister."

***

Gage loaded the last of the luggage into the back of his SUV. It was just after two on Wednesday afternoon, and Rebecca and her sister were already in the vehicle waiting on him. Unless they ran into traffic, they would arrive at his parents' house just in time for dinner.

The last two days had been interesting. His original impression of Megan had been accurate. She was the complete one-eighty of her sister. And as he'd gotten to know her, he liked her more and more. She was fun, easygoing, and able to let her hair down when the situation called for it. He'd seen glimpses of sadness every so often, but for the most part, she was trying her best to move on from whatever had happened with her boyfriend.

On Monday evening, Rebecca and Megan had joined him at one of the local hospitals for a charity "meet and greet" the team's PR rep had set up. While he and some of the other guys shook hands and signed autographs, Rebecca had stood off to one side trying her best not to look like a looming bodyguard. Megan, however, had gravitated toward the children's area that had been set up for the younger kids who weren't interested in meeting a pro football player.

Zach and Kenny had stopped by on Monday night after the event, since he'd skipped out on them on Sunday evening. Megan had found the Monopoly game he hadn't seen in years stuffed in the back of one of the closets in his basement, and convinced them all to play. Even Rebecca had joined the game. She'd smiled and laughed right along with everyone else.

Unfortunately, that night was the highlight of the week thus far. On Tuesday morning, after finishing his swim, he had found both Megan and Rebecca with their heads huddled together in the kitchen. Megan greeted him enthusiastically, joking with him, and asking if he owned a pair of swim trunks. They'd bantered back and forth for a few minutes until she'd thrown an apple at his head. He'd caught it, of course, and then took a huge bite out of it before running up the stairs to his room for a shower. During the entire exchange, Rebecca had kept her back to him. The only acknowledgement she'd given to the conversation between him and her sister was the extreme stillness of her body.

For the rest of the day, either Rebecca had been attached to her sister's hip under the guise of supporting her, or she'd made herself scarce. He'd lost count of how many times she'd disappeared outside to "check the perimeter." It got so bad, he was seriously thinking about having cameras installed outside to cover every angle of his property so she wouldn't have an excuse to run from him anymore. Because that was exactly what she was doing. Running.

When he opened the door to get behind the wheel, laughter abruptly stopped. Rebecca, who was seated in the front passenger seat, quickly turned away to look out the window. Megan was in the backseat, and while she'd stopped laughing, a huge smile remained plastered across her face. "Did I miss something funny?"

Megan opened her mouth to speak, but Rebecca cut her off. "No. You didn't miss anything."

"I see," he said, looking doubtful.

Something in Rebecca's voice—that "I don't want to talk about

119

it" tone—made him think they might have been talking about him. Most other subjects Rebecca was open to discuss. Him? Them? She'd placed those two topics off-limits.

He hadn't pushed her on either lately because of her sister, but that would change. They were going to be spending the next three and a half days with his family, and as far as they knew, Rebecca was his girlfriend. There would be expectations, whether she understood them or not. She was going to be effectively cornered, and he was going to love every minute of it.

It took four hours to reach his parents' house. He spent most of that time answering questions. Megan seemed to have an endless supply of them. "Where did you go to school? How long have you been playing professionally? Do you like it? What's the biggest difference between college and pro?"

The questions went on like this for a while before she turned her inquiries to his family. "How many brothers do you have?"

"Three." He decided to go ahead and fill in the blanks for her, because he knew what she'd be asking next. "Paul, he's the oldest and a cop. He has a little girl, Chloe. His wife, Melissa, died in a car wreck when Chloe was still a baby."

"Oh, that's horrible."

"Yeah, he took it pretty hard, but having Chloe helped. She's a pretty amazing kid." He smiled. "One of my biggest fans. She has a jersey with my number on it she wears whenever she watches me play."

"Sounds adorable," Rebecca said, speaking up for the first time in over an hour.

"You have no idea. She's got all her uncles wrapped around her little finger."

They all laughed. He took a moment to glance over to his right at Rebecca. She was smiling, relaxed.

As if sensing his gaze on her, she turned her head. When she saw him staring, she quickly looked away. He stifled a curse and turned his attention back to the road. What exactly was it that had her so fearful? He'd ask Megan, but he doubted she'd tell him. He'd dropped a few probing questions over the last two days, and other than finding out that neither Rebecca nor Megan had much to do with their parents, he hadn't gleaned much. She was a mystery, and he was determined to solve it.

"So what about your other brothers? You said you had three," Megan prompted.

He cleared his throat and tried his best to push his thoughts of Rebecca out of his mind for the moment. "Next in line is Chris. He builds houses and lives up near Dayton. He recently became engaged. His fiancée, Elizabeth, will be there, too."

"Cool."

Gage smiled.

"And last, but not least, is Trent. He owns a landscaping company not far from where my parents live. He'll be the only one there without a woman," Gage said, winking.

She laughed. "Thanks for the tip." She was quiet for a few seconds. "Paul has a girlfriend?"

"No."

"So Trent isn't the only one without someone," she said in a curious tone, clearly confused.

"Oh, Paul's got a lady."

He saw her questioning look through the rearview mirror. "Chloe. His daughter. Paul doesn't date, or hasn't, anyway, since his wife died."

"He must really have loved her."

"He did," Gage said, his voice echoing a remembered sadness. "They were high school sweethearts."

After that, things grew silent and remained somber all the way to Cincinnati. It was only as they were pulling off the highway that Rebecca spoke up. "I don't think we should lie about my profession."

Gage whipped his head to the side to look at her. "I hadn't planned on it."

She went on as if he hadn't spoken. "Being a cop, if your brother senses we're lying, it could lead to bigger questions we don't need. I think it's safer to stick as close to the truth as possible."

"Agreed," he said, turning onto his parents' street.

"Good. We'll just say that we met while I was on assignment in Nashville. That's not a lie."

He laughed but didn't say anything. If she thought they'd get away with such a simple explanation, she was in for a rude awakening. Maybe it was because she and her sister didn't have much to do with their own parents, but he knew his mom was going to want details about how he met the first girl he'd brought home in almost ten years.

Chapter 16

Rebecca had been so lost in her own thoughts that she hadn't paid much attention to their surroundings. Once they were out of Nashville and she was fairly certain they weren't being followed, she'd let her mind drift, only halfheartedly paying attention to Gage and Megan's conversation until they'd begun to talk about his family.

She'd read it all in the background check Hansen had run on him, but cold facts weren't the same as hearing about the people themselves. The fact that his oldest brother Paul was a police detective had always been a concern.

When she'd called to check in with Hansen yesterday, they'd gone over the details of his family again. Hansen thought a cover story, something mundane like her working at a local store Gage frequented, would be a good idea. The problem with that scenario was that if something slipped, if Paul didn't believe the story, he had the resources to conduct his own background check a lot easier than the average person. They might be able to cover that she was an FBI agent, but there would be holes. Holes that would cause more questions. Especially if he discovered she was currently on administrative leave because of a case.

When she'd ended the phone call with her partner, how to play the situation with his family was still up in the air. She'd been thinking about it ever since, trying to decide what was best. Hearing Megan and Gage talking over the past two hours had finally brought her to a decision. A decision regarding his family, at least. What she was going to do about Gage, and her irrational attraction to him, was still undecided.

All the indecision on her part led to her surprised reaction when they pulled into the driveway of an average–sized, two-story suburban house. After seeing the lavishness of Gage's home, she'd assumed his parents' residence would be similar, in size if not in style. She couldn't have been more wrong.

"Wow," Megan piped up from the backseat. "Not what I expected, but I like it."

She turned to scold her sister for being rude, but then she noticed Gage was smiling, and held her tongue.

"Thought it would be bigger, huh?" he said, winking.

"Yeah. Bigger."

Megan laughed and so did Gage.

Having observed the interactions between Gage and Megan the past two days, Rebecca had to admit she didn't quite understand it. She was glad they were getting along so well, but the way they communicated made her feel somewhat left out. It was stupid and completely irrelevant, considering she was there to do a job and nothing more, but it didn't change her gut reaction. It was that response that had her seriously considering what Megan had suggested. Should she have an affair with him? Have a little fun and get it out of her system?

Gage turned off the vehicle, pulled the keys out of the ignition, and placed them in his pocket before her sister settled down enough for him to continue his explanation. "I was sixteen when my parents bought this place. Once I was signed, I offered to buy them something bigger. They wouldn't hear of it. And my parents—especially my mom . . ." He shook his head. "Once she sets her mind to something, it would be easier to move a mountain than get her to budge."

"I think I'm going to like your mom." Megan smiled. He smiled back, but instead of responding, he stepped out of the vehicle and went to retrieve their luggage.

Rebecca and Megan followed, pulling their jackets tighter as the cooler air hit them. Not only had they traveled almost four hours due north, but it was just after six in the evening and the sun was going down. The temperature must have fallen at least thirty degrees since they'd set out from Nashville that afternoon.

Just as they all started toward the front of the house, the door opened and an older woman stood framed by the doorway. She looked to be in her late fifties or early sixties. There was quite a bit of grey in her hair, but hints of the brown lingered. She had to be Gage's mother.

Rebecca's conclusion was confirmed a moment later when Gage walked up to the woman and picked her up, her feet dangling in the air.

"Hey, Ma!" He smiled, setting her back on the ground.

She swatted his arm, but the smile never left her face. "Stop your foolishness and get in the house already. It's downright chilly out here." He reached down and picked up the luggage again, slinging his duffle bag over his shoulder. Taking a step back, he motioned for her and Megan to go on ahead.

Once inside, Rebecca stopped for a moment to take in her surroundings. The inside of the house was a lot like the exterior. There were no over-the-top signs of wealth or extravagance. Everything was just as she would have assumed it would be for a retired couple living in the suburbs. There was no grand entryway, just a modest-sized living room with two couches and two overstuffed chairs. It couldn't have been more different from Gage's home.

"Ma said you were bringing someone, but I didn't believe it." The new arrival looked to be in his late twenties, early thirties. He was tall, about six feet two inches, with the same dark brown hair and eyes as Gage. Rebecca knew this had to be one of his brothers.

"Can I take your coats?" his mother asked, drawing Rebecca's attention.

"Yes, thank you, Mrs. Daniels."

She waved one hand in the air as Rebecca and Megan took off their coats and handed them to her. "None of that *Mrs. Daniels* nonsense. Call me Mary."

"Thanks, Mary," Megan said.

Rebecca remained silent.

She was busy watching as more people slowly filed into the room, filling up the space. Three additional men had entered, one older, two about the same age as the first. Gage's father and the other two brothers, she assumed. There was also a woman and a little girl. Even though the two were standing together, she had to conclude from what she knew that they were Elizabeth, Gage's brother Chris's fiancée, and Paul's daughter, Chloe. Seeing them all huddled in the small space, observing them, was a little overwhelming.

Everyone stood staring at each other until one of his brothers spoke up. "Well? Are you going to introduce us or not?"

Gage smiled. "Getting impatient there, Trent?"

"Oh, stop it, you two," his mother said. "I'm sure your brother was just about to introduce us properly to these two lovely ladies he brought with him."

The gentle scolding from their mother appeared to do the trick, and they both fell silent as Gage walked to stand behind them.

"I'd like you all to meet Rebecca and Megan Carson," he said, motioning to each one in turn. He then pointed out his family members one by one. "You've already kinda been introduced to my mom, Mary." She smiled. "This is my dad, Mike. My brothers Trent, Paul, and Chris. Elizabeth, Chris's fiancée." She saw Chris's face change when Gage introduced Elizabeth and wondered if something was going on there. It was not the time to bring that up, though. She didn't know these people. "And this little one . . ." Gage said, stepping around Megan and lowering himself to a crouch. The little girl took the invitation and launched herself into her uncle's arms. "This is Chloe."

"Hiya, Uncle Gage," she said shyly.

"Hey, Princess."

Rebecca watched the exchange and felt something tug at her chest. She didn't get the chance to ponder it, though, as the room suddenly became very active.

It was as if someone had blown a whistle giving everyone permission to move around and talk at the same time. Paul, Trent, Chris, and Elizabeth all surrounded Gage as he stood up with Chloe in his arms. The little girl had to weigh close to fifty pounds, but he held her as if she were no more than a five-pound sack of potatoes. Rebecca had known he was strong. He'd carried her up the stairs to his bedroom without difficulty. It was something that she was very much trying to forget.

Mary and her husband, Mike, stood over in the corner out of the way, both with huge smiles on their faces. From what Rebecca knew about the family, it was rare they came together like this. She'd never been a parent, and heaven knew hers were not ones to go by, but she had to imagine seeing their whole family together was a special sight.

Trent looked over at Rebecca and Megan from where he stood beside Gage before walking over to them. He held out his hand in welcome. "I hope it's not too overwhelming for you. Elizabeth says we can be a bit much sometimes."

"I think it's great," Megan said joyfully. Her sister had always been more of a social butterfly. Rebecca preferred sticking to the shadows. Maybe that was why she enjoyed her job so much, and why she and Hansen worked well as partners—he was a lot more of a people person than she was.

Seeming to notice her silence, Trent turned his attention to Rebecca. "Are you always this quiet?" he asked. His tone was light, joking.

She could tell he was trying to put her at ease. It wasn't working. She felt out of place. Somewhere along the line, personal and professional had gotten blurred. She didn't know what the proper response was anymore, the right reaction.

Gage turned his head, looked over at her, and frowned. He set Chloe's feet on the floor, releasing her, and crossed over to where Rebecca stood. "What are you over here saying to my girlfriend?" he asked his brother as he wrapped his arms around Rebecca's waist, pulling her back against his chest. His warmth comforted her, and she took a deep breath. She could do this.

"Oh!"

At Trent's exclamation, Rebecca glanced up at him, wondering what had caused his reaction. He was looking at her. She also noticed that the rest of his family was staring at her—the both of them—eyes wide.

"What?" Gage asked, pulling her even closer, molding her body to his as much as possible through the clothing they wore. The hard muscles of his chest and arms pressed against her back as he stood behind her, his hands resting on her stomach.

"I just . . ." Trent paused and swallowed nervously. "It's just . . ."

"We thought Megan was your girlfriend," Paul stated, and by the faces of the rest of his family, they agreed. For some reason, that stung.

"Why would you think that?" Gage demanded.

"Megan's just . . ." Chris didn't finish.

"Never mind," Mary said, stepping in front of her son. "Gage, why don't you show Rebecca to your room. You can put all your luggage up there for now, at least until after dinner. Megan, would you like to help Elizabeth and me in the kitchen? Dinner should be ready soon, and we still have a few items to put out."

"Yeah. Okay. Sure," Megan answered, looking over at her sister.

Rebecca tried to put on a brave face, letting Megan know it was all right. She must have failed, because she saw her sister frown.

"Come on," Gage whispered in her ear, pulling her attention away from Megan. Without waiting for her to respond, he took her hand, quickly grabbed the luggage he'd deposited on the floor earlier, led her around his family, and up a flight of stairs.

***

Gage was irritated with Trent for making Rebecca feel uncomfortable. Sure, she wasn't the type of woman he normally went for, but so what? Trent didn't have to point that out.

Taking his mother's suggestion, Gage quickly gathered their things and led Rebecca upstairs to his childhood bedroom. His old room was still covered in pictures and trophies from his high school days. It was almost like stepping back in time.

He was the only one of his brothers who'd ever lived in this house. Trent and Chris had already been off to college by the time their parents had moved. Paul had been well on his way to establishing a life in Indianapolis with Melissa. They'd just gotten engaged and bought a house of their own.

Once the door was shut behind them and they were safely inside his bedroom, Gage threw the luggage on the double bed and gathered her into his arms. "Are you okay, beautiful?"

She didn't answer.

Leaning back so that he could see her face, he noticed the blank mask was back. She was looking at him but not, at the same time. He didn't like it. "Look, I'm sorry about what Trent said. He didn't mean anything by it."

"It doesn't matter."

"Of course it does." Gage didn't understand why what had happened downstairs irritated him as much as it did, but he was going with it.

"No. It doesn't." She tried to back away from him, but he followed her step for step until she was pressed up against the door. There wasn't anywhere else to go. "We should get back downstairs."

He could hear a hint of desperation in her voice. No matter what she said, she was as aware of him as he was of her. She wanted him. He just had to figure out how to get past that brain of hers that was always overthinking things.

Deciding to go with his instincts, he cupped her face with his hands, tilting up her head until her lips were right there, ripe for the taking. He took.

To his surprise, she didn't fight it nearly as much as he thought she would. There was only a moment's hesitation from her before she released a sigh and kissed him back. She wrapped her arms around his neck, holding him as their lips and tongues moved together. He had no idea how long they stood there, kissing. It seemed that whenever he had her in his arms, time and everything else outside her failed to register. Somewhere along the line he heard a noise out in the hall. If he didn't end it soon, they were going to be interrupted.

He released her mouth, trailing his lips down her jaw and neck before giving her a gentle bite near the collar of her shirt. She dug her fingers into his neck. He chuckled. "As much as I'd love to continue this, beautiful, we really should get back downstairs."

Her body went rigid under his hands, and she dropped her arms to her side.

"What's wrong?" he asked. "Talk to me."

"Your family is never going to believe we're a couple."

"Sure they will."

She gave him a skeptical look.

"Why do you think they won't?" he asked, continuing to touch her. Even at that moment, standing there having a serious conversation with her, he was thinking how soft her skin was and wondering how she felt where he'd yet to touch.

"You heard your brother. I'm not . . ." She took a deep breath, causing her chest to rise and fall beneath her sweater. His lower half

129

took notice. He tried very hard to ignore it. "I'm not your type."

"That's where you're wrong. You're *exactly* my type." He brushed his lips against hers. "Shall I show you again?" he asked, giving her a half smile.

She laughed. "No."

"Because I'm more than willing to make the sacrifice," he said, half joking, pulling her body more firmly against his.

"Didn't you say something about needing to get back downstairs?"

He sighed, stepped away, and reached for the door handle. Before opening it, he turned his head and met her gaze. "Later, then."

Chapter 17

He could tell she was nervous as they walked back down the stairs to where his family was waiting, even though she was doing her best to hide it. Over the last three weeks, he'd learned her tells. She held her back drill-sergeant straight and her jaw set in an overly serious pose. He loved to tease her, yes, but he didn't want her to feel uncomfortable around his family. Not only would they notice, but he also wanted them to get along. He wasn't going to question why that was.

When they reached the bottom of the stairs, he paused and turned around, facing her. She was two steps higher than he was, so he had to look up. "You ready for this?" he asked, taking hold of her hands.

"Yes," she said, sounding a lot more confident than he knew she really was.

He smiled and pulled her arms around his waist. "Just relax and be yourself." She nodded but didn't speak. Realizing that was all he was going to get, he changed his hold to take one of her hands, and led them both into the dining room.

His family was gathered around the large table. Some were standing, but most had already taken a seat and were very obviously waiting for the okay from their mom before digging in.

Gage recalled times when they were younger where each one of them had tried to help themselves before their mom had given the go-ahead. Each time, no matter which one of them it was, they got a hasty reminder of manners when their mom took whatever serving utensil was nearby and gave their fingers a solid slap. Man, had that stung. Even after watching his brother's endure their mother's wrath, he'd still tested his luck. Now that they were older, they knew better.

One by one, the family noticed their arrival. They all glanced up from whatever they were doing, including Trent, who looked properly apologetic. He gave his brother a small smile, letting him know there weren't any hard feelings. Trent nodded.

Deciding it was probably best to ignore the elephant in the room for the time being, he walked over to the two unoccupied chairs on the right with Rebecca in tow. He released her hand and pulled her chair out for her. She paused, glancing down at it as if it might bite her, before taking a seat. He waited until she was settled before taking his place beside her. Everyone followed suit.

His mom had fixed stuffed chicken breasts for dinner, with rice, two different kinds of vegetables, rolls, and a large bowl of mixed fruit. It was a lot of food, but he knew from experience there'd be little to none left by the time they were finished. They all dug in, and conversation, at least for the time being, was forgotten as they filled their plates and bellies.

Slowly, conversation resumed. Megan sat at the other end of the table talking with Trent, Paul, and Chloe. The little girl seemed fascinated by Rebecca's sister, questioning her nonstop. He heard Paul remind his daughter several times to eat her food, since she kept getting distracted. Megan seemed completely comfortable with the attention. At one point, trying to get Chloe to eat more of her food, she'd made a game of it with her. It had worked better than her father's constant reminders.

Rebecca, on the other hand, ate quietly beside him. She laughed and smiled at the appropriate times, but he could tell it was forced. Apparently, so could his mother.

"So, Rebecca," his mom said. "Tell us a little about yourself. What do you do for a living?"

This got the attention of the entire table. All other talking ceased, with the exception of Megan and Chloe, as everyone waited for Rebecca's answer.

Gage watched Rebecca's defenses go up again. He placed his hand on her leg to show his support. "I'm an FBI agent," she said, without missing a beat.

"How did you two meet?" Paul asked. Gage could see the wheels turning in his brother's head from where he sat.

She covered the hand Gage had placed on her leg with her own. He laced their fingers together as she answered his brother. "I was working on a case in Nashville that brought me to the football stadium. The team was there practicing."

"Sounds like you were both in the right place at the right time."

Paul let the subject drop, but Gage knew it wasn't over. His brother wasn't rude, and their mom wouldn't be happy if he interrogated Gage's girlfriend at the dinner table. More questions would come later.

In order to curb any further inquiry for a while, he turned his attention to Chris. "I hear congratulations are in order."

"Yeah," Chris said, looking a little guilty. "Ma told me she'd let the cat out of the bag. We were going to wait and announce it this weekend, but then Jan found out, and she shared the news with Ma before we could stop her."

"Why you'd keep news like that quiet for so long is a mystery to me," their mom said, exasperated.

"We thought something as important as this should be done in person, that's all."

Jan was an old family friend, and Chris's landlord. Their mom and Jan kept in regular contact, so why Chris thought he'd be able to keep in under wraps, Gage had no idea. As the one who began this conversation though, Gage thought maybe he should take some of the pressure off his brother. He picked up his glass. "I don't know you that well, Elizabeth. Hopefully, after this weekend, that will change. Either way, I haven't seen my brother this happy in a while, so welcome to the family."

Everyone picked up their glasses as well and joined in the impromptu toast. Even Chloe raised her pink plastic cup in the air, a huge smile plastered on her face.

"Have you two decided on a date?" Paul asked.

"We're thinking March," Elizabeth said. "The weather should be warming up by then. Chris also thought it would be before training camp started for you, Gage, and that hopefully, you'd be able to come?"

Gage smiled. "Camp's not till April. Just let me know the date as soon as you have it, and I'll make sure to clear my schedule."

Both Chris and Elizabeth smiled, and Chris leaned over to give her a soft kiss. Gage noticed his mother's silent sigh as she watched the exchange. He was happy for his brother. Chris's first marriage had been a nightmare almost from the start. Even before things had gone south with his brother's ex, he couldn't remember Chris ever beaming like he was at that moment. His whole face radiated his happiness.

***

As she sat and listened to Chris and Elizabeth's wedding plans, Rebecca began to relax a little. She'd known the personal questions would come, and she'd tried to prepare herself. With any luck, she'd been convincing enough. She would be surprised if that was the end of it, though. From the little she'd read on Paul, the man was good at his job, and that usually meant not settling for half answers. No, she knew that either she or Gage would have more questions to answer before the weekend was finished.

Gage continued to touch her on and off throughout dessert, even though he'd released her hand shortly after the toast. Something about having him there, knowing he was supporting her, had given her the boost she needed to answer his mother and brother's questions. She still didn't understand this hold he seemed to have on her, but she was quickly coming to the conclusion that fighting it, no matter how logical it may be, was a losing battle. For whatever reason, fate had thrown them together. At least for a while.

She allowed her gaze to linger on his form at her left. The memory of their kiss upstairs made her lips tingle again. No matter how much she tried to deny it, she wanted him. Even if there was no future for them, Megan was right. Why shouldn't she have some fun? She'd been responsible all her life. Of course, she'd be responsible with Gage as well, but she could do that and enjoy herself at the same time, right?

He caught her gawking at him and smirked. She was encouraging him, and for once, she didn't care.

The evening seemed to drag on forever. After the table was cleared, the men gathered in the kitchen to do the dishes, while the women went into the living room with coffee. Talk continued about the wedding. Even Megan joined in, offering her opinion on flowers and tuxedos.

Rebecca was only half paying attention. It didn't matter anyway. She wouldn't be around come spring. Who knew where she'd be in March? Her job took her all over the United States. Of course, that all depended on whether or not she ever got clearance from psych.

Eventually, the men joined them in the living room. Gage came to sit beside her on the couch, placing his arm behind her and resting it on her shoulders. He pulled her closer, and she let him. She wasn't quite sure how she was going to act on her epiphany exactly, considering they were going to be staying at his parents' house the next few days, but she wasn't too worried about that. It was only a matter of time before Gage would initiate something again. When he did, she would go with it.

Everyone was so caught up in conversation, they didn't realize the late hour until Chloe began rubbing her eyes. Paul checked his watch, and a few others did the same. It was already after ten.

Paul stood, Chloe hanging tightly to her father's neck. "If you'll excuse us, I need to get someone here ready for bed."

Paul began walking out of the room. "Meg . . . mmm." Chloe whined against her father's shirt.

He stopped.

"What? You have to turn your head so I can understand you, sweetheart."

"Meg . . . in." This time she twisted her body and reached for what she wanted. Megan.

"Megan's going to stay down here and talk with everyone else. We need to get you a bath and into bed."

The little girl shook her head. "Sleep with Meg . . . mmm."

Paul glanced over his shoulder at his mom. Then at Megan. "Um . . ."

"I don't mind," Megan said, answering the unspoken question. "I mean, I don't know where I'm sleeping, but it's fine with me if she wants to share."

Mary stood. "I was going to let you and Chloe have the pullout downstairs and let Megan have the couch in here."

He nodded. "I'll take the couch, then, and they can have the downstairs," he said, then turned to Megan. "If that works for you."

"Works for me." She smiled.

"Happy now?" Paul asked his daughter. "We'll go get your bath and get you ready for bed. Then I'll put you downstairs, and Megan can join you when she's ready." The little girl began to whine. "Stop." He didn't raise his voice, but it was enough for Chloe to end her fussing. Before she could say anything more, Paul turned back around and walked up the stairs.

"Well, that was interesting," Chris said.

"Yes, it was. I've never seen Chloe get so attached that quickly before," Mary added.

"She's a great kid." Megan smiled.

"You'll get no arguments from anyone here. Now, if we could only get a few more grandchildren just like her," Mike said, looking pointedly at his sons.

"And on that note . . ." Trent stood. "I should be heading out."

"You're not staying here tonight?" Gage asked.

"Nope. I figured the house was full enough. Plus, I have to run and check on a sprinkler system that's been malfunctioning, first thing. No reason I need to be waking any of you up at the crack of dawn."

Trent leaving sparked another round of activity. There were hugs given by each of the Daniels family, including Elizabeth. The only two left out of the commotion were Rebecca and Megan.

After good-byes were said and Trent was on his way, Chris leaned over and whispered something in Elizabeth's ear, causing her to giggle. "Um. I think we're going to call it a night as well. I know how this house is in the mornings."

Then Gage was standing. "That's not a bad idea." He reached out his hand, encouraging Rebecca to join him. She took it and stood.

Mary, still over by the door, shook her head, smiling. "Megan, why don't I show you where you're going to be sleeping. There's a bathroom down there where you can get changed."

"Sure. I just need to get my things . . ."

"My room is the first door on your left," Gage answered her unspoken question.

"Great! Thanks." Megan disappeared up the stairs.

Chris and Elizabeth were next.

"Do you two have everything you need up in your room, Gage?" Mary asked. Rebecca hadn't been sure of the sleeping arrangements, but it was apparent that Mary had no issues with her boys sleeping with their significant others.

"Yeah, I think we're good, Ma. Thanks."

They moved toward the stairs in time to see Megan on her way down. When she saw them, she gave Rebecca a sly smile. "Don't do anything I wouldn't do," she whispered as she passed them.

Gage heard her and chuckled.

Rebecca ignored her.

She continued to hold onto his hand as they ascended the stairs to his room. Once inside she released her hold on him, not really sure what to do with herself. They would sleep, yes, but what about *other* stuff? Would he try something? She wasn't sure. He was cocky and confident, but she'd also noticed he was more subdued around his family. Maybe that was because they all seemed to have big personalities. She could only imagine what it would have been like growing up in a house when they were all teenagers.

He walked to the bed and opened his duffle bag. Removing a smaller bag, he tossed the larger one into the corner. "Let me check and see if Paul's done in the bathroom."

She stood, motionless, waiting for his return. It was silly she was so nervous. It wasn't as if she'd never been with a man before. It wasn't as if she was going to *be* with Gage. All she knew for sure was they would be spending the night in the same bed and sleeping together, actual *sleeping* together, which was something they'd already done.

Gage was only gone about thirty seconds. "He's drying her off now. They should be finished in a minute or two if you want to get your things. The bathroom's right across the hall. I'm going to run downstairs and use the one on the first floor."

"Okay." She knew that sounded lame but wasn't sure what else to say.

As promised, Paul walked out of the bathroom less than five minutes later with a very sleepy Chloe cradled in his arms. "All yours," he said as he walked past.

"Thanks." Rebecca grabbed her suitcase and hurried into the bathroom. She went through her nightly routine as quickly as possible, not sure how long it would take Gage downstairs, or if someone else might need to use the bathroom after her.

When she emerged fifteen minutes later, she didn't feel any more confident than she had before she'd gone in. She was also fairly certain Gage would already be in the room waiting for her. Taking a deep breath to steady herself, she walked back down the hall and into his room.

The sight that greeted her almost had her turning around, running back down the hall, and locking herself in the bathroom. Gage stood turned away from her, looking at something on one of his bookshelves, in nothing but his underwear. Her mind was suddenly bombarded with images of her hands on his very firm backside, pressing him closer. The mental picture caused her to blush. She turned her back to him before he caught her staring.

"Hey, beautiful," he said, walking toward her. His arms slipped around her waist, pulling her against him.

"Hi," she whispered. With only his underwear and her thin pajamas between them, there wasn't much she didn't feel of his body, even though it seemed to be behaving itself for the most part.

He brushed her hair away from her neck and rested his chin on her shoulder. "You ready for bed?"

"Yes." Her response squeaked out, and she wondered why, just this once, couldn't she be confident like Megan?

To her surprise, Gage backed away, pulling her with him.

When he reached the bed, he released her, pulled the covers back, and invited her to get in before strolling to the other side and slipping under the sheets himself. It was a double bed, smaller than the one she slept in at his house, but there was still a decent amount of room. Or there would have been if he had wasted any time closing the distance between them and wrapping her securely in his arms.

"Goodnight, Rebecca," he said, kissing the back of her neck.

She sighed, allowing herself to enjoy the feeling of him surrounding her. Closing her eyes, she placed her arm over his and intertwined their fingers. "Goodnight, Gage."

Chapter 18

He was holding something soft and warm in his hand. It took him longer than it should to figure out what it was, but in his defense, he'd just come out of one of the deepest sleeps of his life. Opening his eyes, he was greeted with the top of Rebecca's head. Sometime in the middle of the night, they'd adjusted their positions to where he was slightly above her, her head resting just below his chin. From there, he had a clear view of his hand as it cradled her breast. It was the first time he'd touched that part of her, and it only fueled his desire to strip off her clothing and continue his exploration without anything between them.

His lower half was already awake, and his current train of thought wasn't helping. He needed to move. No matter how much he wanted Rebecca, this wasn't the time. His mom was an early riser, and since the sun was already peeking through the curtains, she was most likely awake. His mom might have been open-minded about him being an adult and having his girlfriend sleep in his bed with him, but he didn't think she would be very happy about hearing her son and his girlfriend going at it.

Rebecca moved in her sleep, unconsciously rubbing against his erection. He groaned and held his breath, willing his brain to override his body. One thing he knew for certain. He had to get out of there.

Gently, he removed his hold on her breast before easing away from her body. He was almost free and clear when she rolled over and her hand landed on his thigh, just inches from where he was aching for her. Closing his eyes, he took a deep breath and removed her hand. The woman had no idea what she did to him. He threw on a pair of jeans and practically ran from the room.

Paul was sitting on the couch, rubbing the sleep out of his eyes, when Gage reached the bottom of the stairs. He looked up. "Morning."

"Morning."

"Ma's in the kitchen starting breakfast. I heard her moving around in there a few minutes ago. Chloe asked for pancakes this morning, and you know how Ma can't seem to tell her no."

Gage smiled. "True. But she can pretty much ask any of us for anything and we'd be hard-pressed to deny her."

"Yes, I know," he said in mock disgust before grinning. "It's hard for me to say no to her sometimes. Being her dad, however, means I sort of have to."

"Being her uncle means I don't." Gage chuckled.

Paul's chest shook in a silent laugh.

"I'm going to see if I can swipe some coffee. You want some?"

"Please."

Gage left his brother in the living room and walked into the kitchen. His mom was at the sink rinsing blueberries. She looked over her shoulder and smiled. "Coffee's over there," she said, motioning to the coffeepot on the counter.

"Thanks," he said, taking two mugs from the cabinet and filling them. "Paul says you're making pancakes."

His mom never missed a beat as she spread a towel out on the counter and laid a strainer full of berries on top. Then she reached in a lower cabinet and retrieved a large mixing bowl. "That's right. Everything should be ready in about fifteen minutes. That way I can just pop them on the griddle when everyone's ready."

He walked over and placed a kiss on her cheek. "Thanks, Ma."

She blushed and shooed him away.

Laughing, he picked up the coffee he'd left on the counter and walked back into the living room. Paul was still in the same position. His brother wasn't a morning person. "Here," Gage said, handing Paul his coffee.

"Thanks." He took a sip, cringing a little. "It's been a while since I've had straight black coffee."

"Since when? You always used to drink it black."

A haunted look crossed Paul's face for a moment before he shook it off. "Not for a while."

Although he was curious, Gage didn't pursue it. A lot of things had changed for his brother after his wife died. From the look that had crossed Paul's face, this was probably one of them. Why coffee was one, though, didn't make a whole lot of sense.

"So how'd you and Rebecca sleep?"

Gage took the opportunity to take a drink before he answered. "Good."

"She still asleep?"

"Yeah."

He nodded. "How long have you two been dating? Ma said it was fairly new."

"Doing some digging last night were you?"

"No." Gage quirked his eyebrow, and Paul chuckled, shaking his head. "Okay. Maybe a little. You have to admit, you dating an FBI agent is a little suspicious." Paul blew out a hard breath of air. "You dating *anyone* is suspicious, actually."

Gage grabbed the pillow behind him and lobbed it at his brother. Paul easily batted it away.

"I date."

"What you do isn't dating, and you know it."

Gage shrugged. "Okay. I'll give you that. I don't usually date in the traditional sense."

"Which brings us back to . . ."

He leaned forward, elbows on his knees. "We've been seeing each other for a few weeks."

Paul whistled. "That *is* new."

"Yeah."

"And she's important enough to bring home?"

The question should have been simple, and in reality, it was. "Yes."

Gage didn't try to explain it to his brother. He couldn't explain it to himself. Even though this was supposed to be a ruse, for him it was quickly becoming anything but. Rebecca was unlike any woman he'd ever met. She was beautiful, sexy, and completely and utterly unaffected by his pseudo-celebrity status. No matter what he threw at her, she gave it back to him, even when he was messing with her.

The woman knocked his legs out from under him without even trying.

"Okay," Paul said, bringing Gage back to reality.

"Okay?"

"Yeah. Okay. If that smile on your face is anything to go by, I'm happy for you. It's about time you found someone."

"Thanks," Gage said, holding his mug in both hands.

They sat in silence, drinking their coffee and listening to the rest of the house come awake. It had been a long time since he'd shared a moment like that with his eldest brother. In fact, he couldn't remember the last time they'd talked like this. When he'd been in college, maybe? The eight-year age difference meant that Paul had already been out of the house well before Gage had become a teenager. Since then, they hadn't had many opportunities for things like this.

Sitting back on the couch, he watched as, one by one, everyone made an appearance downstairs. Chloe, the complete opposite of her father, bounced with energy first thing in the morning. She ran up from the basement, a sleepy-looking Megan trailing behind her, and went directly to her father. Jumping in his lap, she proceeded to tell him all about her night sleeping next to Megan.

"You look like you could use some coffee."

Gage's observation was met with a yawn from Megan. "You have no idea."

Gage laughed. "One coffee, coming right up."

When he returned, Chloe had moved on to tell her dad about the animal-shaped pancakes Grandma was making her. Gage loved his niece to pieces and would do anything for her, but he had no idea how Paul did it. Being a parent was difficult enough—being a single parent was another thing entirely.

The four of them were already at the breakfast table scarfing down blueberry pancakes and sausage when Rebecca joined them. Her hair, even though it looked as if she'd tried to tame it, stuck up in abnormal places. He'd never seen her look so disheveled, and he only wished he'd had more to do with it.

She sat down beside him. "Morning."

He leaned over and kissed her. "Good morning."

She looked stunned for a moment, then blushed and glanced down at her empty plate.

Chris and Elizabeth appeared in the doorway before Gage could say anything more to Rebecca. They were quickly followed by his dad.

Within minutes, his mom had a large stack of fresh pancakes on the table. "Dig in."

***

Rebecca was surprised when she woke up alone in bed that morning. She'd been sure Gage would take advantage of the situation. Disappointment washed over her, but she tried not to dwell on it. Maybe he'd needed to get up and use the bathroom or something.

Not sure what the proper etiquette was for waking up in the morning at your boyfriend's parents' house, she put on her jeans and a sweater, along with her bra. Taking it off the night before had been a whim, something she'd rationalized after her decision to give in to her attraction to him. Going downstairs *sans* bra with a houseful of his brothers was not something she even wanted to contemplate. She only hoped her sister was being as conservative. Rebecca wasn't getting her hopes up. Megan didn't always follow convention.

Rebecca found Gage sitting at the table with Paul, Megan, and Chloe. They were already eating. It all smelled delicious, and her mouth began to water. After a big dinner the night before, she shouldn't have been hungry, but she was.

When she took a seat beside Gage, she hadn't expected him to kiss her. She'd been nervous about acting the part of his girlfriend, but somehow it was working. They were supposed to be a new couple, and for the most part, they were acting that way. The problem was, it wasn't feeling all that much like acting. She tried not to ponder that too much. Whatever she and Gage had or didn't have would end with her assignment, simple as that. He had his life, and she had hers.

The rest of the family joined them at the table, and soon everyone was eating and chatting about their lives. Halfway through the meal, Trent joined them. No one missed a beat, automatically including him in the current topic of conversation.

It was a relaxing morning. This whole family thing was new to her, but she was finding she liked it. Mary and Mike Daniels clearly loved each one of their sons. They were active in the conversations, showing concern and excitement where it was needed. Chloe's adoration for her grandparents was clear as day on her face every time she looked up at them and smiled. Rebecca felt a pang of something deep in her chest watching the exchanges. This was what it was supposed to be like. *This* was family.

Once everyone had their fill, they worked together to clean up. One by one, each person disappeared to grab a shower. She was in awe of how smoothly everything ran. Someone would return, freshly showered and dressed, and someone else would go and do the same.

While the synchronized rotating shower thing was taking place, they were each given assignments by Mary. The coming and going of individuals didn't seem to matter to the flow of the work. Rebecca noted how Mary divided the chores. She, Elizabeth, and Mary were at the kitchen counter putting together the turkey, stuffing, and several casseroles. Paul and Chloe, who insisted Megan help her, were given the task of making the pumpkin and apple pies. Gage and Trent were banished to the living room to peel potatoes, while Mike and Chris chopped up the ingredients for a salad and some fruit. Rebecca had never seen so much food, but after watching them all eat dinner the previous night and breakfast that morning, she had little doubt it would all get eaten.

The whole time they were working together Rebecca expected to be interrogated. It never happened. Mary talked to both women, but it was mostly casual things. Nothing that was overly intrusive.

Two hours later, the turkey was in the oven and all the prep was done. She stood off to the side, not really sure what to do next. She had showered, changed, done her hair and makeup, and had helped with dinner, all before noon. What else was there for her to do?

Arms slipped around her waist, surprising her. She must have jumped, at least a little, because she heard his deep chuckle in her ear. "What are you thinking about over here, beautiful?"

She closed her eyes and sighed, deciding to enjoy the feel of him. "Just wondering what's next. I'm assuming dinner isn't for a while yet."

He turned her around to face him. "You're serious."

Rebecca frowned.

"You really have no idea what comes next?"

"No," she said, feeling as if she were missing something.

"Thanksgiving wasn't really a family event at my house."

The look on his face made her pull back a little. She hadn't meant to tell him that.

He held her tighter. "One of these days I'm going to ask you to explain that." She opened her mouth to speak, but he cut her off. "Football. That's what comes next." He pointed to the living room where everyone was gathering. "The pre-game show will start in about . . ." Gage checked his watch. "Twenty minutes."

"Oh."

He looked her up and down, appraising.

Suddenly, they were moving. He'd picked her feet up off the floor and carried her out of the room and around the corner. Then they were alone, in the laundry room. "What—?"

Her protest was silenced when he covered her mouth with his. She didn't resist, giving into the kiss and the feel of his soft lips.

Once he realized she wasn't going to fight him, his grip on her eased. Instead of holding her in place, he caressed her back with his hands, slipping one underneath her shirt. His hands felt amazing on her body, causing her to lean into him even more and pull him closer. Even knowing his family was a mere twenty feet away, she wanted more.

He appeared to agree with her. Gage lifted her up on top of the washer and wrapped her legs around his waist. She felt the press of his body against her as they continued to kiss. Their tongues battled as their hands roamed. Her whole body felt like it was overheating.

"Gage, have you seen—"

Gage and Rebecca froze.

"Oops. Sorry." The smug smile on Trent's face said he wasn't sorry in the least. "I'll just . . ." He backed out of the room, his shoulders vibrating with mirth.

Rebecca lowered her head and turned away, embarrassed. She tried to unlock her legs from around Gage's waist, but he wouldn't let her. "Are you all right?" he whispered, kissing her neck.

"Your brother just caught us kissing."

Gage laughed. "Yep."

She looked at him. "That doesn't bother you?"

He shook his head. "Nope. Why would it bother me that my brother caught me making out with my girlfriend? Do you know how many times I've walked in on my brothers in a similar situation?"

"You've caught your brothers kissing girls in your parents' house?"

He began rubbing his hands up and down her back again. She could tell he was trying to soothe her, but it was distracting. "Not me personally, no. Chris caught Paul in his bed with Melissa once, though."

"Having sex?"

"Yep. Chris said he didn't see much, but it was enough for him to blackmail Paul into letting Chris use Paul's car for the weekend. That and some good ribbing for a while." He relayed the story with good humor.

"Paul wasn't upset?"

"Of course he was." Gage laughed, finally stepping back to allow her to slide off the washer. He didn't release her waist, however, guiding her feet back to the floor. "Trent came home about half an hour later and found them wrestling in the backyard. If not for the threat of our parents coming home, it may have actually come to blows. Paul was pretty protective of Melissa. He was afraid Ma would find out and tell her parents."

"Didn't they like Paul?"

Gage shrugged. "Not so much they didn't like him. More that Melissa and Paul were only eighteen and they didn't want her tied down so young."

"Eighteen *is* young."

"Yeah, but Paul says he knew he was going to marry her, even back then."

Rebecca smiled. "I can't imagine loving someone like that."

"Melissa was pretty special," Gage said, sadness returning. "We all miss her."

"I'm sorry," she said, reaching out, feeling the need to ease his pain.

He leaned into the hand she'd placed comfortingly on his cheek and kissed her palm. "We should get in there before they send a search party again."

Gage said the words but didn't release her hand. He stepped closer until his forehead touched hers.

"We should go," she whispered.

"We should."

They stood unmoving for several minutes before a noise in the next room caused them both to sigh and separate. With one last look into her eyes, he laced his fingers with hers and walked out to join his family.

Chapter 19

Rebecca was never far away from Gage for the rest of the day. His family filled the living room, taking up every available space, including the floor. After watching Gage play for the past couple of weeks, she was able to follow the game without much difficulty. She even understood a few of the calls without having to ask for an explanation.

It was different watching a game on television than in person. One of the major differences was that she didn't know any of the players. Getting to know Zach and Kenny, as well as running into several other members of Gage's team over the past three weeks, made the game more personal. They weren't just anonymous guys out there—they were Gage's friends. To her surprise, Gage knew most of the players on both teams. She supposed that made sense. From what she and Hansen had gathered so far with the background checks, the world of professional football was much smaller than it seemed.

As they watched the game, every so often Gage would make a comment about one of the players. Sometimes his observations were professional, sometimes personal. For the most part, however, he appeared content to lounge back on one of the overstuffed chairs with her on his lap. She'd tried to sit beside him on the couch, but he had refused to hear of it, and she hadn't wanted to make too big a fuss in front of his family.

If she was honest, she liked sitting with him, feeling him tense during a crucial play, or his breath speed up when the team he was rooting for was about to score. At one point, she'd twisted around to face him. "You'd rather be out there on the field playing than sitting here, wouldn't you?"

He'd smirked and pulled her down for a quick kiss. "You'd better believe it. Sitting here not able to do anything is torture."

At halftime, his mom brought in several snacks. Rebecca was still full from the huge breakfast they'd eaten, but Gage, his brothers and father all jumped at the offering. The females in the room nibbled a little at the nachos, pretzels, and chips, but none of them did more than take a few bites here and there. She was seriously beginning to wonder where Gage was putting all the food. The man had no fat on him that she could see.

Gage was a little bummed that the team he'd been rooting for lost. He'd been friends with one of the players in college. After observing him watching the game, it was finally sinking in just how many people he knew and who knew him. Any one of the people he'd come into contact with over the years could be the person they were looking for. People held grudges for different reasons, and those reasons didn't always make sense.

As the second game was starting, Mary announced that dinner was ready, and everyone gathered in the formal dining room once again. Everything had already been laid out, and the table was set. All that was left was to serve the food.

Thanksgiving dinner at the Daniels' house was a lot like the holiday movies on television. There was a lot of talking, joking, and passing back and forth of food. Most of the conversation throughout the meal revolved around the previously watched game, and she learned that all four of the Daniels siblings had played football in high school. She shouldn't have been surprised. They were all tall men with broad shoulders.

The rest of the evening consisted of more football and the pies Paul and Chloe, with the help of Megan, had made that morning. Mary had waited to put the pies in the oven until right when they'd sat down for dinner, so by the time everyone had finished and cleaned up, the pies were finished cooking. Thirty minutes later, they were all back in the living room, watching the second half of what turned out to be a close game and eating warm pie. Rebecca couldn't remember ever having a better Thanksgiving.

When it was time to retire to bed, she was more than willing to climb under the covers with Gage. He opened his arms to her and pulled her close, this time facing him. His expression was serious. She was just about to ask him what was wrong, when he kissed her. It was one of those kisses she could feel down to her toes. She clung to him, eagerly kissing him back.

He groaned as he pulled away, falling back onto the pillow behind him. His eyes were closed and one arm was thrown haphazardly across his face.

Rebecca wasn't sure of his reaction. A moment ago, he was kissing her with such gusto that she was still breathing heavily. She watched the rapid movement of his chest and was drawn by some unknown force to touch him. She reached out, but he caught her hand in midair. "Don't."

She snatched her hand back. "Sorry. I didn't mean—"

Before she knew what was happening, she was flat on her back with him hovering over her. "Don't look at me like that."

"Like what?" she asked, eyes wide. Rebecca had no idea to what he was referring.

He closed his eyes again and took a deep breath. Unfortunately, when he reopened his eyes, he caught her ogling his naked chest again. "That!" When she still looked confused, he lowered himself on top of her, his face buried in her hair. "Like you'd let me have my way with you this very second." He pushed himself up, resting his head on his hand. "I want you, Rebecca. You have no idea how much I want you. "

"I know."

"You know." He laughed.

He reached up and cupped her face with his free hand, massaging her jaw. Warmth spread from where he touched, and she leaned into it, closing her eyes. Her whole body was aware of him, not just where they were connected.

His hand snaked down her neck to her collarbone, causing her heart to once again pick up its pace. Then his weight was gone. She opened her eyes, searching for him.

He hadn't gone far. Gage was lying on his side beside her. Seconds later, he slipped his arms around her waist and pulled her into position, spooning her. Relief rushed through her. For a moment there, she'd thought she'd done something wrong. She closed her eyes once again, sighing. She was beginning to think being in his arms was one of the best places in the world.

***

Friday morning was pleasant. More than pleasant, in Gage's view of things. He'd woken up with Rebecca's arms and legs wrapped around him, and he couldn't resist waking her. They hadn't done much beyond kissing, but he had to admit it was a great way to start the day, even if it only added to his mounting frustration.

After breakfast, his mom surprised them all by announcing that since she wasn't the lone woman in the house, they were going shopping. Elizabeth and Megan were excited with the news and had promptly run to get changed. Chloe, when learning she wasn't going with the women, threw a mini tantrum. He'd felt bad Paul had to deal with the fallout, but he handled it well. Gage was continually amazed by his older brother.

Rebecca, as expected, wasn't thrilled with his mother's proclamation. She'd remained in her chair long after Elizabeth and Megan had disappeared to get ready. When he realized she wasn't planning to move anytime soon, he got her attention and motioned for her to follow him up to their room.

"I think you should go," he said once the door was firmly closed behind them.

She shook her head. "I can't do my job if I'm off shopping with your mom and future sister-in-law."

He stepped toward her, wrapping his arms around her waist. "What if I promise to stay inside the house or with one of my brothers at all times? Paul is a cop, you know." He smiled.

"It's *my* job," she said.

His lips brushed against hers gently. "Your job is to be my girlfriend."

She sighed. "You're evil, you know that?"

He chuckled. "Why is that?"

She altered her position, rubbing up against him. His body took notice, and he tightened his grip on her waist.

"Because you don't play fair," she whispered before covering his mouth with hers and plunging her tongue in between his parted lips. He groaned at the intrusion, greedily accepting what she was giving. It was the first time she'd ever initiated anything with him, and he was ready to enjoy every moment of it.

Unfortunately, a knock on the door pulled him out of his lust-filled haze. He mumbled a curse at the interruption.

"We leave in ten minutes," his mother yelled.

"Okay," Rebecca replied. Even that one word seemed to require effort on her part. She was breathing rapidly, her body still plastered to his, her hands tangled in his hair.

He rested his forehead against hers. "You need to go."

She nodded.

"I promise I'll keep myself safe while you're gone."

She nodded again, her breathing slowly returning to normal.

He felt his gut tighten and knew he needed to leave if she had any hope of getting out of their room anytime soon. Reluctantly releasing her from his hold, he backed away and walked to the door, his gaze never leaving hers.

"Just so you know," he said. "This isn't done. The minute we're home . . ." Even though he didn't finish, he saw her eyes dilate, her hands clench. It seemed for once they were both on the same page.

Rebecca was quiet on Friday evening after spending the day with his mom. She'd come back with a few shopping bags of her own, which surprised him. He was curious, but he didn't ask. All he knew was that she'd taken them directly into the room and put them into her bag. It was strange, to say the least.

On Saturday afternoon, Chris suggested a game of football in the backyard. Everyone played, even his mom. They'd stayed outside until the sun went down and the temperature dropped.

By Sunday morning he was more than ready to go home. He'd loved the time with his family, but whatever this was with Rebecca, he needed to figure it out, and that wasn't something he could do with his parents and brothers so close. Rebecca's sister knew the score, so that was different.

As he was bringing their things downstairs, conversation in the kitchen drew him in that direction. His mom, dad, and Paul were all sitting at the table with serious faces. "What's happened?"

They all looked up.

"It's nothing," Paul said.

Rebecca, Megan, Elizabeth, and Chloe chose that moment to enter the kitchen. They'd all come from the basement and were laughing boisterously. When they noticed the grim expressions of those already in the kitchen, they sobered.

"Something wrong?" Elizabeth asked.

Paul glanced at his daughter but didn't say anything.

"Chloe?" His mom spoke up, getting his niece's attention. She quickly ran to her grandmother's side. "Can you do me a favor and run upstairs? I left a bag of goodies on the dresser in my bedroom for you and forgot to bring it down. Do you think you can be a big girl and go get it?"

Chloe didn't give a verbal answer but took off down the hall and up the stairs.

Once she was out of earshot, Gage leveled a pointed gaze at his brother. "Now, what's going on?"

Paul ran a hand over his head before looking at everyone's expectant faces. "Chloe's grandparents—Melissa's parents—are moving up to Fort Wayne." He sighed. "I knew it was coming. I just didn't think it would happen this quickly. I thought Chloe would at least be in school before they left."

"So what does that mean exactly?"

"It means I have one week to find someone I trust to watch Chloe when I work. Cindy and George lived right down the street, so I could call them no matter what time of the day or night it was. My work schedule isn't exactly normal."

"Did they just call you this morning?"

He shook his head. "No. Cindy told me when I picked Chloe up Wednesday afternoon."

"And you're just telling us now?" Gage couldn't believe his brother would withhold information like this.

"I didn't want to ruin anyone's weekend."

"So you need . . . what?" Megan asked. "A babysitter?"

"What I need is for Cindy and George to stay put for at least another year. Barring that . . . ideally, a live-in nanny? I don't know. I have no idea how I'd swing it, though. I just can't see a babysitter wanting to get woken up at three in the morning when I get called out to a crime scene to come stay with Chloe."

"I can do it."

Everyone turned to look at Megan.

"What?" she asked. "I'm available. Chloe and I get along. I think it's perfect," she added cheerfully.

No one said anything until the sound of little feet on the stairs forced everyone to glance at the doorway.

"I'll go see if Chloe wants to watch some cartoons before you go," Elizabeth said, ducking out of the room.

They all waited until they heard the television turn on and the sound of tiny cartoon voices.

"You'd really be willing to pack up and move to Indianapolis?"

"Sure. Why not? I need a change of scenery anyway, and it will give you time to find the right person without having to worry."

Gage glanced over at Rebecca. He wanted to see how she was processing this new development. To his surprise, she wasn't looking at Megan. Her focus was on Paul. His brother, however, wasn't paying attention to her scrutiny.

At first, Gage didn't understand Rebecca's expression. Then he thought about what he knew of Megan. By her own admission, she always fell for the wrong guys. Was Rebecca worried something would happen between her sister and his brother?

He looked from Paul to Megan, but he didn't see it. Sure, Megan was pretty. Paul, however, hadn't looked twice at a woman since his wife died. At least, as far as he knew. Either way, Gage doubted Rebecca needed to worry.

Paul's chair scraped against the tile floor as he stood and walked over to where Megan was standing near the door. He looked down at her, his face not betraying any emotion.

Megan squarely met his gaze.

He reached out, offering his hand. She glanced down.

"Okay," Paul said.

Megan smiled.

"Okay," she said, taking his hand.

Chapter 20

"Have you lost your mind?" Rebecca asked her sister the minute she managed to get her alone.

"No."

"Are you sure? Because from where I'm standing, it sure looks like you have."

"I don't know what you're talking about," Megan said, removing her arm from her sister's grasp.

Rebecca threw up her hands, frustrated. "You just agreed to move in with a man you've known for all of three days."

"Three and a half."

Rebecca rolled her eyes.

"Look," Megan said. "I don't know what the big deal is. It's not like I'm moving in with *him* exactly. I mean, I am, but I'm going to be taking take of his daughter. It's not the same."

"You don't know him."

"And neither do you." Megan stood defiant, hands on her hips.

Before either sister could say anything more, Chloe ran into the room looking for Megan, effectively putting an end to their conversation.

To Rebecca's dismay, Megan jumped into her new arrangement with both feet as she always did everything. She and Paul sat down at the kitchen table, Paul no longer looking miserable but optimistic, and discussed the details of Megan being Chloe's nanny. It sounded straightforward, but Rebecca still didn't like it. Her sister was vulnerable at the moment, and Rebecca didn't know enough about Paul to feel comfortable leaving Megan in his care.

Rebecca knew she was hovering, but she couldn't bring herself to leave the room. Eventually, Gage ushered her out of the kitchen with an expression on his face that told her not to argue with him. She could have dug in her heels, but how would that have looked?

Probably no worse than me standing guard over my sister.

Suddenly, Rebecca felt the need to get away. She needed space. Without meeting his gaze, she mumbled something about needing some air then walked out the front door as fast as her legs would carry her.

Once outside, the unpleasant pressure in her chest eased a little, and she took a deep breath, trying to center herself. It was already midmorning, so the temperature wasn't bad. She probably should have grabbed a jacket, but it was tolerable. Without caring what kind of clothes she was wearing, Rebecca picked up her pace until she was in a full-out run. It had been days since she'd felt the burn in her legs. With every step, she felt a little better, more in control. She knew she couldn't tell her sister what to do, how to live her life, but she hated seeing Megan hurt.

Eventually, Rebecca turned back toward the house. Her clothes were soaked with sweat, and she needed a shower, but she felt ten times better. She still wasn't happy with her sister's decision, but she was resigned to it. One way or another, Megan would do what she wanted to do. That was always the way it was, and Rebecca doubted that would ever change.

When she walked through the front door, she found Gage, Elizabeth, and Chloe sitting on the floor playing Candy Land. Gage looked up at her, concern in his eyes. He pushed himself up off the floor and came to stand in front of her, rubbing his hands up and down her arms.

"Everything all right?" he asked.

She nodded.

"Are they still in there?" she asked, motioning toward the kitchen.

"Yeah. They're still talking. Are you going to be okay with this? Paul wouldn't hurt Megan, if that's what has you concerned."

"She's my little sister. I worry."

"She's your twenty-three–year-old, fully grown, adult sister, who can make her own decisions about her life."

"I know that—"

"But you still worry," he said, pulling her in for a hug.

"Yeah. I do." She hugged him back, accepting his comfort and not caring how disgusting she felt at the moment.

"Hey," Megan said as she walked into the living room.

Gage released her and stood to the side as she went to embrace Megan. "You're positive you want to do this?"

"It'll be fine, Becca. I promise. Maybe this is what I need to break my cycle of always picking the wrong men. I'll be too busy taking care of Chloe to date much for a while."

Rebecca laughed. "True."

"You'll be taking care of me?" Chloe asked, confused.

Megan knelt down to her level. "Yeah. I'm going to be going home with you and your daddy, so I can be there with you when he has to go to work. Is that okay?"

"You're coming home with us?"

Rebecca could see the excitement growing in her little face.

"Yep." Megan smiled.

Chloe launched herself at Megan, nearly choking her as she jumped up and down with joy. "Daddy, Daddy! Megin is coming home with us!"

Paul leaned against the wall, chuckling. "Yes, I know. I guess I don't need to ask how you feel about that."

"Megin will be my bestest friend in the whole world."

They all laughed.

Mike, Chris, and Trent strolled in from the backyard just in time to hear Chloe. They all looked at each other, confused. "What did we miss?"

***

They didn't end up leaving his parents' house until around noon. His mother had insisted on feeding them all lunch before they got on the road, and Rebecca hadn't wanted to leave until she saw Megan off. Gage could still see the concern written all over her face, but she was trying to be strong.

Once they were finally on the road back to Nashville, Rebecca grew quiet again. He let her be for the first hour of their journey, allowing Rebecca her thoughts. Finally, he couldn't stand it anymore. "What is it exactly that has you so worried about Megan moving in with Paul and taking care of Chloe?"

Rebecca turned in her seat to face him. She'd been looking out the window the entire trip, and he'd been concentrating on the road. Instead of the pensive look he expected to see, however, she was alert. He knew instantly Megan wasn't at the forefront of her mind at the moment.

"I think we're being followed."

"What?" he asked in disbelief. He checked both mirrors. They were on the freeway moving with traffic. He couldn't see anything out of the ordinary, but everyone was traveling home from the holiday. There were too many cars.

She shook her head and turned her attention back to the side mirror. He'd been thinking all this time she'd been wallowing in her emotions and looking out the window at the passing scenery.

"Just keep driving. I'm not sure. It's just there's a car that's been behind us for a while. I didn't notice it until we reached the highway, but that doesn't mean anything."

"What should we do?"

"Nothing at the moment. Like I said, keep driving. If they stay with us, I might try something a little closer to home."

He followed her instructions, trying not to let his anxiety take over. Yes, he knew someone had been following him for a while—the pictures he kept receiving were proof of that—but this was the first time he'd been aware of it while it was happening. The muscles in his arms and shoulders tightened in preparation for a fight, even though he knew the chances of that happening were slim to none.

The tension continued to build as they crossed the border into Tennessee. He was trying to be patient, to wait for her to tell him what needed to be done, but the waiting was getting to him. They'd been traveling for almost three hours already, and all she'd done was stare at the side mirror.

"There's a rest stop a mile ahead. We're going to stop and get some snacks."

She'd been so quiet that her sudden speech made him jerk in his seat.

"You're hungry?" he asked, unable to fathom how she could even be thinking about food. They'd eaten a decent-sized meal before leaving his parents' house. Not to mention someone was following them. How could she be thinking about food at a time like this?

Rebecca met his gaze before going back to the mirror. "No. I do, however, want to get confirmation on our tail."

Oh.

Without questioning her further, he followed her instructions and took the off-ramp.

"Just act normal," she said.

"Normal. Right."

She directed him to an empty parking space close to a small building that housed the vending machines. Putting the car in gear, he turned off the vehicle and reached for the door. She stopped him. "You wait here. If this is your stalker, we don't need a replay of what happened in the club parking lot."

Before he could respond, Rebecca reached down to lift her pant leg. She released the snap on her holster and removed her gun. He hadn't even known she was armed.

After checking to make sure the safety was on, she leaned forward, placed the weapon behind her, and tucked it into the waist of her jeans. She reached for the door. "Stay in the car. I'll only be gone a minute. What do you want to snack on?" She spoke the words casually, as if neither of them had a care in the world.

He looked at her dumbfounded.

She gave him a rueful smile. "I'll just guess, then."

He watched as she stepped out of the SUV and walked to the front. She stopped, turned, and waved back at him, before adjusting her direction and walking swiftly to the building. He was nervous. It was hard to act normal when you knew someone was watching your every move. Rebecca, however, appeared to be calm and collected.

Rebecca wasted no time at the vending machines. She inserted the money, made her selections, and gathered her purchases, all in less than three minutes. That had to be a record. With their snacks balanced in one hand, she walked back to where he waited in the parking lot.

When she was back inside the SUV, Gage started the car and headed toward the exit. She hadn't said anything yet, and her only movement was to place the snacks between them and to reattach her gun to her ankle. Her silence was grating on him. "Well?"

Instead of answering him, she removed her cell phone from her jeans pocket.

Her conversation with Hansen was short, but it gave him his answer. Yes, they were being followed and they were going to try to catch the person in the act. He wasn't used to this cloak and dagger stuff, but he was more than ready to do something, anything at this point. His stalker was messing with his life. He wanted this over. He wanted his life back.

As they drew closer to home, Rebecca redialed Hansen's number and put him on speaker. She gave Gage step-by-step directions, leading him through what felt like a maze to where Hansen would be lying in wait. "Just another two blocks," she said for both men's benefit.

No sooner did the words leave her mouth than the car that had been following them, a dark red sedan, veered sharply to the left and turned out of sight. Rebecca cursed. It was the first expletive Gage had ever heard her utter.

After that, things got a little confusing. Rebecca and Hansen were talking back and forth quickly. Hansen was apparently trying to locate the car that had suddenly decided to end its pursuit.

"Where to?" he asked as soon as there was a break in the conversation.

Rebecca sighed and slouched back in her seat. "Home."

"Home? We're not going to try and look for this guy?"

She turned her head to look at him. "No. Hansen will try to find the car. If he doesn't have any luck, we'll see if we can find any surveillance videos. There's a reason I had you take the route you did. And unless you saw something I didn't, we don't know if the person in that car was male or female."

Gage's fingers clenched and released on the steering wheel. He desperately wanted to punch something.

"I lost 'em." Hansen's voice came through Rebecca's phone.

When she answered him, she didn't sound surprised. She rattled off their route to Hansen, and they made plans for him to come by the house the next day with the recordings. The conversation didn't help Gage's mood. As he pulled up to the gate in front of his house, he knew he had to do something with all this pent-up energy coursing through him, or he was going to explode.

His driveway seemed longer than normal as he drove up the

winding path that led to his garage. The doors opened on cue, and he parked his SUV right beside his Mustang. Turning the vehicle off, he let the keys fall to his lap as he closed his eyes and took a much-needed breath.

Rebecca was motionless beside him, waiting. When he opened his eyes and met her gaze, the questions there quickly turned to something else as she read the look on his face. She opened her mouth to say something, but he didn't give her a chance.

Releasing his seatbelt, he rose from his seat, took her face in his hands, and kissed her. It wasn't gentle. It was anything but. Every emotion he'd felt for the last four hours, combined with his need to have her, collided in that moment.

"I want you." His lips barely left hers before going back to the brutal kiss.

Her hands fisted in his hair as she met his tongue stroke for stroke. At that moment, the house could have burnt down around them. They were completely oblivious to the outside world.

"Come to bed with me," he said, finally breaking the kiss but not his hold on her.

For once, her face displayed all her emotions. Her fingers left his hair and slid down to his chest. She clenched her hands nervously before opening them up again to lie flat. Her right hand rested over his heart, and he knew she could feel it thumping rapidly. All he wanted to do was take her upstairs and ravish her, but he wouldn't do it unless she gave him the okay.

Just as he was beginning to lose hope, she shifted in her seat and leaned in to place a brief but demanding kiss on his lips. "Take me to bed, Gage," she whispered. It was all the encouragement he needed.

Chapter 21

As soon as they were in the house, Gage grabbed hold of her hand and didn't let go. He climbed the stairs up to his room two at a time. It took effort on her part to keep up, but she wasn't complaining. She felt as though everything that had happened between them since her arrival had been leading them to this moment.

Walking through the doorway into his bedroom, he immediately pulled her against him. He thrust his hands into her hair, holding her head in place and kissing her to within an inch of her life. She met every bruising stroke of his mouth with equal intensity. Fire burned through her veins. She wanted more.

Gage didn't waste any time removing her clothes. He released his hands from her head, only to slide them under the hem of her shirt. The fabric bunched under her arms as he pushed it up, revealing her bra. Seconds later, his lips were gone as he pulled the shirt over her head and threw it across the room. Then his mouth was back.

He reached behind her and quickly unsnapped her bra, then worked it down her arms, making her temporarily relinquish her hold on him. Gratefully, she hadn't needed to stop kissing him.

Rebecca ran her palms down his chest and around to his back. She slipped her hands under the hem of his shirt and began to inch it up his torso. Gage had the most amazing chest, broad and toned with just the slightest dusting of dark brown hair. She'd been dying to explore his chest with her hands. She raked her fingernails up over his stomach, causing him to suck in a deep breath and break their kiss.

"You're going to kill me, woman."

She chuckled, her breasts rubbing against the material of his shirt. Little shockwaves moved through her from where they were connected to the junction between her legs. She needed more. She wanted the feel of skin against skin.

As if reading her mind, Gage released his hold on her and removed his shirt. She wanted to stare, to take in his body, but he didn't give her a chance. His right hand came up to cup the back of her neck, tilting her head back, while his left arm wrapped around her waist molding their bodies together. Skin met skin for the first time, and they moaned into each other's mouths.

He backed her up to his bed, their mouths fused together. Rebecca couldn't ever remember feeling so alive. It was as if all the nerve endings in her body had come to life at the same time.

Wanting to feel more, she reached for the button on his jeans and quickly undid them. Realizing what she was doing, he reached to unbutton her pants as well. Arms tangled, and some giggles were exchanged, but they were eventually standing in only their underwear.

Their underwear and her gun.

Bracing her leg up on the bed, she quickly removed her gun and holster, eager to get back to exploring Gage. She made sure the safety was on and placed the weapon on top of the nightstand.

Gage smirked as he leaned in to kiss her again, wrapping her in his arms. He guided her back on the bed, his body poised over hers. Inch by inch, they worked their way to the center of the bed. Their destination would have been much easier to reach had they broken the kiss, but neither seemed willing to do that.

His weight rested on top of her as he held her face between his hands and stared down at her. "You are so beautiful, Rebecca."

When his lips met hers again, they were more gentle but no less potent. What had before been a building inferno was now a slow burn. She wasn't sure which was worse . . . or better. Every lick of his tongue, every nip of his teeth, sent her body screaming for more of him.

She ran her hands along his back, urging him, pleading with

him, to go faster, kiss her harder. When that didn't work, she wrapped her legs around his waist, lifting her hips to brush against him, hoping that once he felt her urgency, her need, he'd do something about it.

He groaned but still refused to pick up the pace.

Finally, she had enough. She needed more. Using her self-defense knowledge, she took hold of his wrists. Exerting an exact amount of force on his pressure points forced him to release his grip on her. The moment she was free, she bucked her hips, and twisted. The result had her freed from his hold and him lying bewildered beside her.

Rebecca immediately climbed on top of him. "What—"

She cut him off with a hard kiss.

"I've had enough of slow."

Instead of being mad, he let out a huge belly laugh. She joined him. Not that she found the situation overly funny. More that his laughter was contagious.

Once their laughter began to die down, he grabbed her hips, grinding her against him. That action put an end to any amusement she'd been feeling. She laid her palms flat against his chest and repeated the motion. Gage moaned and held her firmly in place.

"These," he said, taking hold of each side of her panties, "have to go."

Rebecca smiled, raising her hips. He happily pushed the silky material down her thighs, and she kicked them off.

Figuring it was only fair, she reached for the waistband of his underwear and tugged. He lifted his hips off the bed and allowed her to get rid of the last bit of clothing that was between them.

Reaching into the drawer of his nightstand, Gage removed a condom and opened it. Within seconds, it was covering him, and Rebecca had a flash of curiosity wash over her, wondering just how many times he'd done that, and with how many woman.

He sat up, noticing her distress. "If you don't want to—"

"No. I mean, yes. I do. Want to."

"Are you sure?" he asked, brushing the hair away from her face and looking into her eyes.

She nodded. No matter what had happened in his past, Rebecca knew she wanted this, wanted him. She reached out, running a hand down his chest and lower.

He smiled, jerking his hips up into her hand.

He pulled her down, her mouth to his as he rekindled that fire deep inside. For some reason, it grew faster than it had before. She gripped his shoulders, holding on, ready to embrace whatever came next.

He roamed his hands all over her body. Sometimes they were soft and gentle, at other times strong and passionate. She gasped and all thought left her mind as his fingers disappeared between her legs.

"Are you ready, beautiful?" he whispered against her lips. She nodded, and he slid inside her.

***

Finally making love to Rebecca had Gage on a high unlike anything he'd ever experienced. It was even better than winning the playoff game the year before, and that had been amazing. This was mind-blowing. He'd always enjoyed sex, but it wasn't really anything he thought about beyond that. With Rebecca, it was . . . different. She was different.

As he moved inside her, he allowed himself to ride the wave of emotions coursing through him. The way her breasts grazed against his chest, his hands digging into the flesh of her hips. The feel of her riding him.

He had no idea how long they stayed in that position, with her on top. The woman had stamina. She was driving him to his peak faster than he ever thought possible. Sure, they'd been dancing around each other for weeks, but that was all the more reason to make it last. He was exactly where he wanted to be. He didn't want it to end anytime soon.

Lifting her up, he lay her beside him on the bed, and crawled on top of her. She was breathing heavily from her exertion, her chest rising and falling rapidly. He couldn't resist the urge to take one of her nipples in his mouth.

She held tight to his head, holding him to her chest. Her head was thrown back, her mouth open. He could have stayed in that position all night.

The thought of feasting on her body for the rest of the evening spurred him on as he switched his attention to her other breast. Once again, he could have her in his bed for much more than just sleeping.

He could wake up with her, having made love to her as he'd dreamed about since the first day he'd laid eyes on her. Just the thought had his body responding with excitement. Rebecca rolled her hips, drawing his attention lower. Lifting her lower half off the bed, he gave her what she wanted and thrust back inside her.

She appeared stunned by his abrupt movement but recovered quickly. Her hips rocked in time with his, as he moved his lips up her body until he captured her mouth again. The feel of her tongue darting enthusiastically into his mouth had him holding her tighter.

Much to his dismay, the slight pause in their joining did nothing to stop the growing need for release building inside him. With every movement, every kiss, every touch, he drew closer. Hiking her legs higher on his back, he reached between them.

Gage knew the moment he made contact. Her breath hitched, and her nails dug into his shoulders. Every little thing about her was driving him to the brink. He just needed to get her there first.

Time seemed to stand still as Rebecca's body stiffened, and her cry rang out, reverberating off the walls of his bedroom. Watching her find her release was a beautiful sight. Her cheeks flushed. Her hair splayed against his pillow.

She opened her eyes, meeting his gaze. They were so full of emotion, so unclouded by the usual mask she wore. What he saw in their depths sent him over the edge he'd been teetering on as he reached his climax.

Once his breathing began to return to normal, he eased himself down next to her. She turned her head to look at him, and he brushed several strands of hair from her face. There was something about Rebecca Carson. He wasn't sure what it was exactly, but he knew it was something. She made his pulse race just thinking about her, and if what they'd just done was any indication, they were more than compatible sexually.

"What are you thinking?" she asked, rolling onto her side.

He smiled, still running his fingers along her temple, unable to break the connection just yet. "I was thinking about you. Us. I hope this wasn't a one-time thing. I'm not sure once is enough for me." He kept his voice light, playful. He didn't want her to realize the seriousness of his thoughts.

"Oh," she said. "Um. Well . . ."

He loved seeing her flustered.

"No. It's not a one-time thing. Not if you don't want it to be."

"Good," he said, leaning in to give her a soft kiss.

Rebecca sighed. She placed her hand on his chest before gliding it up to the nape of his neck. With the additional leverage, she pulled herself closer. The movement reminded him that he needed to go clean up, and he reluctantly broke the kiss.

"I'll be right back," he said, giving her one last peck on the lips before climbing off the bed and walking into his bathroom.

Cleaned up, he strolled back into the bedroom. She was lying on her back, gazing up at the ceiling. He took a moment to watch her without her knowledge. She truly was a beautiful woman. The way she cared about her sister. The way she put everything into her job. All those things were part of what made her who she was, and they all appealed to him.

"Hey," she said, catching him staring.

"Hey."

"Everything okay?" she asked as he slipped into the bed.

He pulled her back into his arms, resting her head on his shoulder. He rubbed his hands up her side and down to her hip, feeling the soft skin as he thought of all the ways he could enjoy his time with her.

"Everything's great." He kissed her forehead, hugging her closer.

Something had begun to dawn on him. Rebecca was one of the most persistent people he'd ever met. He couldn't imagine she'd give up until whoever it was had been caught. Once the stalker was no longer a threat, he had little doubt she would pack up her things and return to Knoxville. Return to her old life. Without him.

Unable to hold her close enough, he rolled them over and kissed her. He needed to be with her, feel that connection with her again. No matter what he had told himself over the years, that no woman would ever get his heart, no woman would ever tie him down. He was beginning to realize that, just like everything else when it came to this woman, he wanted her to do just that.

Chapter 22

The sound of Rebecca's phone buzzing roused her from sleep the following morning. Gage's warm body was nestled up against her back, his breath fanning the nape of her neck. She was relaxed. The last thing she wanted to do was move.

Sex with Gage had been amazing. While she'd always thought her previous sexual encounters were good, what she'd shared with Gage had put her other experiences to shame.

Her phone buzzed again, and she reached for it. At some point, Gage had picked up their clothes and laid them on a bench at the foot of his bed. He'd removed her cell phone from her belt, and placed it on the nightstand next to her gun. Her gratitude to him for that small gesture increased. She wouldn't have to leave his warm bed to answer her phone.

Rebecca glanced at the caller ID but didn't recognize the number.

"Agent Carson."

"Good morning, sis."

Rebecca sat up quickly, rousing Gage from his slumber.

"Megan."

She laughed.

"Of course it's me. Were you expecting a call from someone else?"

"No," Rebecca said, brushing the hair away from her face and trying to forget about the very naked man beside her who was intently watching her every move. "I was just expecting you to call last night, not this morning," she said, noticing the sun was already peeking through the curtains. "What time is it anyway?"

"Eight." Gage's voice drifted from behind her.

"Is that who I think it is?" Megan asked, excited.

Rebecca looked over her shoulder at Gage. "Um—"

"I knew it! I'm so happy for you, Becca. So was it good?"

She was suddenly awake. "I'm not going to tell you that."

Megan chuckled.

Rebecca felt warm, so she knew she must have been blushing.

"Fine, don't tell me," Megan said, clearly amused by her sister's discomfort. "I just wanted to let you know that we made it to Indianapolis safe and sound. You'll be happy to know that I have my own room next to Chloe's, and that Paul has been nothing but a gentleman since we arrived."

Rebecca sighed. "I just worry about you, you know. You're always going to be my little sister."

"Becca, I know. And I like being your little sister, really I do, but I think this is going to be good for me."

"I hope so."

"Instead of worrying about me, maybe you should concentrate on that gorgeous hunk of man you have in bed with you. I'm sure he could use some attention." Rebecca could almost see the smirk on her sister's face.

"I'm not—"

"Bye, bye, sis."

"Megan?"

Dead air greeted her and she realized Megan had hung up.

Laying her cell back on the nightstand, Rebecca turned to face Gage. He was smiling.

"You heard what she said, didn't you?" she asked.

"Yep."

"And you agree with her, of course."

"Of course," he said, moving to hover over her.

"Didn't you get enough last night?"

His mouth grazed over hers with the slightest touch, and her lips began to tingle. "Not even close."

It was the last thing she thought about for a while.

Hansen was supposed to come by with surveillance recordings

at ten. It was only his impending arrival that got them out of bed. Gage wanted to share a shower with her, but she refused, insisting they would never make it out in time, and she didn't want her partner showing up and finding her naked. She had no idea how Hansen would feel about what she was doing. It had to be unethical—she was supposed to be protecting Gage. Did that count since she wasn't there in an official capacity? She wasn't sure.

She hurried through her shower and rushed downstairs, wanting to be there when Hansen walked through the door. Much to her disappointment, however, her partner was already there, sitting with Gage at the kitchen island, drinking a cup of coffee. He nodded, acknowledging her, then went back to his conversation with Gage. They were talking sports, of course.

Walking over to the coffeepot, she found a mug sitting there on the counter waiting for her. She smiled. Gage must have taken it out of the cabinet and left it for her.

As she poured her coffee and took a sip, she thought about the man with whom she'd just spent the night. He was such a contradiction. When she'd first met him, she'd wondered if he could take anything seriously. Then she'd seen him play, and her opinion began to change. The more she learned about him, the more she liked him. Not just that he was nice to look at, but that there was more to him than the ladies' man she'd originally pegged him to be. He was sweet and considerate, fun and sexy, both in and out of the bedroom.

Figuring she needed to change the direction of her thoughts before she made it glaringly obvious to Hansen just how they'd spent their night, she twisted around to face the men. Unfortunately, she ended up staring straight into Gage's burning gaze. She flushed and felt that tingle in the pit of her stomach. *How is that possible?* She'd lost count of how many orgasms she'd had in the last twenty-four hours. After the first time, Gage had seemed to make it his mission for her to climax over and over again, until she was begging him to join her.

"I think we may have gotten lucky," Hansen said, pulling her from her thoughts. It was a good thing, too. Thinking about the night before wasn't doing anything to help her current state.

Gage broke eye contact with her and turned his attention to Hansen. "It's about time." His frustration with the situation came through loud and clear.

Rebecca wasn't sure how to take that. Of course he wanted to catch whoever was behind this, but that would also mean the end of their association. She wasn't ready for that quite yet.

"What did you find?" she asked, pushing that thought from her head. First and foremost, she needed to do her job. That was what was important. Whatever was or wasn't going on with Gage had to take a backseat.

Hansen opened his laptop, and she moved to stand behind him so she could see. His e-mail was already up on the screen. Clicking on the second one from the top, he opened the file attachment.

"This one seems to have the best angle. I called and had a friend at the DMV run the license plate on the way over here. It's a rental. The good news is the company should have a record of who rented the vehicle, and maybe even video."

"I want to go with you," Gage said, standing.

"I don't think that's a good idea." Hansen spoke up before she'd been able to form the words. Gage was so eager, so determined. Sadness washed over her.

"Why not? I don't have practice today. No one is expecting me to be anywhere. Not to mention this is my life this sicko has been messing with."

Hansen looked at him calmly, but Rebecca saw a note of sympathy in his expression as well. "If whoever this is sees you tracking their footsteps, they may get scared and run." Gage opened his mouth to say something, but Hansen cut him off. "I know that might sound like a good thing, but it's not. Running now doesn't mean they won't come back at a later date. Right now, you have Carson and me watching your back. You need to use your advantage."

Gage looked to her, and she nodded.

He sat back down, defeated.

"Fine. Do what you need to do. Let's just finish this."

Hansen didn't stay long after that. He downed the rest of his coffee, backed up his laptop, and said a hasty good-bye.

***

For some reason, Gage was irritated. Okay, he knew *why* he was irritated. If not for his stalker, he would have spent the entire morning and probably afternoon in bed with Rebecca. But no, he'd had to get out of his nice, warm, very occupied bed to get dressed, go downstairs to his kitchen, and hear Hansen tell him he had to sit on his hands. The whole situation was grating on his nerves.

Rebecca touched his arm, startling him. He spun around, and pinned her to the refrigerator. She gasped in shock.

"Gage?"

His answer was to pick her up, wrapping her legs around his waist. She threw her arms around his neck, meeting his seeking mouth with equal force.

Her response to his kiss fueled his need to take her again. He didn't think he'd make it up to his bedroom, though, so he carried her to the nearest usable flat surface. The dining room table.

He laid her down and immediately began removing clothing. Gage couldn't remember ever having felt so frantic for a woman before, but as he'd already figured out, everything was different with Rebecca. He needed her naked and him buried deep inside her.

To his great joy, she appeared to feel the same way. She grabbed blindly at his shirt, pulling it over his head and tossing it to the floor as he divested her of her own shirt. Their pants soon followed, and at that moment, he was extremely grateful to his brothers for drilling into his head the importance of always carrying a condom with him. He sheathed himself in protection and pressed forward, feeling as if he'd found peace and chaos at the same time.

Their joining was fast and frantic, even more so than their first time. He put all the desperation he felt into every action as he made love to her. He needed her to feel the depth of emotion he did coursing through him, needed that connection with her.

They both fell over the edge not far apart, her nails leaving painful streaks down his back. He gratefully took everything she gave him, and wanted more. He never wanted to let this woman go.

Their breathing was ragged. He looked down at her, sweat beading on her forehead, her face relaxed in its post-orgasmic glow, and it hit him like a freight train. He loved her.

"What?" she asked, touching his face with her hand.

He kissed her palm.

"Nothing."

He may have realized he loved her, but he wasn't quite ready for her to know that. There was no telling how she'd react to that kind of declaration.

"I think we may need another shower." He ran a single finger across her forehead, down her face and neck. Her body clenched in reaction, which only made his smile wider.

"I think you may be right," she said.

He placed a quick kiss on her lips before stepping back, separating them. Helping her up, he excused himself, disappearing into the half-bathroom off the kitchen. When he returned, Rebecca had put her shirt back on and was holding her jeans. "I thought we were taking a shower."

She stared at him, eyes wide.

"What?" he asked.

Not giving her time to respond, he circled his arms around her waist, twirling her around. He grabbed her ass, pulling her up against his lower half, reminding her of what they'd shared just a few minutes before.

"I thought maybe we could share the shower this time, since there shouldn't be any more distractions for a while." He grazed her neck with his teeth to emphasize his point. She responded by tilting her head back, giving him better access. He was quick to take advantage.

"Shower?" he asked again.

"Uh-huh." She nodded, slipping her fingers into his hair.

Gage didn't bother picking up their clothes. He left them scattered on his dining room floor, and carried Rebecca back upstairs to his bathroom. No matter what else happened between them, he planned to make their shower a memorable one.

Chapter 23

Hansen walked into the rental car agency where the vehicle that had been following Carson and Daniels was registered. It was located near the Nashville airport. The moment he'd realized where the address would take him, he'd wondered if it would only be a stop on his journey. In his experience, most rental companies used their airport location as the main hub. They registered all or most of their vehicles out of that location and then shuffled them around as needed. Until he spoke with them, there was no telling from which location the car had actually been rented.

Being that it was early on a Monday afternoon, there was no one else in the place except him and two employees. One was behind the small desk. The other was over at the coffee machine. They both glanced up when they heard him enter.

The woman behind the counter smiled. "Hello. Do you have a reservation?"

"No, I don't," he said, showing the woman his badge. "I'm hoping you can help me, though."

His announcement gained the attention of the man, who joined the woman behind the counter.

"Is something wrong?" he asked.

Hansen wasted no time getting to the point. He also wasn't going to get involved in whatever type of power trip the man had in mind. "One of your vehicles might be involved in a case we're working. I need to know who the vehicle was rented to yesterday."

He handed over to the woman the piece of paper with the license plate number they'd taken from the vehicle.

The man stood looking over her shoulder as she typed the information into the system. He could tell she was annoyed, but she didn't say anything.

"Here it is," she said. "Let me print it out for you."

She left the desk and walked to the back of the room where a printer was set up on a table against the wall. The man continued to scrutinize the computer screen in her absence.

"What kind of case?" he asked as the woman returned with the printout and handed the information to Hansen.

"I'm sorry. I can't reveal information regarding an ongoing investigation."

The man's brow wrinkled. He didn't like that answer very much.

Hansen ignored him and scanned the paper.

Mark Fuller.

The name didn't ring any bells. He'd run close to one hundred background checks in the past three weeks, but this guy hadn't been one of them. It could be an alias. That would mean a fake ID, since rental companies required a driver's license. Or they could have been going down the wrong direction this entire time and stumbled across their first solid lead. He wouldn't know until he did some more digging.

"Was the vehicle rented from this site?"

The woman typed something else into the computer.

"No. It was rented from our north side location."

Hansen nodded.

"Do you happen to know if they have surveillance video?"

This time the man spoke up again. "We all do," he said, pointing to a camera poised in the corner at the rear of the room.

"How long do you keep the videos?"

"We keep them on site for a week, and then they're mailed to corporate. I don't know how long they keep them."

"Is it possible you could give the other office a call and let them know I'm on my way there?" He directed his question to the woman, since she seemed to be more helpful and less antagonistic than the man. "It would help if they could have the tapes pulled by the time I arrive."

"Yes, of course," she said, picking up the phone.

Fifteen minutes later, he was on his way. The manager of the north side location had been notified of his impending arrival. Hopefully, once Hansen saw the tapes, he would recognize this Mark Fuller, and he could pay him a visit, get some answers. Maybe, just maybe, they'd be able to wrap up this case, and he'd be able to return home in time to celebrate his wife's birthday. He missed her, as he always did when he was away. Talking to her every night only did so much when what he really wanted to do was have her in his arms.

***

Rebecca could no longer feel the bones in her body. The man was completely insatiable. He'd rarely stopped touching her all day. Even when they weren't having sex, some part of him was in contact with some part of her.

The need for food had roused them out of bed a couple of times, but even then, he'd made it a sensual experience. He'd slipped one of his T-shirts over her head and led her downstairs. Together they'd cooked a simple meal of eggs, bacon, and some fruit. She'd sat beside him on the stool at the kitchen island, but that hadn't been satisfactory for him. Gage had pulled her stool as close as possible, and then lifted her legs over his so she was practically sitting on his lap. He'd then proceeded to feed her. Rebecca felt like she was in a dream. Did people really do this? Was this real?

Eventually, they'd made it back upstairs, where he'd continued to touch her until she could no longer stand it. She'd thrown him on his back and reached into his drawer for a condom. There was only so much a girl could take.

After that round, he had suggested they watch a movie. She'd been all prepared to get out of his bed and go down to the basement where his entertainment center was, but he had stopped her, saying he had no plans to spend any more time than he had to today out of his bed. They had curled up against his pillows, eating popcorn and watching something on pay-per-view.

When the movie was over, she'd put her foot down when he'd started to go downstairs to get them food. She felt like she wasn't pulling her own weight in this . . . *whatever* this was, between them.

It was beginning to feel more like a relationship than a fling, and she didn't want to think too much about that yet.

When she came back in the room, he had his laptop open. He looked up at her, smiling. "Hey."

"Hey," she said, walking toward him with the tray of food.

She climbed on the bed, setting the tray on the nightstand.

"What are you doing?"

"Need to study up for this week's game," he said, motioning toward the screen.

He was watching video of a football game.

Rebecca started to lean over to get a better look, but then stopped herself. *Fling, remember.* She sat back and picked up the tray, setting it across her lap.

"You had some leftover chicken, so I made us stir-fry."

He leaned over to give her a kiss. "Thank you."

Gage took the bowl she offered and went back to his video. She picked up her bowl and began eating her food, trying not to be in the way.

Five minutes passed before he glanced up at her again. Setting his bowl on the stand beside him, he took the bowl out of her hand and laid it alongside his.

"Hey!"

His only response was to place a hard kiss on her lips and take the tray from her lap and set it on the floor. Then he pulled her against his side, picked up both their bowls, handing her one, and went back to his video as he resumed eating.

"There. That's better."

She wasn't sure how to react, but Gage didn't give her much time to process everything before he started talking to her about what was on the screen. Over the next two hours, she watched his face light up as he talked about football stats and player history. She couldn't help getting caught up in his excitement.

By the time they turned off the lights, Rebecca was exhausted. She was also sore. Never in her life had she had a sex marathon, and that was exactly what the past twenty-four hours felt like. She wasn't complaining, though. The day was turning out to be one of the best of her life, and she hated to admit it, but the great sex wasn't the only thing standing out in her memory.

Gage pulled her against him, tucking her into his side and

resting her head on his shoulder. "Good night, beautiful."

She cuddled closer.

"Goodnight, Gage."

His alarm woke her the next morning, and she sat straight up in bed, startled. Once she realized where the noise was coming from, she allowed the tension to leave her body. She turned around just in time to see Gage reach over to turn off the alarm. Even with such a simple movement, she could see the power in his muscles. She'd gotten to know his body well. She knew the power those muscles contained. She'd felt it.

He noticed her staring.

"See something you like?" He smirked.

She blushed. "Maybe."

"Maybe?" he asked, lunging for her.

She tried to escape, but he caught her. He started tickling her, and she couldn't contain her laughter.

"Stop," she begged.

"Admit you like looking at my body." He was smiling from ear to ear.

She shook her head, trying to deny it, but the effect was lost given her hysteria.

He continued his assault.

"Fine. Fine! Yes! I like . . . your body."

He stopped.

"See. That wasn't so difficult."

"If you say so," she said, still breathing hard. Part of her wanted to turn the tables on him, but honestly, she hadn't laughed so much in years. It felt good.

Gage leaned down to give her a soft kiss.

"Why is it so hard for you to admit you have desires just like the rest of us?"

Rebecca felt the unease creeping back. She didn't want to talk about this.

She closed her eyes and felt his weight leave her. Why was he bringing this up? She didn't want Gage feeling sorry for her. That wasn't what their relationship was about.

His hands trailed up her arms, his lips on her neck. A sigh escaped along with some of her agitation. How could this man produce so much varying emotion in her?

Gage climbed back on top of her, straddling her just above her waist. He lifted her arms above her head, holding her wrists together, first with two hands, then one.

She forgot all about her arms as he slides lower and he continued to work magic with his lips on her neck. Too late, she realized something was being wrapped around her wrists. She opened her eyes, looking above her. He'd tied a scarf to her wrists and attached it to the bedframe. She pulled, but the binding didn't give.

Rebecca felt herself start to panic. "Let me loose."

"Take a deep breath, Rebecca. I'm not going to hurt you."

"Then why?"

"Well, I want you to stop thinking so much and just let go," he said, kissing her right behind her ear, his hands moving slowly back down her arms and shoulders.

She didn't like how her body reacted, like it didn't care he'd tied her to his bed.

"And you think tying me to the bed is the way to accomplish that?"

He laughed.

She was not amused.

"Yes."

"I don't agree with you."

"I'm not surprised," he said, smiling.

She tugged again at the scarf.

"Rebecca, stop."

She looked up at him, eyes wide.

He sighed.

"I want to have a conversation with you, and well . . . I'm not all that sure you won't try to run, and I don't trust that you won't use one of those fancy moves on me, so . . ."

"So you thought you'd tie me up?" she asked, her voice rising.

"It seemed like a good idea." He shrugged, going back to what he was doing. Gage moved his assault lower, down her collarbone to her breasts. He'd become very well acquainted with them recently.

"Let me loose." She tried to put some force behind her words, but they lacked any semblance of authority. His lips were completely distracting her.

"Not until we talk."

"Fine. Talk."

Rebecca was trying to stay calm, not letting the panic take over, and to concentrate on what his mouth and hands were doing.

"I promise, I'm not going to hurt you."

She clenched her fists, digging her nails into her palms. Gage hurting her was quickly becoming the last thing on her mind.

"I want you to tell me about your family," he whispered against her skin.

"What?" She glanced down at him in disbelief, momentarily pulled out of her pleasure-filled haze.

He didn't look up, just continued to lick and nip at her flesh. "I want to know about your childhood, how you grew up."

She moaned and closed her eyes as he took one of her breasts into his mouth.

Her back arched up off the mattress, silently pleading with him for more.

Rebecca didn't like talking about her parents. There weren't many pleasant memories there. It was just easier to forget.

Gage released his hold on her breast and crawled up her body until he was face-to-face with her. He brushed his fingers along her jaw, her cheek, her temple. "Tell me. Please," he whispered against her lips.

He was torturing her, and he knew it.

She took a deep breath, trying to center herself. If she stuck just to the facts, maybe she would be okay.

As she began to talk, Gage returned his lips to her neck, his hands took hold lower. She had to think and really concentrate on her words.

"My father was into all sorts of illegal . . . things. He wasn't . . . picky about it. Cars, drugs . . . petty theft . . . you name it." She needed to focus. "Claimed he did it to put food on the table." She took a deep breath. Unfortunately, it didn't help as Gage shifted above her, bringing their bodies closer together. "He was . . . in . . . and out of jail . . . a few times. That was back before they had the . . . three strikes rule." His hand grazed over her stomach and dipped down between her thighs, and she gasped. "When he was behind bars . . . our mother would . . . pine for him. She'd go see him every weekend and spend her weeknights getting drunk."

"You had to take care of your sister," he whispered in her ear, sending shivers down her spine.

It wasn't a question, but she answered him anyway, wishing so badly she could touch him. "Yes."

"I'm sorry. I understand now why you're so protective of her."

There were no more words for a while as he continued to caress her with lips, tongue, and hand. More than anything, she wanted to touch him, to give back what he was giving to her. "May I have my arms back now?" she asked, almost pleading.

He shook his head. "Nope. Not yet."

"What . . . else?" She gasped as his hand slipped between her legs again.

"Why did you take this job? Why be my bodyguard?" he asked, his teeth grazing her neck, sending a shot of electricity down to where his fingers were lingering, teasing.

She tensed.

He paused his hand's ministrations and leaned up to whisper in her ear. "Stop thinking, beautiful, and just tell me." He kissed a trail down her neck to her collarbone. "Please," he begged as he slid one finger inside.

Moaning at the pleasant intrusion, she closed her eyes and tried to form the words she needed. The ones that would get him to release her without her having to reveal too much. "I was on a case . . . and it went badly." Her back arched off the bed, and a strangled moan left her lips as he continued to do the most devilish things to her with his hand. "They put me on admin . . . administrative leave. I was going . . . stir crazy. Hansen . . . Hansen asked for my help."

She felt him smile against her neck before he leaned up onto his elbow and used his free hand to release her.

Rebecca placed her hands on either side of his face, forcing him to look at her. She was breathing hard, but she needed to get the words out. "If you ever do that again . . . I will lay you flat out on the floor."

He smiled.

"Maybe I'd like you to."

"Maybe you need to be thinking of ways to make me forget your little transgression."

Gage chuckled and rubbed his nose against hers. "I think I already am. I have one more question, though."

"What?" Thinking was becoming progressively more difficult.

"Your parents. Do you or Megan have any contact with them now?" She dropped her hands to her side and closed her eyes. "Hey. Look at me."

Rebecca opened her eyes. His face was full of concern, and she felt the anger begin to churn in her belly. It was the last thing she wanted to feel.

"No," she choked out. "I don't. When I joined the FBI, my dad saw it as a betrayal. Mom took his side. I haven't spoken to them since my graduation from college."

"And Megan?"

"She used to talk to Mom once in a while, but eventually, Mom kept bringing me up, trying to turn Megan against me, so Megan stopped accepting her calls."

He brushed his fingers through her hair absentmindedly. She could tell he was deep in thought.

"Can you do me a favor?" she asked.

"I will do anything you want, beautiful."

"Kiss me." It came out more like a command than a request.

Gage didn't seem to care.

"Gladly," he murmured as his lips connected with hers. All thoughts of her parents faded into the background as Gage reminded her of all the wonderful things he could make her feel.

Chapter 24

Gage finally dragged himself out of bed just before nine o'clock. It was difficult to leave the warm comfort of his bed, especially when it had the added bonus of Rebecca in it, but he couldn't be late for practice. Laps and a stern lecture from his coach the last time weren't things he wished to repeat anytime soon. As it was, he had to forgo his morning swim. A small sacrifice, all things considered. Besides, he'd gotten his morning cardio in without having to leave his bedroom. Maybe one of these days he could convince Rebecca to join him in his pool, although he doubted there'd be much swimming involved.

Much to his dismay, they had to shower separately in the interest of time. Their last shower was something he was hoping to repeat. He did engage, however, in a long, lingering kiss that included some groping before he had to go inside the stadium. Rebecca had a way of giving all of herself to a task, and that included kissing. Once she'd gotten over whatever hurdle there'd been in her head, she'd gone into it full throttle. He loved it. Their make-out session in the parking lot wasn't nearly enough, but it would have to do until he could get her back home.

Even forgoing a combined shower, he was cutting it close as he walked into the locker room. He hurried and changed into his practice gear before jogging down the hall and out through the tunnel that led to the field. It was going to be a brutal day. Their coach always pushed them extra hard when they came back from a bye week. He didn't want them slacking and going into Sunday's game unprepared after the time off.

Gage made it to the field with only a minute to spare. His coach saw him, frowned, and glanced down at his watch, shaking his head. Everyone on the team knew he had a girlfriend. It didn't take a lot to put two and two together and figure out that he was running late due to extracurricular activities. He joined the rest of the offensive line as they huddled around the offensive coordinator to go over the practice schedule for the day. There was to be an extra hour of scrimmages along with some intense footwork. If the guys on defense had anything to say about it, he'd be sporting some bruises by the end of the day.

Ignoring some of the smirks he got from a few of his teammates as they spread out to begin their warm-up, he tried to get his mind in the game and off Rebecca. This week would be another tough game, made more challenging by the fact that they were coming off a bye. Texas was playing strong this year. They played hard, fast, and liked to put points on the board. Gage and the offense would have to keep up, or be left in the dust.

Kenny and Zach flanked him as he started to stretch. He knew the ambush was coming, and they didn't disappoint.

"Are we ever going to see you at the club again?"

"Yeah, man. Two weeks in a row now you've skipped out on us."

Gage shrugged and continued with his stretches. "You guys came over last Monday. You know about Rebecca's sister."

"Yeah. Megan," Kenny said with a predatory smile.

"Watch it," Gage said.

"Oooooh. Protective," Kenny joked. "Sorry, man. Didn't know it was like that."

Gage sighed, lay back, and began doing crunches. "It's not *like* anything. She's my girlfriend's sister. End of story. I just know how you are when it comes to women." He tried to keep his tone light, but for some reason the idea of Megan hooking up with Kenny bothered him. Maybe Rebecca's protective streak was rubbing off on him.

"Okay. If you say so."

"I do."

Everyone concentrated on their workouts for the next several minutes. The silence was charged, and Gage felt bad. A month ago, he would have been right there with Kenny in his assumptions. Given his previous relationship with the female population, he really couldn't blame his friend. Kenny wasn't ready to settle down. Of course, Gage hadn't been either until recently.

"How are things with Angie?" he asked Kenny, trying to change the subject as they flipped over and began a set of push-ups.

"Not much to tell. We've hooked up a couple of times. You know the deal."

"So nothing long-term there?"

Kenny laughed. "No. Not even close. What about you, Zach? How'd your date with the bartender go?"

Zach's smile said it all. "Tonight's her night off. I'm taking her to a comedy club downtown."

"So things are getting serious, then?"

"Not quite as serious as you and Rebecca, but . . . yeah."

"Wow. I'm going to start feeling like the third wheel," Kenny said, flopping down on his back.

"Stop chasing tail and find a girl, then," Zach said, only partly in jest.

Gage smiled, but that unease began to settle in again. After realizing he loved Rebecca, he couldn't imagine her walking out of his life. He had to figure out a way to get her to stay or at least give a relationship between them a chance. He had no idea how that would work with both their jobs, but there had to be a way. The problem was how did he tell her he wanted her in his life—permanently—without sending her running in the opposite direction?

Practice was long, and he hadn't been wrong about the bruises. They were already forming. To add to it, their coach asked him to stay after for a few minutes. It didn't take a mind reader to know that their conversation would be about his new relationship. Sure enough, Gage had gotten a nice little pep talk reminding him that he needed to stay focused and keep his mind on Sunday's game, something he already knew and was desperately trying to do. His coach never came out and said anything about Rebecca and his relationship with her, but he did hint that, with playoffs in sight, it might not be the best time to spend his energies elsewhere. He knew his coach meant well and was just looking out for the team as a whole, but there was no way he would cool it with Rebecca. Especially when it might be all the time he had with her.

When he walked into the locker room, most of the guys were already out of the showers and getting ready to leave. He quickly stripped out of his gear and headed for the hot steam that would ease the ache in his muscles. One of his teammates, a defensive back, nodded to Gage as he turned on the spray in the far corner and began washing off the grime.

One by one, the other guys left the showers, leaving him alone. Gage closed his eyes and leaned back against the tile wall, letting his mind drift a little.

"Mr. Daniels?" A familiar male voice yelled into the shower area. "You in there?"

"Yeah." Gage pushed off the wall, and reached for the handle to turn off the water. "I'll be out in a minute."

It had taken him a few seconds, but he recognized the man's voice as one of the stadium's security. Grabbing his towel, Gage wrapped it around his waist and walked out into the locker room where the man was waiting.

"Everything okay?" Gage asked, reaching for another towel to dry his upper body. The security guard stood there, relaxed. Whatever it was, it couldn't be that bad.

"This came for you up in the main office. They also wanted me to let you know that Mr. Donovan said he wants to see you before you leave."

Of course, he does.

Gage took the envelope from the man and thanked him. No doubt Tim wanted to see if this was another note from his stalker.

Just looking at the handwritten letters on the front of the envelope, he knew it was. It was too much to hope that whoever was behind this had been spooked by nearly being caught on Sunday. No, whoever his stalker was, he or she wasn't giving up. He knew Hansen had insisted this was a good thing, but Gage wasn't so sure. He just wanted it to stop. He also wished he understood the motivation behind it all. Maybe if he did, he could figure out who was doing this.

Not bothering to open the letter, he laid it on his bench, dug his cell phone out of his locker, and dialed Rebecca's number. She answered on the second ring.

"You're late." Her voice was serious, but he could hear the

levity there, too.

He chuckled.

"I know. Coach needed to talk to me after practice."

"Okay. Are you on your way out now, then?"

"No." He positioned the phone between his ear and shoulder, so he could finish drying off and slip his jeans on. "Mr. Donovan wants to see me." Gage paused, knowing she wasn't going to like this next part. He didn't either. "And I got another envelope."

He could almost see her sitting up, suddenly at attention. The sound of a car door opening made him realize she must have already been in his SUV waiting for him.

"What does it say?"

"I don't know. I haven't opened it yet."

"Where are you?"

Her breathing pattern had changed, and he knew she must have been jogging or running.

"I'm fine. I'm still in the locker room."

"Are you alone?"

He glanced around, even though he knew all the other guys had already gone, including the security guard. "Yes."

"You're closer to the players' entrance than you are to Donovan's office, aren't you?"

"Yes. Rebecca, calm down. Nothing's going to happen to me here. There are security cameras everywhere."

"Gage, just please do this. For me." Hearing her pleading finally broke his resolve.

"Okay. I'll meet you there in less than two minutes," he said, taking a clean shirt out of his bag and putting it on over his head.

He stuffed his dirty clothes into his bag and tossed the letter on top before zipping it up, throwing the bag over his shoulder, and heading out of the locker room. She was freaked. He just didn't understand why. This wasn't the first time he'd ever been in the locker room by himself, and it wouldn't be the last. Sure, they'd gotten shot at in the parking lot outside the club, but that had been out in a public place. He couldn't see anyone breaking in and doing anything here. It would be too easy to be caught, and whoever this was didn't strike him as someone who wanted to be found out.

When he reached the door leading to the players' parking lot, he saw Rebecca pacing. She must have used her pass to let herself into the building.

"Hey."

She hurried to close the remaining distance between them and wrapped her arms tightly around his neck.

"Whoa. Are you okay?" He held her tight. Her reaction was a little over the top. As he held her, though, he realized she'd thought him to be in danger. Maybe her reaction meant she felt more for him than she was admitting.

"I'm fine," he assured her. "Other than being a little sore from practice, I've never been better."

She stepped back, checking him over visibly for any injuries. Once she appeared convinced that he was indeed unharmed, she collected herself and went into professional mode. He didn't like seeing her so freaked out, but he wasn't a big fan of "Agent Carson" either. He wanted . . . he *needed* his Rebecca.

"Do you have the envelope?" she asked, all of the previous emotion gone.

He shifted the bag off his shoulder, opened it, and handed her the letter.

Somewhere between her question and his giving her the envelope, she'd slipped on a pair of latex gloves. She flipped the envelope over, examining it, just as she had the last time. Once she seemed satisfied with whatever she was looking for, she ran her finger under the seal to open it.

When Gage saw the contents, it registered that this one had felt lighter than the others, and with good reason. The envelope contained a single photo of Rebecca walking across a street. The picture had been taken earlier that day, most likely when she was going from the players' parking lot to the café that morning.

He was so caught up in the picture, not understanding its meaning, that he almost missed the small piece of paper that had come along with it. It wasn't until he saw Rebecca's hands clench that he glanced up to see what had stolen her attention. He looked back down and read the note. Unlike the other handwritten notes, this one was typed in bold, black letters.

GET RID OF HER!

Chapter 25

The words jumped off the page at Rebecca, and things started to fall into place for her. At least, as far as the photos Gage had been receiving. All of them had included him with various women. Before, she'd thought it was an interesting bit of information, but she'd viewed it as more a comment on his lifestyle choices than anything else. After this current photo, she was thinking it was intentional. Whoever it was, they weren't honing in on Gage specifically, but more his relationships with the female population.

Who would care who Gage dated, though? Or more accurately, who he slept with? An ex-girlfriend, perhaps?

Gage ripped the paper out of her hands and held it in front of him. His face was intense, almost scary. Although she knew she should take the paper back, guard it as evidence, his expression stopped her. They had the photo and plenty of other notes. That would have to be enough.

"Do you have any idea who would have a problem with the women in your life?" she asked.

"What?" He glanced up at her in disbelief.

"All the photographs you've been sent have one thing in common. All of them, with this one exception, have been of you and women you've had some type of relationship with."

"I don't think I would consider sex a relationship."

She winced. Even though she knew that's what they had—*all* they had, really—it hurt a little to hear him say it.

"Be that as it may, the women appear to be the one constant."

"What does that mean?"

Instead of answering his question, she asked one of her own. "Who would be bothered by who you date? Even though whoever this is has been keeping watch, this is the first time they've pointed to a specific person and told you to get rid of her."

"You," he said, pointedly. "They're telling me to get rid of *you*."

"I know."

There was pain in his eyes, hurt. She wanted to comfort him. The tips of her fingers itched with the need to touch him, but she held back. As much as she wanted to hold him and have him hold her as well, at that moment he needed her as an FBI agent, not a girlfriend.

"I know I've asked this before, but is there an ex-girlfriend? Maybe even someone who has had a crush on you for a long time but hasn't said anything?"

Gage ran a hand through his still-damp hair. "I don't know. There was a girl I dated for a while in college, but it was never really that serious. Everything else is high school stuff. I can't see any of them doing this."

"A crush?"

He shook his head, the note clenched in both hands. "Not that I'm aware of."

Footsteps could be heard coming down the hallway toward them, and they both looked up in the direction of the noise.

"We should go see Donovan."

Gage didn't respond other than to take her hand and start walking. They passed the guard they'd heard on their way to the elevator. He smiled and nodded as he passed them.

Once inside the closed space of the elevator, Gage backed her up against the wall and gave her a hard kiss, holding her hips firmly in his hands. It was over almost before it began, but it conveyed more meaning than words could have at that point. The doors opened, and she stood there stunned for a moment before shaking herself back to reality and the business at hand.

After two short raps to Donovan's door, a voice called for them to enter. The team's owner sat behind his large wooden desk. He smiled, but it didn't reach his eyes.

"Come in," he said, motioning to the seats in front of his desk.

They sat down, Gage never letting go of her hand. Donovan noticed.

"I see you two are getting along better. That's good."

"Everything's great." Sarcasm dripped from Gage's words, and Donovan frowned.

"Another envelope was delivered today," Rebecca said, jumping in before something happened between the two. Gage was already on edge, she could feel it, see it in the way he held his body. He didn't need to start a fight with his boss on top of everything else.

"May I see it?"

Rebecca took the picture and held it up for Donovan to see.

"I'd rather you not touch it, Mr. Donovan. It will make fingerprinting's job a lot easier."

"Oh yes, of course," he said, leaning across the desk to take a closer look. When he realized what the picture was of, he glance over at her, eyebrows raised in question.

"It seems the person wants me out of Gage's life."

Donovan sat back in his chair, folding his hands in his lap.

"You got all that from a picture?"

Gage abruptly stood up, slamming the typed note onto the desk.

When Donovan read the note, he visibly paled.

"Oh."

"As you can see, this changes things," Rebecca said, laying a hand on Gage's arm, urging him to sit back down.

"Yes, I suppose it does. What happens now?"

"Nothing."

"What?"

Both Donovan and Gage looked at her with wide eyes.

"If we do anything now, we give the stalker what they want. If he or she is agitated by our lack of compliance, there is more chance of them taking a risk, and slipping up."

"Or doing something more reckless and getting my star quarterback hurt or killed."

Rebecca shook her head, disagreeing. "I don't think that will happen. Gage is rarely alone. And based on this new evidence, I'd say I'm more at risk than he is for the time being."

Gage reached for her hand again, holding it tight in both of his.

"Are we any closer to catching whoever it is?" Donovan asked, ignoring Gage's reaction.

"We are. My partner is in the process of following a very promising lead at the moment. If all goes well, we may have a suspect in custody soon."

Donovan released a deep breath. "That's good to hear."

After a few more probing questions, to which she provided vague answers, Rebecca and Gage left Donovan's office and headed back to the players' parking lot.

By the time they reached Gage's SUV, she was beginning to worry about him. He hadn't said a word on the way down, and he'd refused to let go of her hand for any length of time. She'd had to request he release it long enough for her to remove her gloves after placing the envelope, picture, and note in a plastic bag Donovan provided. As soon as the gloves were off and tucked back inside her back pocket, he took hold of her hand once more. She'd again had to ask him to let go so she could check the vehicle and they could get inside. He quickly fastened his seatbelt once they climbed in, and reached for her hand.

Finally, she couldn't take it anymore. "Are you all right?"

He stared at her, eyes full of something she didn't want to put a name to. "Someone is targeting you because of me. No. I'm not all right."

"It's my job, Gage," she said, trying to keep her voice calm.

"Is that all I am to you? A job?" He unbuckled his seat belt and took her face in his hands. "Is that really all we have between us? A job?"

Rebecca swallowed, nervous. She didn't want to lie, not after everything. The intensity in his eyes scared her a little. So did the ache in her chest, the pounding of her heart. Gage was rapidly becoming extremely important to her. She didn't know how to process all her emotions, but she was certain this thing with him was no longer only a job.

"No," she whispered.

He brushed his fingers gently across her cheek. "I . . ." Gage cleared his throat. "I don't want anything to happen to you. I'm not sure I could stand it."

His kiss was barely there. She kept trying to deepen it, but every time he'd pull back just enough to break the seal of their mouths then go back to the same gentle pressure. Eventually, she gave up and enjoyed what he was offering.

***

Gage had been on the verge of telling her he loved her. It had been there, on the tip of his tongue, but he bit it back. After the day's events, he needed to feel her, hold her, and make love to her. His biggest fear, even bigger than finding out his stalker had fixated on her, was that he would tell her how he felt and she would shut him out.

After making a detour to drop the newest letter off to Hansen, he broke a few speed limits driving them home. They'd barely made it into the house before he swept her up in his arms and carried her upstairs.

Their lovemaking was slow, deliberate. With every touch of his hands, every kiss of his lips he tried to convey his feelings for her. This wasn't about sex. Not for him. This was about showing her what he couldn't say. He only hoped she understood the message.

It was after seven by the time they walked back downstairs, him in a pair of jeans and her in one of his T-shirts. He really liked seeing her in his shirt. Too bad she hadn't forgone her panties as well. Although he'd tried to persuade her, she wouldn't budge. He let it go but couldn't completely dispel the vision he had in his head of her bent over the kitchen counter in nothing but his shirt. Just the thought had him ready to go again.

He suppressed his urges and helped her make dinner. They sat together at the dining room table and ate. It was there he asked her about her meeting with Hansen earlier in the day.

"Was Hansen able to find anything out about the rental car that was following us?"

She took a bite before she answered. "The vehicle was registered under the name of Mark Fuller. He ran the license number and was able to compare it to the surveillance video from the rental location. They match, which is good, but as of yet, Hansen hasn't been able to find a connection between you and Fuller."

Gage racked his brain, but the name Mark Fuller didn't ring any bells.

"He was the guy following us?"

She shrugged. "That's the assumption. At least until we have more information."

He thought about that for a minute. "What happens now?"

"Hansen's trying to track down the guy. He's got some friends at the local police department, so he was able to put an APB out on him and the car since it still shows as rented to Fuller. He was also planning to swing by his residence today and see if he had any luck tracking him down. Hopefully, once we have him in custody, we'll start getting some answers."

They finished their meals, and retired upstairs to Gage's bedroom. Slipping under the covers, he pulled her into his arms. Kissing the top of her head, he asked if she'd like to watch a movie. She surprised him by suggesting a game of twenty questions instead.

"What's your favorite color?" she asked.

"Red."

"I've never seen you wear red."

"Is that another question?" He chuckled.

She thought about it for a minute then sighed. "No."

He smiled.

"What made you join the FBI?"

"There was a girl who went missing in my hometown when I was sixteen. She was about Megan's age at the time, and I couldn't imagine anything like that happening to my little sister and not being able to do anything about it. I knew right then that I wanted to be part of finding missing children."

"Is that what you do mostly? Find missing kids?"

"Is that another question?" She smirked.

He laughed.

"Yeah, I guess it is."

"Then, yes. That's mostly what I do. Sometimes I'm put on other assignments, but finding missing or abducted kids is what I enjoy doing. Even when the ending doesn't turn out the way I hope, at least I can give their families some closure."

He noticed a change in her as she spoke. "Did something happen?"

She rolled away from him, putting space between them for the first time since they'd climbed back into bed.

"Hey. Talk to me. What happened?" He moved behind her, gathering her back into his arms. Every muscle in her body was tense, and he was scared she was going to bolt.

"It was about two months ago," she whispered.

He held her tighter, trying to comfort her, knowing whatever she was about to tell him was difficult for her.

"A six-year-old girl went missing. There was a custody dispute, and her father took her."

She didn't say anything for several minutes. "They called you in to find her?"

"Yes."

Silence filled the room again as she gathered her thoughts. This time, he just lay there and let her think.

"We found her two states away in Georgia. Her father was wasted, empty whiskey bottles everywhere."

Her voice took on a dead quality that ran his blood cold. He could tell she was distancing herself, and something told him the worst part was yet to come.

"He wouldn't let her go. I tried everything I could think of, but he wouldn't release her. I had no choice . . ."

"You had no choice about what?" he prompted when she seemed to lose herself to her memories.

"He had a gun to her head, and I could tell he was going to pull the trigger. I had to shoot him first."

Things began to make sense to him. She'd told him she was on leave from the FBI, which was why she'd taken the job to protect him. Given the time frame, he had to assume her leave was directly related to the shooting. "I'm sorry," he murmured into her hair.

She didn't respond.

He remained silent for a while, absorbing what she'd told him. Eventually, she broke the silence by asking him another question. This one about football. The emotionally charged conversation closed, at least for the time being. They lay there for the next several hours, questioning each other until they both began to yawn. He turned out the lights and drifted off to sleep, temporarily forgetting about the person threatening his happiness.

His phone ringing startled him awake the next morning. Turning over, he glanced at the clock. Six forty-five. He fumbled for the phone. "Hello?"

"Sorry to wake you, Gage, but I'm in the airport getting ready to fly out to Los Angeles. I wanted to catch you before I boarded the plane."

"Yeah. Sure, Mel. What's up?" Gage asked, trying to wake himself up. He needed some coffee.

Rebecca rolled over beside him. She looked a lot more alert than he felt. Her eyes questioned him, but she didn't speak.

"The photographer from your underwear shoot called late last night. Apparently, there's something wrong with some of the shots. He's pushing to do a reshoot."

Gage groaned. He'd hated that shoot the first time around.

"When will you know?"

"My flight leaves in a half hour. I'm supposed to meet with him over lunch. I should know more then. How about you stop by my office tomorrow after practice? I should have all the details at that point and be able to tell you how we need to proceed. Hopefully, this is just an artist making a big fuss about nothing."

"Okay," Gage said. "I'll see you tomorrow afternoon."

Mel disconnected the call, and Gage flopped back on his pillow.

"Everything all right?"

He sighed.

"We have to go see Mel tomorrow, and I might have to fly out to LA in the near future. Knowing my luck, it will have to be after Sunday's game. Just what I want to do with my day off," Gage muttered.

He glanced over at Rebecca. She was lying on her side, her head propped up with her hand, and the sheet pooled around her waist, leaving her breasts exposed. An evil grin spread across his face. Reaching out, he pulled her closer. Maybe being awoken early had its advantages.

Chapter 26

After practice Thursday afternoon, Gage drove them to Mel's office. The day had gone much better than the one previous with one exception. Hansen had yet to track down Mark Fuller or the car. He'd ended up sleeping in his vehicle the previous night in an attempt to catch Fuller coming home, with no luck. Currently, he was planning a stakeout of the suspect's place of employment.

They pulled into the lot outside Mel's building, and Gage found a parking spot. It was a crisp December day, and Gage threw his arm around her shoulders as they walked the short distance into the building. She froze for a moment, glancing around, and he almost released her.

"Everything good?"

She smiled.

"Yes, everything's fine, but could you put your arm around my waist instead? That way my arm is free in case I need to use it."

In case, she needs to reach for her gun.

He did as she requested, happy she'd not wanted him to remove all contact.

The interior of the building hadn't changed much since the last time they'd been there. The only difference was the addition of a few garlands and wreaths hung over the doors and windows. He also noticed a poinsettia sitting on a table beside the elevator. Those were the only concessions to the season. It was nothing like the elaborate way his mom decorated for Christmas. Then again, this was a business, not a home. He wasn't sure yet if he'd get to go home for Christmas that year or not. He always hoped, but it was never a guarantee.

Even though Mel was expecting them, they had to wait since he was in the middle of a call. His receptionist offered them something to drink, but they declined. Gage wanted to get this over with. He didn't want to fly back to LA and prance around in his underwear before a camera again. Once had been more than enough.

When they were called back, he kept his hand locked with Rebecca's as they walked through the adjoining door to Mel's office. His manager sat behind his desk, waiting. He smiled at Gage. When he noticed Rebecca, his smile decreased slightly. Maybe Mel didn't want to discuss business in front of someone he didn't really know. He hadn't said anything after the last time, not that it would have made any difference, but he could have thought it was a one-time thing.

By the time they'd taken a seat he was all smiles again.

"Gage, it's good to see you again. And you . . . Rebecca, isn't it? I wasn't expecting you to be joining us again this afternoon."

"I hope that's not a problem, Mel. We were planning to go to dinner after, and since it's not far from here, it just made sense." They hadn't planned to go out tonight at all, but he figured a little white lie to his manager was easier than trying to come up with another reason to explain why Rebecca was there. He knew it must have looked odd to Mel. Gage had never had a girlfriend in all the years he'd known him. He'd certainly never brought one with him to a meeting, yet he'd brought Rebecca with him twice. Mel had better get used to dealing with Rebecca, however, if Gage had anything to say about it.

"Oh. No. It's fine with me if it's okay with you."

"Good," Gage said, smiling. "Now, what did you find out about the pictures?"

Mel frowned. Gage knew he wasn't going to like the answer.

"There appears to have been an equipment malfunction. The first batch of pictures is fine, but the second batch . . ."

"What's wrong with them? I didn't notice anything different after the break."

"The cameraman isn't sure. All he knows is that when he developed the images, all of them had tiny black spots. All the pictures from your afternoon shoot have to be redone."

Gage hung his head and sighed. Never again would he do an underwear ad. Unfortunately, he was already under contract for this one. How in the world had he let Mel talk him into this?

"When?" he asked, looking up at his manager.

"You'll catch a flight Sunday night after the game. I know it will be late, since it's an afternoon game, so I made sure they wouldn't expect you at the studio before noon. Here is your plane ticket. Your flight doesn't leave until ten, so unless you go into double overtime, you should have no trouble catching it."

Gage looked over the ticket. Everything appeared to be in order as far as he could tell.

"There will be a town car waiting for you at your hotel at eleven. They are also to have everything wrapped up no later than four. It will put you back in Nashville after midnight, but I promise no early wake-up calls."

Mel laughed at his own joke. The best Gage could manage was a weak smile.

His frown quickly returned and stayed there as they walked back to the vehicle. Once they were on the road again, Rebecca reached for his hand and gave it a squeeze to get his attention. He glanced over at her.

"Want to talk about it?"

"Not really."

She nodded.

Not feeling ready to go home, he decided to run with his lie to Mel and drove to his favorite restaurant. Rebecca didn't comment on their change in direction.

The hostess greeted him by name when they walked through the door and led them to a table. It wasn't until after they'd ordered their food that he noticed her watching him.

"What?"

She leaned back in her seat and folded her hands in front of her on the table.

"I'm not going to like this, am I?" he asked.

She frowned.

"I don't know."

"Well, whatever it is, lay it on me. More bad news isn't going to make much difference at this point."

"I'm wondering if maybe Hansen should go with you to Los Angeles."

He sat up straight.

"What? Why?"

She sighed and met his gaze.

"I just think . . ." She took a deep breath. "I'm afraid you're reading more into this, into us, than you should. Maybe some distance . . ."

Gage scooted his chair closer to her, eating up the space between them.

"No."

"No?" She looked at him with wide eyes.

"No. I'm not reading more into us than I should. And no, Hansen is *not* going to go with me to Los Angeles."

"Gage—"

"No!" His voice echoed through the restaurant, and people turned their heads to see what was going on at their table. He lowered his volume but not the intensity. "No. If I'm going to LA, so are you." She opened her mouth to protest, but he cut her off. "I have no idea where this thing with us is going, Rebecca, and neither do you, so stop running scared."

"I'm not—"

"What do you call it, then? Rebecca, whatever it is between us . . . this doesn't happen every day. Hell, sometimes it doesn't happen in a lifetime. I'm sorry this scares you. Maybe it's because of your parents. I don't know. But what I do know is that I'm not letting you turn your back on something that could be great."

***

Rebecca couldn't move.

Gage held her captive by his words. Her mind screamed at her to get up and leave, but her body refused to move.

"I love you, Rebecca."

No. He doesn't love me. He couldn't.

She shook her head, trying to dislodge the words he'd spoken from her head. They weren't true. They couldn't be true. He wasn't supposed to love her. This wasn't supposed to happen. It was supposed to be sex. Nothing more. It couldn't be more. He was all wrong for her. She had a plan. A good plan. He wasn't supposed to ruin it.

Food appeared in front of her. She pulled her hands out of Gage's grasp to start eating. The food was tasteless in her mouth, but she ate it anyway. It was something to do, something to distract her from the mantra on a repetitive loop in her brain.

About halfway through her meal, Rebecca realized Gage hadn't touched his food yet.

"Aren't you eating?"

He frowned and pushed his plate away.

"Suddenly, I'm not hungry."

She lay down her fork and turned to face him. Her knees bumped into his as she moved. Warmth spread through her at the contact. Her chest felt heavy, her stomach empty, despite the food she'd just eaten. She wanted to reach out and feel his arms wrap around her as they'd done so many times over the last week. Instead, she kept her hands in her lap, clasped tight together, safe from her impulses.

"You should eat. You had practice today, and you have to be hungry."

"I think I'll survive without food for one night."

She frowned.

Then he placed his hands on her face, touching her, making her feel all the things she didn't want to feel. Her eyes closed of their own volition. She leaned into his touch before she could stop herself.

"Please, Rebecca. Please, just give us a chance. That's all I'm asking. I know you're scared. I am, too."

As good as this felt, him touching her, she had to be strong. She had to end this. It was the only way.

She snapped her eyes open, took hold of his wrists, and removed his hands from her face.

He sighed and dropped his hands onto his lap. She'd never seen him look so defeated. It didn't look right on him. She missed that cocky grin of his. The overconfident man who cornered her at every turn. The man who made her overheat from the inside out every time he touched her. The man she was going to willingly push away for both their sakes.

She stood.

"I'm ready to leave if you are."

Gage stared at her for a long minute before standing. He threw some money on the table for their meals. She wasn't even sure he counted it.

He walked beside her in silence out to the SUV. She stayed focused enough on their surroundings to keep him safe, but inside, she felt like she was going to be sick. After checking under the vehicle, they climbed in and drove home . . . back to his house. Out of the corner of her eye, she saw his fingers clutch and release the steering wheel as he drove, but he didn't speak.

Once back at the house, she excused herself so she could check the perimeter. She was grateful when he didn't fight her on it—she needed some time to herself.

As she walked slowly around the outside of his house, she realized just how comfortable she'd become there. Comfortable and stupid. She felt the tears start to fall down her cheeks, and she didn't try to stop them. She would solve this case for him, make sure he was safe. Then—no matter how hard it was for her—she would say good-bye.

Chapter 27

It was dark by the time Rebecca let herself in through the back door. The main floor was quiet, the lights dimmed. She set the alarm then went to locate Gage. She wasn't prepared to come face-to-face with him yet. She hoped she'd be able to confirm he was safe and in the house before retiring to her bedroom for the night—without him seeing her.

She almost walked right past him. He was sitting in the corner of the living room. With the lights so low, she hadn't seen him. Unfortunately, there was no hope of avoiding him. He was staring right at her.

"I'm going to make sure the house is secure before calling Hansen. I want to see if he was able to track down Fuller."

Gage stood.

He took a step toward her then stopped.

"That's all you have to say?"

"Gage, don't do this." Rebecca was hanging on by a thread as it was. She didn't need to rehash everything. There was no way she'd be able to keep it together, and she didn't want him to see her cry.

Before he had a chance to say anything more, she turned and ran up the stairs as fast as her feet would carry her. She heard his footfalls behind her and knew he was following. Thankfully, she was able to open her door and slam it shut, locking him out seconds before he reached her. He banged on the door with both fists, calling her name, but she ignored him. Using what she'd learned growing up, she closed her eyes and blocked out the noise around her. Redirecting her thoughts, she concentrated on her new goal—taking a shower. She walked straight for her bathroom, and turned on the water. Stripping out of her clothes as quickly as possible and flinging them carelessly on the floor, she stepped into the shower letting the water wash away the fact that her heart was breaking.

After thirty minutes, her skin was starting to wrinkle, but the ache in her chest hadn't eased. *It will get better*, she told herself. It had to.

Rebecca dried off, and walked naked back into her room. She ran a hand over the bed she'd not used in over a week. It seemed huge and empty, but she knew she'd better get used to it. There would be no more sharing a bed with Gage.

Walking over to the dresser, she removed a pair of pajamas and put them on mechanically. She felt disconnected from her body. All her limbs were attached and functioning properly, but it was all on autopilot.

Determined to get her mind off Gage, she sat down at the small desk where she had set up her laptop. She logged onto her e-mail, hoping that Megan had sent her something to distract her. Luckily, she had.

Megan loved sending her pictures. This time the photos were of her room at Paul's house. Rebecca had to admit it was nice. Nothing extravagant, but it was perfect for Megan. On the table beside her bed was the framed picture of the two of them as teenagers that her sister always carried with her. Seeing it made Rebecca smile.

She scrolled down further and looked through the other pictures Megan had attached. Paul's house reminded her of Gage's parents' house. It was nice but simple, practical. There wasn't anything lavish in sight. Considering Paul's profession, it made sense. Cops, even detectives, didn't make that much money.

Thinking about Paul's job led her back to her own. She needed to go downstairs and check that the house was secure before she could climb into bed and try to fall into the oblivion of sleep. Unfortunately, she knew Gage would still be awake, and she was going to do everything she could to avoid another confrontation that night. She would have to wait him out. He had practice the next day. He had to go to sleep at some point. When he did, she would sneak downstairs and make her rounds.

Hoping Hansen had good news, she picked up the phone and dialed.

It took him a while to answer, and when he did, she could barely hear him through the background noise.

"Hang on!"

Slowly, the noise began to fade.

"You still there?"

"Where are you?"

"Yeah, thanks." He paused, and then the background noise was completely gone. "Sorry. I'm at a club downtown."

"I take it you haven't found Fuller yet."

"No. His manger said he took the week off. He is scheduled to work on Monday, so at worst, I'll corner him then. One of the other employees heard me asking about Fuller and said he frequents this club. I'm hoping to get lucky. If not, I'll be back on stakeout duty tomorrow at his residence."

Rebecca sighed. She leaned back in her chair and closed her eyes.

"I'm going to be honest, though, Carson. I think there's something we're missing here."

"What do you mean?" she asked, opening her eyes and standing. She couldn't bear to sit anymore. A nervous energy was coursing through her body.

"Fuller works at a fast-food joint. From what his manager said, he's an average employee. I can't see him having the means to follow Daniels around or plant explosives on his vehicle. The shooting . . . I could buy that. It doesn't take all that much to get a gun if one's determined, but explosives?"

"You don't think he's our guy?"

"No, I don't. That doesn't mean I don't think he might have some information that can help us. The vehicle following you two was registered to him. If he wasn't driving it, hopefully he knows who was."

"Agreed. Anything else?"

"No. On your end?"

"Gage has to fly to Los Angeles Sunday night after the game for a promotional photo shoot."

"You need me to tag along as backup?"

As much as Rebecca wanted to say yes, she knew it would be

better if Hansen focused his energies on finding Fuller. At this point, it was the best lead they had.

"No. You need to find Fuller."

"I'll call you once I find him. You just watch Daniels and yourself. After what this person's already pulled, I wouldn't put anything past them."

She walked to her bed and sat down after hanging up with Hansen. They had to find Fuller. Somehow, her gut was telling her he was the link, and she'd learned to follow her instinct, like every good law enforcement officer.

Glancing at the clock, she realized it was already after eleven. She walked to the door, and listened for any sound from Gage on the other side. Nothing.

Slowly, she peeked out into the hallway His door was closed. She breathed a sigh of relief and padded down the stairs with as much stealth as she could. Less than ten minutes later, she was back in her room, behind a locked door, free and clear.

She leaned back against the door and stared at the empty bed across the room. The pain in her chest returned, and she did her best to will it away. It didn't work. Putting one foot in front of the other, she crossed to her bed and crawled under the covers.

***

Gage heard Rebecca as she tiptoed down the stairs. He was tempted to follow and corner her. Make her admit that she felt something for him, too. Maybe it wasn't love—not yet—but it could be. He knew she cared for him, at least. She'd admitted as much.

He didn't follow her, however. His bed was cold and empty without her, but he lay there and endured it. Telling her how he felt had been a risk. He'd known that, and he was paying the consequences.

Even as he lectured himself, he knew she'd not really given him much of a choice. Something had happened, and she'd already started to pull away. Maybe she'd realized she was falling for him, too. He hadn't gone into this expecting to fall in love and neither had she. Love had blindsided him, but in the best possible way.

Rebecca was stubborn. It was one of the things he loved about her. Unfortunately, it was also one of the things that infuriated him.

He hadn't been lying when he said he believed they could have something great. Love was a risk, but it was one worth taking with the right person. Gage was positive Rebecca was that person.

Friday morning came all too soon, and he was back at practice. Rebecca returned to the routine of avoidance she'd adopted before they'd spent Thanksgiving with his family. She woke up early—he had no idea what time since he'd been up before seven—and checked the outside. After that, she shut herself in her room until it was time to leave for the stadium.

Gage wished he knew what to say to break through whatever wall she'd put up this time, but he was at a loss. He didn't have much experience with relationships. Plus, Rebecca was the complete opposite of the other women he had dated. He could almost guarantee that what would have worked with them wouldn't work with her anyway.

The drive to the stadium was tense. He wanted to touch her, to hold her hand like he had before, and he almost did. Her posture was defiant, almost daring him to push the boundaries she'd set once again. More than anything, he wanted to do just that, but it wasn't the time. Unlike before, he knew what it was like to get lost in her. If he started, he wasn't sure he'd be able to stop.

His hand reached out to her automatically as he turned to go. She took a step back and tilted her head to the side. He dropped his hand and walked into the stadium, while she stood watch beside his SUV.

Somehow, he managed to stay focused on practice. Being able to blow off some steam helped. His receivers were, once again, commenting on the power he was putting behind his throws.

"Hey, ease up, man. You're gonna burn my hands off at this rate," one of his receivers complained as he jogged back into the huddle.

"Can't take the heat, Kelly?" Kenny asked.

"Stop it, guys. Let's run the play again, but this time cut to your right. I want to practice some sideline passes."

Kelly groaned but went to take his place on the field.

Gage walked up behind his center, and moments later, the ball was in play. Four defenders pressed hard against his offensive line trying to get to him and the ball. He was aware of them, but his focus was on his receivers. One was over the middle. He was completely open. The other two were hugging the sideline, just as he'd called it, but they were also playing man-to-man coverage. It would have been smarter to throw it to the open receiver, but Gage wasn't in the mood to play it safe. He hurled the ball through the air toward Kelly. The ball landed right on target, square in the middle of his chest, seconds before the safety tackled him.

Kelly rubbed his chest as he stood. Gage smiled. It wasn't the best way to relieve his irritations, but it was all he had at the moment.

Practice lasted another two hours before they broke for the day. He showered, changed, and then walked out to the parking lot to meet Rebecca. She was in the car waiting for him, like any other day.

She watched him walk across the parking lot and even smiled politely when he slid behind the wheel.

He'd had enough.

"How long are you going to shut me out?"

"Can we just get back to your house, please?"

Gage gritted his teeth and started the vehicle. Something was going to give when they got home, one way or another. He couldn't just sit on his hands and do nothing. He had to try.

As soon as they were inside the house, she walked toward the stairs.

"I'd appreciate it if you'd join me for dinner. I'll come get you when it's ready."

She looked at him, curious.

"You have to eat," he said.

"All right."

He nodded.

She turned on her heel and climbed the stairs to her room.

Gage took a deep breath and jogged to his refrigerator. It was fairly well-stocked, with the basics, anyway. The problem was, he had limited knowledge. Knowing what he needed to do, he dug his phone out of his pocket and dialed.

"Hey, Ma. I need your help."

Chapter 28

Two soft knocks sounded on her door just after six o'clock. She took a deep breath and tugged at the bottom of her blouse, even though it was already lying perfectly in place. Rebecca walked to her bedroom door and opened it.

Her breath caught in her throat when she saw Gage standing on the other side. He was wearing a black dress shirt and pants. The silky shirt clung to the muscles of his arms and chest, and the dark colors gave him a mysterious quality, making his brown eyes look even darker. He looked incredibly sexy. She wanted to run her hands up and down the front of his shirt before circling her arms around his neck and kissing him. Never in her life had she met a man with such potent appeal.

Rebecca turned around, pretending to grab something on the dresser. She needed a minute to get a grip on her reaction, or she was going to jump into his arms. That wouldn't be helpful. It wouldn't make things easier.

Yes it would, she argued with herself.

No. She had to stick with the plan. She had to think long term. Gage wasn't . . . right . . . for her.

The first time she'd reminded herself of Gage's incompatibility with her life plans, she'd believed it. At the moment, however, she was starting to doubt herself. That hadn't happened in a long time. Rebecca was used to making a decision and sticking to it. Gage was changing everything.

"Dinner's ready." He held out his hand for her, waiting for her to take it.

She stared down at his hand, debating whether or not to go along with whatever he had in mind. Rebecca met his gaze with her own, full of questions.

"It's just dinner, Rebecca."

Dinner. Right.

Reluctantly, she gave him her hand. He wrapped his warm fingers around her palm, and she felt the heat travel up her arm and through the rest of her body. She closed her eyes, trying to get her bearings.

"You ready?"

She opened her eyes and looked at him.

"Yes. I'm ready." He smiled and squeezed her hand, before leading her down the stairs.

When they walked into the dining room, Rebecca stopped abruptly. She blinked twice, thinking she might be seeing things. When she reopened her eyes, everything was exactly the same. There were two place settings at one end of the table, each with a neatly folded napkin, along with two lit candles. The lights had been lowered to create an intimate feel with the candlelight. She felt the muscles in her throat contract.

"Gage . . ."

"Too much?"

She looked again at the scene in front of her, the obvious work he'd put into it, and felt the pressure in her chest return.

"I don't know," she whispered.

She focused on him again, scrutinizing his face, his eyes. He watched her, waiting for . . . something.

"What is it you want from me?"

He took a step toward her. "I want you to have dinner with me. That's it. Just dinner."

"That's it?" she asked, skeptical.

He smirked. "Okay. That's not all I want, but if that's all you'll give me, I'll take it."

"Gage, I—"

His finger pressed against her lips, silencing her, and she felt her skin react at his touch.

"Dinner."

She nodded.

Throughout the meal, Gage was a perfect gentleman. Knowing she didn't drink alcohol, he poured them both water to go along with the chicken, vegetables, and rice he'd made. He kept the conversation casual, asking her a lot of questions about college and her job with the FBI.

It reminded her of the game of twenty questions they'd played while lying in his bed. Unfortunately, that was the last thing she wanted to be reminded of right then. Gage was amazing. He was handsome, charming, and he had a softer side that she had a feeling most people didn't get to see. Of course, he was also one of the cockiest men she'd ever met. Instead of that being a turnoff, she found she liked it. It was part of who he was.

The sound of his fork hitting his plate with a little more force than was normal brought her attention back to him. He was frowning.

"What's wrong?" she asked.

"I was going to ask you the same thing. You seem to be thinking really hard about something, and I don't think it's anything good by the look on your face."

She sighed and placed her own fork down on the table.

"What is it that you want from me?"

"I told you. Dinner."

Rebecca shook her head. "No. I mean, what is all this supposed to mean?" She gestured to the romantic setup.

Gage laid his napkin on the table off to the side and leaned forward in his chair. He reached for her hand. She tried to pull back, but he held on tight, not letting her get away.

"I know what I said the other night scared you." She opened her mouth to protest, but he stopped her. "It made you uncomfortable. Is that better?"

When she didn't answer, he continued. "You asked what I want from you. What I want is for you to consider giving us a chance. A chance beyond your job to protect me." She opened her mouth again, but he went on without allowing her to get a word into the conversation. "I don't want you to say anything right now. I don't want you to make any decisions. I just want you to think about it. Think about making this thing between us official."

He held her gaze for the longest time, and she wondered if he would kiss her. The air around them grew thick with tension, and she knew if she followed her instincts, she would be immediately in his arms enjoying his mouth, his hands. He'd made love to her on this table before, and she knew he wouldn't hesitate to do it again. All she had to do was give in to what he wanted.

Things weren't as simple as following her gut in this instance, however. This wasn't about a case anymore. This was her life. Her future. She couldn't gamble with it. Her childhood had been full of instability. She didn't want that for her future.

Gage didn't seem to expect a verbal answer from her, and she didn't provide one. After several minutes, he released her hand, pushed back from the table, and walked into the kitchen, leaving her alone with her thoughts.

He returned a few minutes later with two decorative glass bowls filled with chocolate ice cream. He placed a bowl down in front of her before sitting down beside her again. She looked down at the ice cream as if it were going to jump out and bite her. Making her dinner was a simple gesture, but it was one that no one had ever done for her before, before Gage. Her heart constricted, almost painfully, as she glanced up at him. He was watching her, a look of longing in his eyes.

After several minutes, he picked up his spoon and took a bite of his ice cream, breaking eye contact. She picked up her own spoon and did the same.

***

When Gage had decided to cook a romantic meal for Rebecca, he wasn't at all sure how it would go. All he knew was that he had to do something. He wasn't one to wait around for things to fix themselves. He was a doer, and always would be. Whenever there was something he wanted in life, he went after it.

Calling his mom had been a necessity. His cooking abilities were limited, and they tended to fall into the nonromantic variety. He didn't think cheeseburgers ranked very high on the romance scale. His mom stayed on the phone with him until he was certain everything was the way it should be. Once the food was finished, he set the oven on low and placed their plates inside to keep warm before going up to change.

Dinner went over about as well as he'd expected, but at least he was able to say his piece. He wanted her in his life. Gage only hoped, once she thought it through, she could see how good they were for each other.

Saturday morning came earlier than he would have liked. He awoke, showered, and dressed, wondering if he invaded her thoughts as much as she did his. Football had been his life for over ten years, longer if he counted all his pre-high-school time in the Pee-Wee League. It was what drove him, defined him. Over the years, women had come in and out of his life, but very few had made a lasting impression.

When Gage came downstairs, he found Rebecca standing in the kitchen toasting a bagel.

"Morning." He smiled.

She looked up from her task, her eyes cautious. "Morning."

Her stance was tense, as if she were waiting for him to pounce. Although he wanted nothing more than to pull her into his arms and kiss the living day lights out of her, he didn't. Keeping her in his peripheral vision, he walked over to the refrigerator, took out the orange juice, and poured himself a glass. He grabbed a bagel out of the bag and took a bite, leaning against the counter.

She went back to her bagel but kept him in her sights. He couldn't say he blamed her. If he had his way, she would be wearing a lot less clothes, and he would be having something much more desirable to eat for breakfast than a blueberry bagel.

As his thoughts drifted, he raked his gaze over her form. Her slacks hinted at the curves beneath, curves of which he had intimate knowledge. Although he would have preferred her in jeans, at least she'd worn one of her sweaters and forgone the suit jackets she favored so much. The slacks he could deal with. Her jackets . . . they covered up her backside too much for his liking. She had a fine ass. It shouldn't be hidden.

"What time do you have to be at the stadium?"

He knew she knew the answer already, but he responded to her anyway.

"Eleven."

She nodded and took a bite of her bagel. It didn't escape his notice that she was avoiding eye contact with him. Her gaze held firm to the coffee mug sitting in front of her on the counter.

"You know, it's going to be pretty difficult to protect me when you can't even look at me."

She glanced up at him, eyes wide. Then she seemed to get a hold of herself. She stood up straight, picked up her coffee, and leveled a hard stare in his direction. "Are you questioning my ability to do my job?" she asked, taking a sip and setting the mug back down.

He smirked.

"Not at all. Just making an observation."

"I see. And do you foresee unexpected danger within the walls of your home in the near future?"

He smiled wider. He couldn't help it. Bantering back and forth with her had quickly become one of his favorite things.

"No."

"Given that assumption, is there a reason why I should be watching your every move at this exact moment?"

No matter how much he knew he shouldn't, Gage couldn't back down from her challenge. He laid the remainder of his bagel on the counter along with his glass and stalked toward her. A flash of fear crossed her features then it was gone, hidden away under that mask of hers. Gage wanted to break through that façade. He'd seen the passion, the fire underneath when she let herself go.

She didn't back away. Then again, he hadn't expected her to. He stood in front of her, placing his hands on the counter, effectively trapping her. Her chest rose and fell with exaggerated breaths, the only sign of her discomfort. She held perfectly still, almost as if she were afraid to move.

He leaned in, his lips skimming the skin of her cheek as he whispered in her ear. "I'd prefer it if you were always watching me, beautiful, but I'll take what I can get."

Gage stepped away, watching her cheeks flush, her chest rise and fall with each breath. She couldn't hide her responses from him no matter how hard she tried. He reached for his bagel, popped the last of it in his mouth, and strolled toward the stairs, a huge smile on his face.

Chapter 29

Rebecca was drained. It was Sunday night, and they were aboard their fourth plane in two days. Traveling didn't normally bother her. With her job, she was used to it. Then again, she was also used to sleeping at night. That hadn't been happening. The little bit of sleep she had gotten was full of dreams of someone chasing her. She would wake up in a cold sweat, her heart pounding in her chest.

Gage sat beside her, more subdued than she was used to seeing him. It was the first time since she'd known him that his team had lost a game. He seemed deep in thought, pensive. The game had come down to the last three seconds. The entire stadium had been on its feet, holding their breath as the ball was snapped. The kicker had made contact with the ball, sending it soaring through the goal posts. Knowing Gage, he was probably running through the game in his head, trying to figure out what he could have done differently. In that respect, they were alike.

She looked out the window at the night sky, wondering which state they were flying over at that moment. Their plane was due to land in Los Angeles around midnight local time, which would make it right around three in the morning back in Tennessee. Too bad the three-hour difference wouldn't help her catch up on her sleep.

Even if they were able to sleep in, Rebecca doubted she would be able to take advantage of it. She suspected she would be sharing a bed with Gage. The hotel they had stayed at on Saturday night had been booked for the team and had two double beds. She'd learned from Gage that the players were always assigned roommates and given rooms with two beds. The room in LA had been booked by his manager, and only for him. Why would there be two beds?

Over the past two days, she had nearly broken more times than she could count. Keeping herself from touching him was a lot harder than she'd originally thought. How she would manage lying in the same bed with him she had no idea. Sitting there, seeing him with his brow wrinkled in concentration, she wanted to run her fingers along the puckered ridge and provide comfort. She knew it was only a game, but she also knew how hard he worked and that it was important to him.

Rebecca closed her eyes, trying to distance herself, but it didn't help. She could still feel him beside her. The impulse to touch him increased with every second.

"You okay?" he asked, startling her.

"Yeah. Yes," she said, sitting up straighter in her seat. "I'm fine. Just tired."

He frowned.

"You haven't been sleeping."

"I . . ." She took a calming breath. "No. Not really."

Gage didn't touch her, but he might have. His gaze bore into her as if he could see into her soul. "Me either."

"Excuse me." The flight attendant interrupted the moment, breaking the spell.

Rebecca swiftly turned her head back to the window, allowing Gage to address the woman.

"We're going to be dimming the lights in a few minutes for those passengers who'd like to sleep through the flight. Is there anything I can get either of you?"

Gage paused before he answered. She could almost feel his gaze through the back of her head, but she refused to turn around and face him.

"No, thank you. I think we're good for now."

"Okay. Just press the call button if you should need anything." The woman spoke with a little too much cheer. She was probably leaning into him, letting him know there was more on offer should he be interested. Rebecca couldn't blame her. Gage was gorgeous. Add to that his being a professional athlete in the prime of his career . . . the man was hard to resist, which was exactly the problem.

They encountered a handful of reporters at the airport, but other than asking for a few pictures they mostly left them alone. The local papers in Nashville had already publicized their relationship, so their being together wasn't really newsworthy. Not on a national scale, anyway.

The hotel was right in downtown Beverly Hills, and quite a bit nicer than anything Rebecca was used to. It was late, especially since it was after four in the morning Nashville time. Luckily, they had nine hours before the town car was due to take Gage to his photo shoot. She only hoped she would be able to get a few hours of actual sleep in that time.

Gage walked to the large front desk and checked them in under his name. Other than a few employees, they were the only people in the large lobby. After signing some papers, the man handed Gage two key cards, and a bellboy appeared to take their luggage. They followed him to the elevators, Gage placing a light hand on the small of her back as they stepped through the metal doors. Everything inside the hotel was clean and polished. Not even the elevator doors had smudges.

The bellboy took them to the fifth floor and led them to their room at the end of the hall. He opened the door and then stepped aside, allowing Gage and Rebecca to enter first.

She had to admit, the room was beautiful. It had a contemporary feel, but with enough color to make it comfortable. There was a balcony directly behind a small sitting area. She could only imagine the view at sunset.

Rebecca stood to the side as Gage tipped the bellboy then shut the door after him, leaving them alone.

"Are you hungry? I could order room service."

"Won't the kitchen be closed by now?" She hated to admit it, but she was starving. They had been offered food on the plane, but her mind had been in such a jumble she hadn't been able to eat much. Plus, that had been four hours ago.

He picked up a menu from the coffee table and handed it to her. "Order whatever you want and then double it. Have them charge it to the room. I'm going to jump into the shower."

She listened for the bathroom door to close before turning her attention to the menu. There were no prices, which made her a little uneasy. It was a reminder of how different their worlds were. Gage hadn't blinked at the extravagance of the hotel, and she doubted he would react if she ordered fifty-dollar cheeseburgers. He seemed to be at home no matter where he was. He adjusted to his surroundings whether they were posh or basic. He . . . fit.

Rebecca picked up the phone and called downstairs to place their order. The man on the other end of the line informed her it would be delivered to the room in about twenty minutes. After placing the menu back on the coffee table, Rebecca walked out onto the balcony. Most of the city was sleeping, but she could still see cars moving about on the streets. She was alone, yet surrounded. It was an all too familiar feeling.

At dinner on Friday night, Gage had asked her to consider a relationship with him. A real relationship. There was no denying what her heart wanted. Her head was holding her back. She knew herself well enough to know that she didn't do things halfway. With the men she'd dated in the past, she'd gone into it looking for a long-term partner, a husband. She didn't play games. Gage was the first man she'd broken her rules for, and he was the only one who'd stolen her heart.

A knock sounded at the door, and she walked back inside to answer it. An older woman stood in the hallway holding a tray, her smile way too bright for that time of night. Rebecca took the food, laid the tray down on the table against the wall, and went to get the woman a tip.

"Thank you," Rebecca said, handing her several bills.

"Anytime. Have a good night, ma'am."

Rebecca closed the door, her hand pressing firmly against the wood. She turned around, about to pick up the tray and carry it over to the sitting area, when she noticed him. Gage leaned casually in the doorway wearing nothing but a towel wrapped around his hips. Droplets of water dripped slowly down his shoulders and chest. All thoughts of food were forgotten.

Rebecca lifted her gaze to meet his. He was watching her, waiting. The next move was hers. She knew what he wanted. She knew what she wanted. The only question was whether or not she would take that step.

Blocking out the voice that was telling her she shouldn't give in, Rebecca crossed the distance between them, throwing her arms around his neck and pulling his face down to hers. Her tongue plunged into his mouth forcefully, her fingers burrowing their way into his damp hair. She was taking everything he was willing to give her, and it still didn't feel like enough.

She felt his hands pull at her clothing. He seemed as desperate as she was to get rid of the barriers between them. Piece by piece, her clothes dropped to the floor, until the only thing separating them was the thin fabric of her panties, his towel discarded along with the rest of her clothes.

Her hands slid down his chest, enjoying the feel of muscle beneath the tips of her fingers. She scraped her nails over his nipples. He responded by digging his fingers into her hips, grinding her against him.

She gasped, breaking the seal of their lips. He reached from behind, moving her hair out of the way and holding her at the angle he desired before attacking her neck with his mouth. Rebecca dug her fingers into his back, trying to hang on as wave after wave of sensation took over. She couldn't think, only feel.

The next thing she knew, she was being lifted, her legs encircling his waist. She knew he was taking her somewhere, but she didn't much care where as long as he didn't stop what he was doing.

In what felt like an eternity later, she was laid down on the cool sheets of the bed. Gage was poised over her, his lips and tongue continuing to work their magic on her neck and collarbone. The material of her underwear was still in place, separating them. Reaching down, she pushed the fabric down her hips. He brought his right hand down to help rid her of the last obstruction.

The feel of his skin pressing against hers was indescribable. How had she willingly gone for days without feeling this? She needed him inside her, wanted to feel the pleasure that only he could give. Her fingers tugged at his hair, urging his lips to return to hers.

His mouth sought hers vigorously. All the hunger she felt was given back to her and then some. He kissed her with bruising force, and she reveled in the sheer emotion behind every kiss, every touch.

When he finally entered her, it was as if something inside her clicked into place. All the feelings of detachment and separation, of isolation and uncertainty, were gone. With him, she felt full, not only physically but also emotionally. The rush of emotions overwhelmed her and sent her clinging to him as she fell over the edge into the most intense orgasm of her life.

She continued to hold onto him as he found his own completion. He collapsed on top of her, his body weight more than welcome. Her fingers drew small circles on his shoulders, feeling the damp skin beneath that had nothing to do with his shower.

Gage pulled out of her, shifting his weight to the side so as not to crush her, but never released his grip on her. He laid his head on her chest, his arms wrapped around her, holding her tight as if willing her not to pull away from him. She responded by hugging him closer. He didn't have to worry about her going anywhere. She wasn't sure she could leave him if she tried.

Rebecca lay in bed with his head cradled to her breasts. She listened to his breathing slow as he drifted off to sleep, and felt her own eyelids growing heavy for the first time in days. Tonight, one thing had become clear to Rebecca. Although she wasn't sure how a relationship between the two of them would work, she knew they had to try. She couldn't attempt to gloss over the truth anymore. She loved him. Whether or not he fit into the plan she had made for her life didn't matter. He was the man she wanted to spend the rest of her life with. She just had to figure out how to tell him.

Chapter 30

Hansen had spent almost the entire weekend parked outside Fuller's house with no luck. His neck was cramped from sleeping in his car, and he was badly in need of a shave and a good meal. The fast food and convenience store fare was starting to turn his stomach. He never thought he would crave leafy greens, but they would be a nice change from the grease he'd consumed over the last three days.

It was already noon, and there was still no sign of Fuller at his house. Hansen checked his notes for what felt like the hundredth time. Fuller was due at work in a little over an hour. Figuring he might have better luck there, he started the car and pulled away from the curb. He would have just enough time to swing by the hotel, shower, and change. Hopefully, in an hour's time, he would be face-to-face with the mysterious Mark Fuller.

Forty-five minutes later, Hansen was feeling much better. It was amazing the difference a shower and shave could make. He'd even stopped in the hotel restaurant and picked up a salad, which he was eating while parked across the road from Fuller's place of employment.

By one o'clock, Fuller hadn't made an appearance, and Hansen was starting to think the man had skipped town. He was about to pick up his cell and call Rebecca to let her know the stakeout had been a bust, when a car drove past and pulled into the restaurant parking lot. The man inside had sandy blond hair, same as Fuller. He took his time exiting the vehicle, but once Hansen got a good look at him, he was certain it was his guy. Making sure his gun was in his holster and his cuffs easily accessible, Hansen jogged across the street.

Fuller took his time strolling across the parking lot to the front entrance of the restaurant, apparently not at all concerned that he was already ten minutes late for work. Hansen caught up with him two steps from the door.

"Mark Fuller?" he asked.

The man looked up at him, appraising. "Who's asking?"

Hansen removed his badge from his pocket and showed it to Fuller. "I have some questions I'd like to ask you."

Fuller's eyes went wide a split-second before he took off running. Hansen was instantly grateful that his wife had insisted he get in better shape. Otherwise, he never could have kept up with a man at least twenty years his junior.

The chase lasted for roughly three blocks before Fuller started to slow, then stumble. Hansen was on him before he picked himself back up, slamming him down to the pavement, and reaching for his cuffs. He kept his knee in Fuller's back until he heard the satisfying click of metal as the handcuffs closed over the man's wrists.

Standing, Hansen flipped the man over and helped him to sit up.

"I haven't done anything."

"Then why did you run?" Hansen asked, towering over Fuller.

"Why wouldn't I run? Everyone knows you cop types harass people just for the fun of it."

Hansen laughed. He'd been sitting in his car waiting for this man for days. Maybe all the isolation was going to his head, but the thought that he had nothing better to do with his time than chase after some conspiracy theorist struck him as hilarious. Fuller looked at him as if he'd lost his mind. Maybe he had.

When he finally got himself under control, Hansen picked up a small wooden crate someone had discarded in the alley and set it down a few feet in front of Fuller. Hansen sat down, his hands folded in front of him.

"As I said before, I have some questions for you."

"I told you I don't know anything. I'm going to be late for work."

"You were already late for work when you pulled into the parking lot. I doubt you're highly concerned. Now, where have you been for the last week?"

The man's mouth opened in shock. "You've been watching me? Oh man . . ."

"Answer the question."

"Are you gonna call the cops and have me arrested?"

"No. Not yet. Right now, I'm trying to figure out what you know, and then I will decide if I turn you over to the local police."

"Is this about the car I rented?"

Hansen smiled. *Now we're getting somewhere.* The guy wasn't as stupid as he let on.

"Why did you rent the car? You aren't driving it."

Fuller shook his head. "It wasn't for me. Look. Some guy came in while I was working last week. He said he had a job for me. I was suspicious at first, so I asked him if it was something illegal. He swore to me it wasn't. He just needed a rental car, but since his license had been suspended, he couldn't do it himself. Told me he had to go see his sister who was sick, and the only way to get there was by car. I almost told him no, but the money was hard to resist. I don't make much flipping burgers, you know."

"So this man, he paid you to go rent a car for him. Then what?"

Fuller shrugged. "Then nothing. I just rented the car and drove it back to the restaurant. The guy met me here, paid me, and then took the car."

"So why did you disappear for a week?"

"It's been a while since I've had some cash. I decided to have a little fun. Enjoy myself."

"So this guy still has the car?"

"Yeah, as far as I know. He had me rent it for two weeks."

"Do you think you could recognize the man if you saw him again?" Hansen asked, standing.

"Yeah. Not every day some dude offers you cash to rent him a car."

Hansen pulled Fuller to his feet.

"Good. You and I are going to go look at some pictures."

***

The first thing Gage noticed when he woke up was that he was not alone in bed. His arms were wrapped around Rebecca, his face lying between her shoulder blades. She was still sound asleep, her naked body flush with his. He hugged her closer, using one hand to brush the hair away from her neck. It felt good to touch her again like this, to be with her so intimately.

His thoughts drifted back to the previous night. He'd walked out of the bathroom to hear voices at the door. It hadn't crossed his mind to consider what he was wearing, or not wearing. Spending years using communal showers had rid him of any level of modesty a long time ago.

What he hadn't expected was Rebecca's reaction. He'd watched various expressions cross her face before she'd practically run toward him, throwing her arms around his neck and kissing him. Gage had wasted no time removing her clothing and carrying her to the bed. They'd been apart too long. All he wanted to do was feel that completion he'd only ever found when connected to her in the most primal of ways.

He ran his hand down her side to her hip. Her skin was smooth under his palm. She looked so peaceful as she slept. There was even a tiny smile gracing her lips. He could only hope she was remembering last night. It wasn't something he was likely to forget anytime soon.

A knock on the door drew his attention. Rebecca stirred and turned her body toward him, stretching, giving him an unobstructed view of her breasts. The woman had no idea how tempting she was.

"What time is it?"

Gage glanced at the clock on the bedside table. "Almost ten. We forgot to set the alarm last night." He ran his finger down her cheek, and smiled when she blushed.

The knock sounded again, louder than before, and he sighed.

"I need to get that."

She started to get up. "I should—"

His kissed her, and she sank back down onto the bed.

"Stay. I'll go see who it is and get them to go away. Probably the hotel manager making sure we have everything we need or something. Wouldn't be the first time," he said, slipping out of bed.

He plucked a pair of jeans from his bag and threw them on, not bothering with underwear. Gage hoped to go another round before they had to leave for the photo shoot. If he had his way, they wouldn't leave the hotel room until they had to catch their flight home. He didn't think Mel would be too happy with him, though, if he blew off the reshoot.

His bare feet padded across the carpet to the door. As he went, he picked up their discarded clothes and tossed them into the bedroom so they wouldn't be visible from the door.

Whoever was on the other side was getting impatient. They knocked again, even louder.

"Hold your horses. I'm coming," Gage yelled.

Reaching the door, he noticed the tray of food they'd ordered last night sitting untouched. His stomach grumbled a protest, reaffirming the visual reminder that they'd foregone food in favor of other activities. He was about to lift the cover to see what she'd ordered them, when another knock came.

He sighed and glanced through the peephole.

Mel?

Gage opened the door to his manager, who was all decked out in a suit and tie.

"Mel, what are you doing here?"

"Well, good morning to you, too, sunshine," he said, pushing his way into the room. "I brought you some breakfast and coffee."

Gage rubbed a hand over his face in frustration and shut the door. Mel had already made himself comfortable in the sitting area. He guessed the plan of making Rebecca see stars again was out of the question.

As if she'd heard him call her name, Rebecca appeared through the bedroom doorway. She had dressed, but her hair still had that wild quality to it, probably from him running his fingers through it all night. He smiled at her, but she didn't smile back. Something in her eyes worried him. Unfortunately, there wasn't anything he could do about it at the moment.

"Oh. Hello, Rebecca. I didn't realize you would be here," Mel said.

Gage thought he detected a little irritation in his tone, but he had no idea why. Rebecca was his girlfriend. Hopefully, after what transpired last night, she was going to be in his life for a very, very long time. Why wouldn't she come with him to LA?

Rebecca's frowned deepened. "Yes. Gage invited me to come along to keep him company."

"I'm surprised you were able to get time off work with such

short notice."

She shrugged and walked over to where Gage stood. "My job is flexible."

Gage knew exactly what his manager would ask next, and he wanted to halt that line of questioning before it reached that point. He laced his fingers with hers, squeezed her hand, and led them to the couch next to Mel.

"Thanks for breakfast. We didn't get in until about one, and we were both exhausted. Did you fly in this morning?"

Mel was still watching Rebecca, but he answered Gage's question. "Yes. My flight landed about two hours ago. I stopped by the studio to make sure everything was set up properly this time, and then came here. The last thing I want is for something to go wrong again. This is your first national ad. It will put you on the map outside the sports world."

"I don't want to be on the map outside the sports world. I like things the way they are," Gage said, taking a sip of his coffee and then offering it to Rebecca.

A look crossed Mel's face that Gage didn't understand, but then it was gone. His manager checked his watch and then stood to leave. "I'll give you two a few minutes to freshen up and finish breakfast. I'll meet you downstairs at eleven, and we'll take the town car over to the studio together."

"Okay," Gage said, standing to see his manager out.

Mel opened the door and paused. "I take it she's coming with you to the studio."

Gage frowned.

"Of course. Why wouldn't she?"

Mel smiled, but it seemed off.

"No reason. I'll see you downstairs in less than an hour."

Gage watched as Mel walked down the hallway to the elevator. Closing the door, Gage turned to find Rebecca standing behind him. He reached out to her, but she stepped back. Were things going back to how they'd been?

He reached out again, but she shook her head.

"Hansen called."

The reason for her hesitation became clear. It made the rejection a little easier to take.

"And?"

"He's got Fuller down at the local police station looking at photos. Someone paid him to rent the car. If he can ID someone, we should have our man."

"Man?"

"Yeah. Man."

Chapter 31

After Mel left, Rebecca went to take her shower while Gage ordered them breakfast. His manager had brought a single cup of coffee and a breakfast sandwich. Given neither of them had eaten any of their meal the night before, they both wanted something more substantial.

The hotel's bathroom was small compared to what she'd become used to at Gage's house, but it was still bigger than what she had in her apartment in Knoxville. She tried not to think about that too much as she stepped into the shower and began to lather her hair.

Deciding she wanted to give a relationship with him a chance was all well and good, but the fact remained that they lived and worked in different cities. He couldn't move and neither could she. There was no professional football team in Knoxville, and there was no FBI office in Nashville. Two hours didn't seem like a lot, but when it came to trying to juggle a relationship, who knew? Just the thought of sleeping in separate beds again gave her a nauseous feeling in the pit of her stomach.

She tried to push those depressing thoughts aside as she reached for the soap and started washing her body. As her hands glided across her breasts, down to her belly, she remembered the last time she and Gage had showered together. Too bad they didn't have time this morning. It was an experience she couldn't wait to repeat. Maybe if it hadn't been for Mel's interruption, things would have gravitated in that direction.

Thinking about Gage's manager again halted all her sexual fantasies. Something about the man was off. She just couldn't put her finger on it.

Reaching between her legs to clean herself, she froze. Her fingers were covered in creamy goo. She closed her eyes and leaned back against the cool tiles. *Condom.* They'd forgotten to use a condom.

Movement from inside the bedroom caused her to spring into action again. She couldn't think about forgotten condoms right now. Other things had to come first.

When Rebecca emerged from the shower, Gage took his turn. Once they were both dressed, they sat in the small seating area eating the bacon, eggs, and pancakes he'd ordered and discussing Hansen's phone call. Knowing it was a man narrowed down the suspect list but not by much. There was still the possibility it was a fan, someone not in Gage's immediate circle of acquaintances.

The more they talked about it, the more Rebecca's mind kept returning to their visit from Gage's manager, Melvin Maxwell. He'd never been one of her favorite people, but the trip to his office the previous week combined with his responses that morning had her pushing him up on her list of suspects.

She had no proof other than something about him rubbed her the wrong way. It was enough to put her on guard. It wasn't enough, however, for her to say anything to Gage. If she were wrong, she didn't want to cause problems between him and his manager. No. She would watch and wait. Hansen should have something soon. If it was Maxwell, it was better she kept him close for when they had the proof to nail him.

Before they left the room, she made sure she had her gun in place at her ankle, loaded and ready to go. Gage watched as she made sure everything was working properly before strapping it in place. He raised an eyebrow but didn't comment.

They were halfway through the lobby when she spotted Maxwell standing near the doors. He was on his phone, engrossed in conversation. She knew the minute he spotted them. He frowned, and his eyes narrowed slightly. One thing was obvious. Melvin Maxwell didn't like her being there one bit.

"Right on time," he said, disconnecting his phone call and glancing down at his watch.

"You did say eleven." Gage must have noticed Maxwell's irritation as well. His hand, which had been gently caressing her back as they walked across the hotel, moved to grip her hip.

"Yes, I did," he said, smiling. "Are you both ready, then?"

"Let's get this over with," Gage said, moving toward the entrance.

Rebecca dragged her feet, and he glanced down at her. She ignored him and addressed Maxwell. "After you," she said, smiling her sweetest smile.

Maxwell cocked his head to the side, appraising her. She thought he might try to protest, but then he turned and walked out the door. They followed.

"What was all that about?" Gage whispered in her ear.

She shook her head. Even if she was able to explain it to him, she couldn't. Maxwell was too close, and they weren't likely to shake him for the remainder of the day.

The ride to the photo shoot was tense. Gage could feel her anxiety and was reacting to it, so she tried to relax. She doubted Maxwell would do anything to jeopardize the shoot, even if he were the stalker. He'd put too much work into keeping his identity concealed.

A small woman with bright red hair greeted them as they exited the car. She looked over at Gage, and her gaze lingered appreciatively. Rebecca took hold of his hand, staking her claim.

"It's good to see you again, Jenny."

The young woman took in their linked hands, and her cheery expression faltered.

"Is everything set up and ready to go?" Maxwell asked, cutting through all the pleasantries.

"Oh. Yes. Dane has everything ready. All we're missing is Gage." She smiled again, flirting. Rebecca didn't like it, but she figured she would have to get used to it if she was going to have a future with him.

Thinking about the future reminded her of what she'd discovered earlier. What would happen if she were pregnant? How would he react? She knew he loved his niece, but there was a big difference between being an uncle and being a father. Was he ready for that? Was she?

She tried to focus on what was going on around her as they

walked into the darkened studio. There were lots of cords and panels, lights and umbrellas. The whole place looked like a disorganized maze.

Gage gave her a soft kiss on the cheek before following Jenny back behind one of the panels to change, leaving her alone with Maxwell. He didn't say anything. Then again, neither did she.

Rebecca watched Gage step out from behind a completely different panel wearing nothing but a pair of gray boxer briefs. His back was to her, and she couldn't help but admire the way they fit. Her man was quite the specimen.

Rebecca smiled. *Her man.* It felt really good to think of him as hers.

He walked to a lighted spot in the center of the room and turned. Gage squinted, looking into the darkness. She knew exactly when he spotted her. He smiled that cocky grin of his she'd come to love.

A few seconds later, an older man, maybe in his early fifties, stepped into view with a camera, drawing Gage's attention. The man was talking, but it was too low for her to hear what he was saying. Gage nodded and turned to the side. After several adjustments, the older man lifted his camera and began taking pictures.

She'd lost count of how many pictures were taken when the man said something else to Gage, and he walked off to the side behind the panel he'd emerged from earlier. He was gone for only a few minutes before returning. The new underwear was black. She honestly couldn't say which she liked him in more. He looked hot in both.

The entire time she'd been standing there watching Gage's photo shoot, Maxwell had been on and off the phone with various people. Some sounded like clients. Others, she didn't catch enough of the conversation to tell. She was trying, discreetly, to keep an eye on him without him knowing. The man was perceptive, however, and when he hung up from his latest phone call, he called her on it.

"You seem very interested in my conversations."

"Not really." She shrugged, trying to downplay the fact that he'd caught her spying.

"Oh, but I think you were. The question is, why?"

Rebecca turned away from him, facing the bright lights where Gage was currently lying on a bed with his hands behind his head. "Your phone calls were disrupting my concentration, that's all. I'm trying to watch Gage's photo shoot." That was a girlfriend-type thing to say, right?

He stepped up behind her, and she tried not to react. That was until she felt something pressing into her lower back.

"Who are you?"

"I don't know what you mean. I'm Gage's girlfriend."

"Maybe, but I doubt that. I've known Gage since his senior year of college, knew he was going to be a star with that throwing arm and his good looks. The women ate him up in college. Even the moms. He had them all drooling. Not even he saw his potential."

"But you did." Everything was starting to fall into place for Rebecca.

"Yes. I did."

"What changed?"

"Smart girl." Even facing away from him, she could almost see the creepy smile.

Gage hoisted himself from the bed and jogged back behind the panel to change again.

"Let's take a walk," Maxwell said, pressing the gun into her back. The barrel dug into her skin.

Rebecca didn't hesitate. Her first priority was to keep Gage safe. That was her job. Having confirmed where the threat was coming from, the best thing to do was to get Maxwell as far away from Gage as possible.

She stayed silent until they were outside. The town car was gone. They weren't scheduled to be finished for a couple of hours yet. There were a few people about, but no one close.

"This way," he said, guiding her down the length of the building.

"You're the one who sent the pictures. The one who wanted him to get rid of me."

"Shared that with you, did he? Too bad he didn't listen."

"But why?"

He snorted and pushed her to walk faster.

"You're distracting him. He has everything he needs to succeed—talent, looks. But instead of taking advantage of opportunities, he's busy chasing after sluts like you. I'd thought the others were bad, but you . . . I knew you were going to be a problem that first day he showed up in my office with you in tow."

They reached the corner that would remove them from view. She had no doubt that he intended to kill her. He'd tried to scare her off with the picture and letter. Since that didn't work, he'd moved to what he felt was the next logical step. Apparently, Maxwell didn't believe in paying women off. To him, death was obviously the easier option.

Just as they were turning the corner, she heard Gage's voice. He must have noticed she was gone, and was coming after her. Foolish man.

She wasn't the only one who heard Gage's voice. Maxwell heard it, too, and his response was to shove her into the alley with enough force to separate them. It was the first opportunity she'd been given to go on the offensive since they'd been outside, and she took advantage of it.

Using the momentum from him pushing her, she fell forward, dropping to the ground onto her hands. She kicked out her right leg in a sweeping motion, knocking Maxwell's feet out from under him.

He stumbled backward, hitting the pavement hard, but didn't release the gun as she had hoped. Instead, he refocused on her, ignoring the sound of footsteps rapidly approaching, and pointed the gun.

Rebecca reached for her firearm, releasing it from its holster in record time, but she wasn't quick enough. Maxwell fired his gun, sending a burning pain through her upper arm.

Luckily, it wasn't her shooting arm, and her gun was already in her hand by the time the bullet sliced into her flesh. Gritting her teeth, she lifted her gun, aimed as best she could through the pain, and fired before he could finish the job he'd started.

The gun fell from Maxwell's hand, landing with a thud onto the pavement. His eyes were wide, as if in shock, before his head fell backward and he collapsed onto the ground.

Her arm flopped to the ground, her fingers still gripping the gun. With the threat eliminated, the adrenaline that had fueled her actions dissipated quickly, leaving the pain in her arm to take over. Her vision began to fade in and out, darkness tempting her.

The last thing she saw before her eyes closed was Gage's panicked face as he came around the corner.

Chapter 32

"Rebecca!"

Gage ran to her side, his hand immediately going to the wound on her shoulder. There was blood everywhere, and there was nothing around to use to try to stop it. He tried his hand, but it didn't work very well. The red liquid continued to seep at an alarming rate through his fingers.

"What happened?" Jenny's panicked voice drew his attention away from Rebecca. He focused in on the scarf she was wearing around her neck.

"Give me your scarf."

"What?" she said, bewildered.

"Give me your scarf!"

He vaguely registered her fingers trembling as she unwound the scarf from around her neck. Once it was free, she thrust it in his direction and stepped back as if it were a snake about to bite her.

Lifting Rebecca's arm, he wrapped the thin scarf tight around her bicep. It didn't take long for the scarf to change color from its original powder blue to red, but at least the bleeding appeared to have slowed.

"Do you have a cell phone on you?"

"Um . . . I—"

"Cell phone? Yes or no?" His voice was cutting, but he didn't have time to deal with Jenny. Rebecca was hurt and bleeding. She needed medical attention.

Jenny fumbled in her pocket for what felt like an eternity given the seriousness of the situation, before handing him her phone. He snatched it from her and began dialing. Thankfully, the operator answered almost immediately.

"Nine-one-one, what's your emergency?"

"I need an ambulance. She's been shot." Gage tried to stay calm, but all he could do was think about the possibility of Rebecca dying. He couldn't lose her. Not when he'd just gotten her back.

"Someone's been shot, sir?"

"Yes!"

"Okay. What's your location?"

Gage had to turn to Jenny for help with that one. She was still staring wide-eyed at the two people lying on the ground in front of her, but she spouted off the address without hesitation, which he relayed to the dispatcher.

"Okay, sir. Police and ambulance are on their way. What is your name?"

"Gage. Gage Daniels."

"And can you tell me where the shooter is, Gage?"

"He's right here. He was shot, too. She shot him."

"So there are two victims. Are they both still breathing?"

"She is." Rebecca's chest moved up and down. It wasn't the smooth motion it usually was, but it told him she was still breathing, still alive.

"What about the shooter?"

"I don't know, and I couldn't care less. She . . ."

"She what, sir?"

"She was protecting me."

"Gage, what do you mean, she was protecting you?"

"She's FBI. She must have realized Mel was . . . and followed him out here or something. Oh, Rebecca, why didn't you tell me? Come get me. Something?" He wasn't talking to the operator anymore. His fingers grazed the side of her cheek, leaving streaks of blood from where he'd touched her wound earlier.

"One of the victims is an FBI agent?"

That drew his attention back to the phone. "Yes. She was undercover. Protecting me."

The next ten minutes were a blur for Gage, which involved someone throwing a robe over his shoulders, paramedics, police officers, and a lot of curious onlookers. Someone was taking pictures, but he was too focused on Rebecca to care. He kept touching her, trying to get her to open her eyes, to talk to him, but nothing worked. Her eyes remained closed.

One of the police officers recognized him, and it worked in his favor. They loaded Rebecca into an ambulance quickly after checking that the scarf he'd put around her arm was doing its job. He wanted to ride with her, but they wouldn't allow that. Instead, one of the officers—the one who had recognized him—offered to let him ride to the hospital with him.

Before he hopped into the police cruiser, Jenny appeared with an armful of his clothes. He hadn't even thought about the fact that he was only wearing the underwear from the photo shoot. When he'd walked out from behind the panel after changing into yet another color of underwear, he'd searched for Rebecca in the darkness, just as he had the times before. When he hadn't seen her or Mel, he had gone searching.

The ride to the hospital was quick. Sirens blared as they sped through traffic lights. Gage held tight to the clothes in his hands and kept glancing back at the ambulance behind them. He must have looked as frazzled as he felt because the officer didn't ask him any questions.

They pulled up to the entrance of the ER, the ambulance still following them, and Gage jumped out of the vehicle. By the time he had Rebecca in his line of sight again, she was surrounded by people. Everyone had a hand on her, checking for various things. He knew he needed to stay back and let the doctors do their job, but that only made him feel even more helpless than he already did.

Mel. He couldn't believe it. And why?

"Sir, are you the one who called this in?" asked a small woman in colorful scrubs.

"Yes."

He saw the paper and pen in her hands. She needed information on Rebecca, and he had to give it. There was no one else.

"What do you need to know?"

The woman ushered him inside the hospital and into a small administrative room. Rebecca had already been wheeled behind a set of large doors. He could no longer see her.

"I need to get some personal information on her."

"All right."

"Her full name?"

"Rebecca Carson." He paused. "*Agent* Rebecca Carson. Shit. I need to call Hansen." The woman looked confused. "Her partner. I don't have his number." He paused again. "Her phone. I need her phone. She would have had it on her."

The woman noticed his growing distress and gave him a sympathetic smile. "It's all right. They'll have to remove all her belongings and clothing before surgery anyway. I'll have them brought down to you."

"Yeah. Okay." He pressed down hard on his legs, willing them to stop bouncing up and down.

"Now, what is your relationship to the victim?"

"She's my girlfriend."

The woman hesitated for a moment. While she was considering her next question, Gage's attention was drawn by a commotion in the hall. When he looked out, he saw another stretcher being brought in with his manager on it. His face was covered with an oxygen mask attached to a pump, and there was another medic with his hands on his chest counting out compressions. It looked like Mel was in a lot worse shape than Rebecca, but Gage couldn't bring himself to care. The woman he loved was fighting for her life because of that man. *His* manager. A man he'd trusted.

"Sir?"

He turned his attention back to the woman.

"Do you know if Rebecca is allergic to any medicines?"

"No. Not that I know of."

"Any medical conditions we should know about?"

He shook his head.

"Pregnant?"

Gage opened his mouth to say no and then stopped.

"I don't know. Maybe." The words came out not much louder than a whisper. Realization hit him like a ton of bricks. Last night had been amazing, wonderful, and completely spontaneous. Even still, he'd been sexually active since he was sixteen, and never once in all those years had he ever forgotten to use protection. Not once. The thought of being inside her had overruled anything else, including thoughts of digging a condom out of his bag.

"All right. I'll get this information up to the doctors. Do you have contact information for her next of kin?"

"Um? Oh. Yes. Her sister. Megan. I . . ." Gage reached for his phone, but realized it wasn't there. He'd taken everything out of his pockets when he'd gotten undressed, and placed it in the drawer. Jenny must not have thought to retrieve those items. "I don't have my phone on me. I'll use Rebecca's phone to call her sister. She would want to know."

The woman nodded. After writing a few more things on the paper, she walked him down a long hall to a set of elevators. The doors opened several minutes later, and they stepped inside.

"They've taken her up to surgery. You can sit in the waiting room up there, and the doctor will come out and talk to you once it's done. I'll have them bring you her things so you can call who you need to."

He nodded.

"An officer will also be up to talk to you. They'll need to get a statement from you on what's happened."

"That's fine. I just . . . I need her to be okay."

She gave him a sad smile as the elevator doors opened. They walked out onto a floor that looked almost exactly like the one below.

They rounded a corner, and she pointed out another set of doors. "The waiting room is right through those doors. You need to check in with the nurses' desk, let them know who you are and who the patient is. There are vending machines there if you're hungry and bathrooms . . . if you'd like to change."

Gage glanced down, and for the first time since this whole thing happened, he cracked a little smile. "I guess I should put on some clothes, huh?"

"Unless you'd like to give all those ladies in there a show." Her smile no longer had that edge of sadness.

Gage thanked her and walked into the waiting room. The officer who had given him a ride earlier was there waiting for him. He stood off to the side as Gage went to the desk and registered as he'd been instructed.

When he was finished, he walked over to the officer. "Mind if I put some clothes on first?"

The officer smirked. "No. Go ahead. I'll wait."

"Thanks."

Gage's clothing seemed to weigh him down even more as he walked back into the seating area and toward the officer. He noticed a few people staring at him, but he wasn't sure if that was because they recognized who he was, or because they'd seen him earlier talking to the cop. At the moment, he wasn't sure he cared either way.

The officer stood as Gage approached. He was holding a plastic bag. Rebecca's things. He handed the bag over to Gage, and they both took a seat.

"I need to ask you some questions, Mr. Daniels," he said, taking a notebook out of his pocket. It seemed like everyone had questions for him when all he wanted to do was lie in a bed, holding the woman he loved and making sure she was safe and well.

"Sure," Gage said, clearing his throat.

For the next half hour, Gage explained how he'd met Rebecca and what had been going on with his stalker. The officer took everything down in his notebook, asking questions to clarify when needed. There were a few questions Gage couldn't answer. He didn't know why Rebecca had gone outside with Mel, and he didn't know what had led up to them both shooting each other.

As they were wrapping up, Rebecca's phone rang. Gage had to dig it out from the bottom of the plastic bag in order to answer it. He checked the caller ID. It was Hansen.

"Hello."

There was a long pause on the other end before Hansen responded. "Daniels?"

"Yeah. It's me." He couldn't disguise how weary he felt.

"What happened? Why are you answering Carson's phone?"

Gage ran a hand through his hair and slumped back in his seat. The officer stood and handed him a business card. "Call me if you think of anything else."

"Thanks."

"Where are you?" Hansen's tone regained Gage's attention.

"At the hospital. Rebecca was shot. She's in surgery."

"Maxwell."

"Yeah."

"Is he in custody?"

"I don't know. She shot him, too. I saw them bringing him in, but I have no idea where he is now."

Gage listened to what Hansen was saying, trying to answer his questions the best he could, but after a certain point, all Hansen's words started running together.

When their conversation ended, he stared at the phone for several minutes before he made the call he was dreading. Gage knew his brother's number by heart. He hoped someone was home.

"Daniels residence." Megan's voice was cheerful as she answered. He knew he was about to change that.

"Megan. It's Gage."

"Hi, Gage. How are things? Is my sister treating you right?"

"Is Paul home?"

"Oh. Yeah. He's here. Sorry. You probably want to talk to him. I'll just go—"

"No! I mean . . . I need to talk to you. Not Paul." He took a deep breath. "Rebecca's been shot." He heard her gasp.

"Is she okay?"

"I don't know. She's in surgery now. Does she have any allergies? Medications she's allergic to? They asked me, and I didn't know."

"No. Nothing that I know of, anyway."

He nodded even though she couldn't see him.

"I think you need to come be with her. Can Paul get you to the airport?"

He heard movement in the background. He figured Paul must have gathered something was going on based on Megan's end of the conversation. Gage could hear her talking to someone, most likely his brother, but it was muffled. The next voice that came on the phone wasn't Megan.

"What's going on?" Paul demanded.

Gage sighed. He knew that tone. Paul was in cop mode. The problem was that Gage wasn't in the mood for his big brother's protectiveness.

"Megan can explain to you on the way. She knows most of it. Can you drive her to the airport? I'll get her a flight and text you with the information. I think she needs to be here for her sister."

Paul muttered a curse.

"I'll get her there, but you are going to have some explaining to do, little brother."

"Fine. Whatever. Just not now."

240

"Gage?" Megan asked, getting back on the phone.

"Yeah?"

"Take care of my sister, okay?"

"I will." Gage only hoped it was a promise he would be given the opportunity to keep.

Chapter 33

Rebecca's eyes were heavy, as if something was weighing them down. She could hear beeping in the background, and there was a smell that she couldn't quite place. Her arm ached as if someone had punched her. She groaned.

"Becca? Becca, are you awake?"

Megan?

She tried to open her eyes again. It took all her concentration, but eventually she was able to open them enough to see her sister leaning over her. Megan's face was etched with worry. It didn't take long for even Rebecca's muddled mind to put two and two together. She'd been injured and must be in a hospital.

She tried to speak, but her throat felt like she'd gone without water for days. Maybe she had, since she had no idea how long she'd been lying there.

"What . . .?" She cleared her throat. "What . . . happened?"

"You were shot. Do you remember?" Megan's hand gripped Rebecca's.

She searched her brain, trying to recall what had transpired. The details were a little fuzzy, but she remembered.

Gage. He'd been the last thing she'd seen as unconsciousness claimed her. Where was he? She attempted to turn her head, but couldn't see him.

"Gage?"

Megan frowned.

"He had to fly back to Nashville this morning."

Disappointment filled her. He wasn't here. He'd left.

"He didn't want to leave. I pretty much had to kick him out," Megan said.

"Why ... would you ... do that?" Her voice sounded raspy. "Can ... I have ... some water?"

"Oh," Megan said, reaching for a pitcher sitting on one of those rolling carts next to the bed. "Sorry. The nurse said you'd probably be really thirsty when you woke up. I wasn't thinking."

Her sister held a straw to her lips, and she took a sip. The cool liquid felt good as it went down. After a few short pulls on the straw, Rebecca was tired. She fell back against the pillow.

"Why did you make Gage leave?" Her voice still didn't sound right, but it was better.

Megan pulled a chair up beside the bed and sat down. She tucked her legs underneath her and folded her arms, just like she'd done when she'd been little.

"It's Wednesday."

Wednesday? But ... it had been Monday. She'd been out for two days?

Her sister must have read the confusion on her face. "You lost a lot of blood and went into shock, so they had to give you a transfusion. They sedated you for twenty-four hours so your body could heal."

"Oh." The reality of how badly she'd been hurt hit her full force.

"His coach had already called several times, and yesterday he told him that if he wasn't there for practice on Thursday they were going to fine him some insane amount of money. I couldn't let him do that. The doctors said you were out of the woods. It was just a matter of you waking up. I told him I'd keep him updated and call him when you woke up so he could talk to you. Do you think you're up for it?"

He hadn't wanted to leave.

The disappointment ebbed and was replaced by an eagerness to hear his voice again.

"Yes. Please."

Megan smiled and reached for the phone. She'd just picked up the receiver when the nurse walked into the room.

"I see you're awake. It's good to have you back with us," she said, walking over to the bed and reaching for Rebecca's wrist to take her pulse. "How are you feeling?"

"Tired."

"That's to be expected. Any pain?"

"My arm is a little sore, but nothing I can't handle."

The nurse gave her a knowing look. "I'll up the pain medication a little. You need to get your rest, and if you're hurting, that's going to be difficult."

"I don't want to go back to sleep yet."

The nurse ignored her and continued to do whatever it was she was doing. "The sooner you get better, the sooner you get to leave." The nurse picked up her chart and made some notes before strolling back to the door. "I'll let the doctor know you're awake."

As soon as the nurse left, Rebecca turned back to her sister. "Gage?"

Megan smiled, but instead of reaching for the phone, she picked up the cup of water again and held the straw to Rebecca's mouth. "Drink."

Rebecca frowned but obeyed.

After setting the cup back down on the tray, Megan reached for the phone. "Just so you know . . . I want an invite to your wedding."

"What? I—"

Rebecca didn't get to finish her sentence because Megan pressed the phone up to her ear. She glared at her sister, who responded with an innocent expression. Rebecca rolled her eyes.

"How is she?" Gage's agitated voice came through the phone.

"It's me. I'm fine," Rebecca said.

"Rebecca. You're awake, beautiful."

"Yeah. I just woke up."

"I'm sorry I had to leave. I didn't want to. I—"

"I know. Megan told me."

He sighed. "How are you feeling? Are you hurting?"

"Not much."

He was silent for a long moment. "I wish I were there."

"I wish you were, too," she whispered.

"Have they said when you'll get to come home?"

"No." She yawned, suddenly tired. How was that possible? She didn't want to hang up. Didn't want to let go of the feeble connection she had to him. "Haven't seen the doctor yet."

"You're tired."

"I'm all right." She tried to reassure him.

"You need your rest."

"Don't hang up." She knew she sounded desperate and whiny, but she didn't care.

"Okay. I'll stay on the line until you go to sleep. How about that?"

"Thank you."

"Anything thing for you, beautiful." She could hear the smile in his voice.

She sighed.

"Now, close your eyes and rest. I'm right here."

The next few days were a challenge. Rebecca wasn't used to being confined to a bed or not having use of her arm. She was up and walking as soon and as often as they would allow her.

Two local agents from the Los Angeles field office stopped by on Wednesday night to get her statement. Even though she wasn't on active duty, she was still an agent who had been involved in a shooting. It was from them that she learned Maxwell hadn't survived. Her bullet had punctured his neck, a little higher than she had aimed, but effective nonetheless. He'd bled out before they'd loaded him onto the gurney.

The local agents had already spoken with Hansen. While she was stuck in the hospital recovering, he was busy wrapping up the loose ends in Nashville. All the local agents needed was her side of what had happened with Maxwell on the day of the shooting. Recounting the story, she realized she hadn't given Maxwell enough credit. She hadn't seen him as a real physical threat, and he'd proven her wrong.

On Thursday morning she spoke to Hansen. He and some agents from the Knoxville office had combed through Maxwell's apartment. They found journals dating back fifteen years and covering each and every one of his clients. The journals went a long way to explaining the how and why.

Gage hadn't been the first client Maxwell had stalked, but he'd been the most high profile. Maxwell had logged who they dated, where they went, and any other special details about them. It was rather frightening. He seemed obsessed with controlling their lives, convinced it would boost their careers. Anything he deemed detrimental to that had to be taken care of, and in whatever fashion he deemed necessary.

There were records of Maxwell sending letters to other clients, much like he had with Gage. The difference being that when those clients had received the letters, they'd curbed whatever undesirable activity Maxwell had pointed out. Gage hadn't conformed, and Maxwell had become frustrated.

There was mention of the explosives the security guard had found on Gage's SUV. The bomb had been meant to scare off the woman he'd been with the previous night, but the explosives hadn't gone off at the right time. The shooting outside the bar in Nashville had been yet another scare tactic, meant to send Rebecca fleeing in the opposite direction. Her showing up in LA must have been the last straw in Maxwell's view, and he'd decided to handle things in a more permanent way.

When she shared that bit of information with Gage during one of their Skype conversations, he was livid. She honestly believed that if Maxwell weren't already dead, Gage would have tried to kill him. As it was, she spent almost an hour calming him down. It was only when he noticed through the webcam her shifting in pain that his tone changed from angry to concerned.

On Friday, she met with her surgeon. He said everything appeared to be healing nicely and gave her the okay to leave the hospital. Her arm remained in a sling that didn't allow much movement, but at least she would have a little more freedom to come and go when and where she wanted. He also informed her that she wouldn't be able to fly home for at least another week, until after her sutures were removed.

Megan had called Gage when the doctor arrived in her room, just as she had been doing for the last two days. When he heard the doctor's pronouncement, he refused to stay silent.

Rebecca knew Gage was stubborn. She'd seen it firsthand in his pursuit of her. He bombarded the doctor with questions, trying to find a way to get her back to Tennessee earlier than the additional week the man was insisting upon. The doctor refused to budge, however, citing her safety. Apparently, cabin pressure on an airplane and surgery didn't mix well.

The doctor said his good-byes, promising to get her discharge papers going. He gave her the phone number to his office, telling her to call and set up an appointment for the following week to have her sutures removed. She wasn't happy about having to stay, but at least it was only another week. The next Friday, she could fly back home.

***

Gage stood inside the small building next to the tarmac the following Friday afternoon. Rebecca had been to see her surgeon the previous day. He'd removed her stitches and given her the okay to fly home. It was a good thing, too. He'd been distracted ever since he'd been forced to return home without her. It was pure luck they'd won last week's game. If not for their defense, they wouldn't have.

That week in practice, he'd been no better. He wanted Rebecca home, and finally, he was getting his wish. He had arranged with Tim to use his private plane. Gage would have loved to fly out there to bring her back, but it hadn't been possible. He was already in hot water with his coach. Rebecca was always at the forefront of his mind. She overrode practice, his team, and even the paparazzi who had taken to following him and camping outside his house. He'd traded one stalker for a dozen.

A small plane landed on the runway and began taxiing toward the small hangar.

"Sir? As soon as the plane stops, you can go out on the tarmac to meet them." The airline attendant explained.

"Thanks." Gage smiled. He waited until the plane came to a full stop and then picked up the bouquet of flowers he'd brought with him before walking outside.

The cold winter wind stung his cheeks. Thank goodness for the sun—that made it tolerable. It was hard to believe Christmas was only two weeks away. It felt as if the last month had gone by so fast.

One of the ground crew pushed a small stairway up to the plane. A few moments later, the door opened. Gage held his breath, not able to contain his excitement to see her again.

Megan appeared first. She saw him and smiled. Halfway down the stairs, she turned to look back inside the plane, tilting her head in his direction. She laughed, shook her head, and practically skipped the rest of the way down.

"Hey, Gage."

"Hey." He spared Megan a brief glance, and then looked back up at the entrance to the plane.

Seconds later, Rebecca took a tentative step out of the opening. All thought about the cold left him the moment he saw her. She was paler than normal, and her left arm was tucked close to her chest instead of inside the arm of the thin coat she was wearing. He smiled and walked toward her, closing the distance.

Carefully, she made her way down the stairs. She took that final step onto the ground, and he wrapped his arms around her. "Welcome home, beautiful."

She sank into him, exhaling. Her right arm circled his waist, pulling him closer. "Hi."

He turned his head and found her lips with his own. The kiss was tempered by their environment and her injury, but it was sweet all the same.

"I missed you."

"I missed you, too," she said, gazing up at him. She looked tired.

"Let's get you home." He reluctantly stepped away from her. Handing her the flowers, he went to get the luggage.

When they arrived home, Gage told Megan to make herself at home, and then helped Rebecca up to bed.

"I can do it myself, you know," she said when he began helping her undress. "I'm not helpless."

He smiled. "Yes, but this way is a lot more fun."

She laughed. "You never change, do you?"

"Nope."

He stopped undressing her and met her gaze, all levity gone.

"I hope you can handle that. Not just now. I mean . . ."

He swallowed. Why was this so difficult?

"Rebecca, this week has been . . ." He stopped and started over. "Nearly losing you—for a second time—made me realize some things. I don't like being apart from you, for one. I'm not sure how we'll fix that completely given both of our jobs, but I do know that I want us to spend as much time together as possible."

"Gage, I—"

"Let me finish, please."

He paused, taking her good hand and lacing their fingers together.

"I love you, and I want us to spend the rest of our lives together. I don't care if that means following each other around the country. I'm willing, if you are."

Rebecca was silent, her eyes brimming with tears.

"Say something," he pleaded.

"I love you, too."

He smiled. "I was hoping you'd say that."

Gage cupped her face gently with his right hand, caressing it softly as he brought their mouths together again. "Marry me," he whispered against her lips.

She froze, and he pulled back. His hands never left her, but he couldn't hide the hurt on his face.

"What's wrong?"

She glanced down, then back up at him. The look in her eyes told him she was afraid. He couldn't understand why, though.

"I need to tell you something."

"Okay," he said, still not able to stop touching her.

"Sunday night we . . ." She took a deep breath, and he saw her wince. "We didn't use a condom."

"I know," he said. "They asked me at the hospital if you could be pregnant. That's when I realized. I'm sorry."

She shook her head. "It's not all your fault. I was there, too. I should have said something. Gage . . . I had the doctor do a blood test while I was there yesterday. I know it's early, but I wanted to check anyway. I needed to know."

He nodded.

"It was positive."

A shot of fear pulsed through him, followed by an image of a little girl with Rebecca's hair and eyes. He was going to be a dad. Gage smiled, but his expression faltered when he realized she was still nervous.

He took her face in between both his hands. "I know it probably isn't ideal, but I want you forever, Rebecca. I want a home with you, kids, and everything else that comes with it."

"You still want to marry me?" Her voice was full of uncertainty.

"Is that what has you worried? Did you think I'd be upset?"

"I didn't know."

"I'm not upset." He smiled, placing a soft kiss on her lips. "So what do you say? Do you think you can put up with me for the rest of your life?"

Rebecca laughed. "Yeah. I think I can."

Epilogue

Rebecca stood in front of a floor-length mirror nervously biting the inside of her cheek. The white dress she was wearing was simple, but elegant. It could have easily passed for a semi-formal evening gown. She'd seen a similar one in red worn by one of the player's wives at the team Christmas dinner Gage had taken her to in December. The dress she wore tonight, however, wasn't an evening gown meant for a night out on the town. It was her wedding dress.

She pressed her palms against her still flat stomach, thinking of the baby growing inside. Gage wanted to get married as soon as possible before the baby was born. Maybe it was vain of her, but she hadn't wanted to walk down the aisle once she started showing. That, along with Gage's game and practice schedule, and Chris and Elizabeth's upcoming wedding in March, left very little time for them to work with.

It took some organizing, and a bit of miracle working, but they'd managed to get everyone to Las Vegas on Valentine's weekend. Rebecca glanced down at the new ring on her left hand. It was a simple platinum band to match the engagement ring Gage had given her on Christmas Eve.

Reaching behind her, she slid the zipper down, and removed her wedding dress before hanging it behind her on a hanger. Her hair had been pinned back from her face for the wedding, but she knew she wanted it loose tonight. Gage loved to run his fingers through her hair when they made love.

She felt her body warm at the thought of tonight. It had been Wednesday, three days, since they'd been together. They'd left early Thursday morning for his parent's house, and given her bouts of morning sickness, sex in the morning was usually off the menu. That night, they'd been peppered with questions from his family and Megan. They'd only told them the previous weekend at Sunday dinner they were not only getting married, but going to have a baby as well. Since then, they'd been flooded with questions and ideas from what they wanted as wedding gifts to starting work on the baby's room.

Once they'd arrived in Vegas late Thursday night, Rebecca was exhausted. Since she'd gotten pregnant, she seemed to get tired easier. She didn't completely understand it, but her doctor said it was normal.

Friday was just as busy. They'd met with the hotel's event coordinator in the morning, and then the women had taken her out for a day of shopping and food while the guys whisked Gage away to do who knows what. She didn't ask, and to be honest, she wasn't sure she wanted to know.

After running a brush through her hair, Rebecca washed her face and took another look at herself in the mirror. She wasn't one to wear lingerie, but she figured tonight would be a good night for it. When she'd gone shopping on Black Friday, her sister had convinced her to go into a lingerie shop with her. Somehow, Rebecca had ended up buying a pink lace and satin corset with matching panties. It was tight, and not all that comfortable, but she had to admit it looked good. She only hoped Gage liked it.

Hearing the door to their suite close, Rebecca knew Gage was back. She'd had a bad bout of morning sickness earlier in the day, probably a combination of the baby and her nerves over the wedding, and had eaten through all of the ginger cookies she'd brought with her. When Gage found out upon them entering their hotel suite after the reception, he'd insisted on running to the store and getting them for her. She had no doubt he could have easily picked up the phone and had room service deliver them, but since finding out she was pregnant, Gage had become extremely hands on when it came to her and the baby. It was nice, although, a little overwhelming at times.

"Rebecca? You okay in there?" he asked through the closed

bathroom door.

"Yeah. I'll be out in just a minute."

Taking one last look at herself, Rebecca grabbed the pink satin robe she'd picked up two weeks ago. Maybe it was strange, but she felt more awkward and nervous in the lingerie than she ever did naked. Tying the ends around her waist, she reached for the door.

When she walked into the bedroom, Gage was standing next to the bed, lining up five boxes of cookies. His back was to her, and she took a moment to admire his broad shoulders. It was hard to believe he was now her husband.

"Did you get enough boxes?"

Gage turned around quickly, and she heard him suck in a sharp breath upon seeing her. Definitely a good sign.

"I wanted to make sure you had enough."

She nodded. "That should last me for a few days at least."

He didn't move, and neither did she. "I can always go out and get more if you need them."

He gave her appearance a slow appraisal. She saw the rise and fall of his chest increase in speed as he continued to take her in.

Rebecca had no idea how long they stood there staring at each other before he finally spoke. "Is that new?"

"The robe is."

Gage looked up, meeting her gaze. He swallowed. "And underneath?"

"I've had it for a while, but I've never worn it before, so I guess you could say it's new, too."

She watched as he closed his eyes for a brief moment, and then he was across the room in less than a second, pressing her against the wall. He threaded his fingers through her hair, as he brought their mouths together for a searing kiss. "I need to see you."

She reached up toward his neck, and began unbuttoning his shirt, as he lowered his lips to her neck, and began working to untie the belt at her waist. "I hope you like my surprise."

"What—" The words died in his throat, and she knew he'd felt the lace beneath the robe.

He raised his head, and pushed the robe from her shoulders. The silky material fell from her body leaving her torso covered in pink lace and satin. It was dainty—feminine—in complete contrast to what she usually wore, both in and out of bed.

Her chest rose and fell under his gaze as she waited for his reaction. He looked up at her. She waited, unsure, hoping he liked it.

Before she had time to react, Gage bent down and swept her up into his arms without warning. She gasped and wrapped her arms around his neck, holding on tight.

"What are you doing?"

He didn't answer, just walked her over to the bed, and placed her gently onto the mattress. She propped herself up onto her elbows, as she watched him remove the rest of his clothing, before he joined her on the bed.

As he towered over her, she saw his eyes dilate, and heard his breathe quicken. He leaned down and brushed his lips over the top of her breast causing a shiver of anticipation to run through her entire body. "You certainly surprised me, Mrs. Daniels. Now, let's see if I can return the favor."

Keep reading for a preview of
Crossing the Line

To learn about Sherri's upcoming releases, sign up for her newsletter at http://eepurl.com/J4vDb

Preview – Crossing the Line

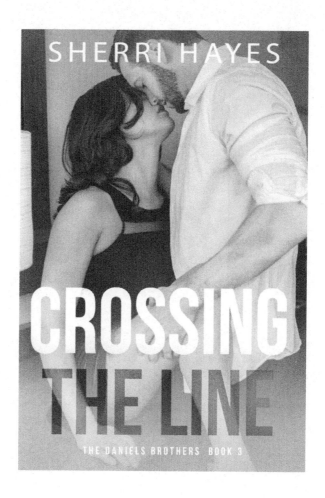

Chapter 1

"Did you see me, Daddy? Did you see me?"

Paul Daniels bent down and lifted his five-year-old daughter, Chloe, into his arms. "I did."

He gave her his best smile, not that she noticed. Chloe was too excited to pay much attention to anything for long. Paul thought nothing could top the excess of energy his little girl displayed the day Chris and Elizabeth called to ask her if she'd be their flower girl. He'd been wrong. Three months ago, Chloe had been full of questions about the unknown—she'd never been to a wedding before. Today, she was bouncing off the walls, and her smile matched his new sister-in-law's in pure joy.

It was as if he hadn't commented at all.

"And Eliz'beth's dress is sooo pretty. Isn't it pretty, Daddy?" Chloe didn't wait for his response this time either, before she continued. "Now she's my aunt." She concentrated to make sure she got it right. Megan had been working diligently to help Chloe improve her speech before she started school in the fall.

Paul searched the crowd of people bustling into the reception hall for the woman in question, as Chloe squirmed wordlessly making her desire to be put down known. He lowered her feet to the floor, and watched as she slipped in between two wedding guests while he continued to scan for Megan.

Megan was the younger sister of his baby brother Gage's wife. Paul had met her when she'd come to Thanksgiving with her sister.

Little had he known what a savior she'd turn out to be. She'd brought life back into his house. Life that he hadn't realized was missing.

She'd rescued him when he'd been in desperate need of someone to watch Chloe. Hours before he'd loaded Chloe into the car to set off for the holiday with his parents, his in-laws had announced they were moving almost two hours away. For four years, they'd lived nearby and were able to take Chloe whenever he was called in to work. His job as a homicide detective meant that he could be called out at all hours, and he couldn't leave his young daughter alone. Megan had fit the bill by offering to move to Indianapolis and into his house as a live-in nanny. She'd saved Paul from having to spend countless hours searching for an alternative.

As if knowing the direction of his thoughts, Chloe weaved through the people in her path until she was beside her nanny. Megan smiled when she caught sight of the little girl, and she circled her arms around Chloe's shoulders, lifting her off the ground, and twirling. They were both laughing—happy. The two of them had clicked from the beginning, and his chest clenched almost painfully watching the two of them together. It should have been Melissa standing there twirling Chloe, but he couldn't be upset that it was Megan. She'd put her life on hold for them—helped them out when they'd needed it most. Paul wished he could be as carefree.

His brother, Chris, wanted to give his fiancée, Elizabeth, the wedding of her dreams, right down to the ceremony being held in a quaint little church not far from where they lived in Springfield, Ohio—and it was. Elizabeth had walked down the aisle in a long white gown, his brother in a tux. Everyone who meant something in either of their lives was present. It was . . . perfect.

Unfortunately, it brought back too many memories for Paul. Memories that were raw and painful. Almost fifteen years ago, he'd been where his brother was—marrying the love of his life. He didn't begrudge Chris and Elizabeth their happiness. No, he was grateful. His brother had had a rough time of it after his first marriage fell apart. For Paul, it was a sharp reminder that he no longer had his wife at his side. She'd been taken from him by a drunk driver.

Starting to get choked up, Paul cleared his throat, and made a beeline for the bar. He didn't drink often, and never when he had to drive afterward, but tonight he didn't have to go anywhere but upstairs to his hotel room. Chloe was here, of course, so he couldn't go overboard. He just wanted to numb some of the pain.

Paul leaned his elbows on the bar as he waited for the petite blond bartender to finish with the drink she was making for another guest. He thought the guy standing patiently waiting for his drink was one of Chris' employees. Paul was also fairly certain that the guy was single by the way he was openly eyeing the young woman from head to toe. She was pretty— Paul wasn't blind, after all. Unfortunately, there was no spark. There never was. Not since his wife, Melissa.

Six months after Melissa's accident, he'd tried. He'd left Chloe with Melissa's parents and gone out to a club. It had been loud and he'd felt out of place, but he'd met a woman he found attractive and went for it. They'd ended up at her place an hour later, clothes on the floor, with him hovering over her.

He hadn't been able to go through with it, though. As he reached for a condom, he'd seen Melissa smiling up at him, her chest vibrating as she attempted to suppress her mirth while he fumbled trying to roll the rubber down his erection. It was an old memory, from when they were teenagers, but it had stung all the same. He'd gathered his clothes, dressed, and apologized, leaving the woman, whom he only knew as Karen, lying naked on her bed staring after him.

The bartender handed over the drink she'd made, and then turned to Paul without giving the other man a second glance. Looked like he wouldn't be getting that after-closing booty call.

She turned to Paul and smiled. "What can I get ya?"

"Scotch. Neat."

Her smile got wider. "Coming right up, handsome."

Paul glanced over his shoulder, and caught sight of his mom and dad. They appeared to be engrossed in a conversation with two people he didn't know. His dad looked in Paul's direction, and Paul quickly turned back around. The last thing he needed was his dad zeroing in on his less-than- festive attitude.

The bartender placed the half-full glass of scotch down in front of him. She made sure to lean in a little closer than normal. "Here you go."

"Thanks." Paul picked up the glass and took a drink. It burned as it went down his throat, which was good. Anything was better than the knife twisting in his gut.

"So how do you know the bride and groom?"

Not wanting to be rude, Paul answered her. "I'm the groom's brother."

"Older or younger?"

Paul laughed, before backing away. "Thanks again for the drink."

He made it halfway to the corner he'd scoped out as a decent hiding place, before he was waylaid by his brother, Trent. "Hey, man." Trent looked down at the drink Paul had in his hand, and raised his eyebrow.

"Something wrong?"

"I was going to ask you the same question. Since when do you drink anything but beer?"

"I like to mix it up sometimes." Paul didn't add that those "sometimes" usually involved his wedding anniversary and the anniversary of his wife's death. Chris' wedding didn't fall on either of those occasions, but Paul was making an exception.

"Since when?"

After taking another sip of his scotch, Paul narrowed his eyes at his younger brother. "Did you have a reason for coming over here other than to give me a hard time?"

Trent frowned, but let it go. For now, at least. "Megan and Chloe were looking for you. Chloe wants some pictures of you, Megan, and her together. Chris and Elizabeth don't have a problem with it, but they wanted to make sure it was okay with you before they agreed to anything."

The last thing Paul wanted to do was pose for more pictures, but there were very few things he'd deny his daughter. Pictures of the woman she'd grown extremely close to over the last four months wasn't one of them. "It's fine."

Again, he saw that look of doubt cross his brother's face. "Okay . . ."

Paul ignored Trent's curiosity. "Where?"

"Out in the lobby. The photographer has been taking some pictures in front of the fountain."

Not waiting to see if Trent would come up with more questions regarding his odd behavior, Paul took off toward the fountain.

Before entering the lobby, he took one last gulp of his scotch, feeling the heat. He could do this. For his daughter, he could do this.

Setting his now empty glass down on a nearby table, he plastered a smile on his face, and went to find Megan and Chloe.

***

Megan Carson held tight to Chloe's hand as she continued to flutter about without a care in the world. They were in the lobby waiting on Paul. At least, Megan hoped they were waiting on Paul. It hadn't escaped her notice that he'd been tense all throughout Chris and Elizabeth's vows. And a couple of times she noticed him getting a look on his face. She couldn't help but wonder if he was thinking about his wife.

He'd smiled and laughed along with everyone else, but she could tell his heart wasn't in it. She now knew him well enough to know the difference. And she'd guess his family did, too. Although, technically, Megan was his family now as well—ever since her sister married his brother.

Chloe squealed, and pulled harder on Megan's arm. "Daddy!"

Releasing the little girl's hand, Megan stood back and watched Paul scoop up his daughter. Seeing them like this gave her a warm feeling. He smiled at Chloe, and this time it didn't look fake or forced. Then again, whenever it came to Chloe, Megan didn't question Paul's love or willingness to do anything for her. Chloe was the apple of his eye—a tangible reminder of his dead wife.

"I was told there's a picture that needs to be taken out here." Paul tickled his daughter's sides.

She giggled. "Yes, Daddy. I want a picture with yous, and mes, and Megan."

Paul glanced down at Megan, and she took in his warm brown eyes. She loved when they sparkled with joy, as they did in that moment. No one could do that to him but Chloe. Not his mom or his brothers. Not even her. No matter how much she wished otherwise.

The photographer approached them with his camera hanging from a strap around his neck. "Ah, good. Everyone's here, yes?"

He quickly corralled them into the correct position, with Megan and Paul flanking Chloe as the three of them sat on the edge of the fountain. To an outside observer, they'd look like a normal family. Appearances could be deceiving, though, and in this case, they were way off. Megan was Chloe's nanny, nothing more. She took care of Chloe when Paul was working, making sure she had everything she needed, and that the house wasn't a disaster when he came home.

That was where it ended. Occasionally, Paul would allow Megan to cook dinner for them, but it was rare, and usually only on days when he knew he wouldn't be home until after six. Paul took taking care of his one and only child seriously. She was his responsibility, and while he allowed Megan to take over when he had to leave, he didn't take advantage of her presence in their life—although sometimes she wished that he would.

With the pictures over, Chloe ran back into the reception with an announcement that she was going to find her grandmother—Paul's mom— leaving Paul and Megan behind.

"Thank you."

She looked up at Paul. He towered over her, at just over six feet to her much shorter five foot five. "You know I'd do anything for Chloe."

He was ultra-serious again. "I know, but you don't have to. You're not working tonight."

Megan frowned. He had that melancholy look she noticed crossed his features all too frequently. "Are you all right?"

It was Paul's turn to frown. "Of course. Why wouldn't I be? It's my brother's wedding."

His answer didn't ease her concern. Paul was a good guy—the best guy she'd ever met in her twenty-three years. He put every other man who'd crossed her path to shame, with the exception of Gage and the rest of his brothers and father. The Daniels men had certainly upped her standards in the opposite sex.

"I don't know. You just don't seem like yourself tonight."

Paul waved off her observation. "It's been a long day, that's all."

Yes, it had been a long day. Megan and all the other Daniels women, including Chloe, had met at the spa a little after eight that morning. They'd all gotten their hair and nails done while the guys did whatever guys did to get ready for a wedding. Since then, they'd all been going strong. Megan didn't think that was the problem, but she let it go. For now. "It has been a long day."

In what seemed like an effort to steer her away from any further questioning, Paul held out his arm, and motioned toward the reception. She took a deep breath, and smiled, allowing him to deflect. Whatever was going on with him today, she figured it had to do with his wife. One thing she'd learned about Paul in the four months she'd known him was that he was still very much in love with Melissa. It didn't matter that she'd been dead for over four years. She was still alive in his heart.

Once back inside, Megan was hijacked by her brother-in-law, Gage. "Would you please talk to your sister?"

Megan laughed. "What's up, Becca?"

Her sister, Rebecca, gave her husband a disapproving headshake. "Nothing, except Mr. Overprotective here doesn't think I can do anything on my own."

"I'm trying to be a gentleman." Gage huffed his response, but at the same time, he wrapped his arms around Rebecca's middle, pulling her up against him. It still amused Megan to see how Gage had changed since falling in love with her sister. He'd gone from the cocky playboy to the overprotective husband and daddy-to-be.

Rebecca leaned in to him. "I do not need for you to walk me to the bathroom. I'm not a child." She paused. "And before you say it, I'm not going to get sick. I haven't had a bout of morning sickness in over a week."

Gage kissed her temple and inhaled. "I'm sorry, beautiful, but you know how much I worry about you."

Megan watched her sister—her sister who could take down a man three times her size with her bare hands—melt in her husband's arms. "I guess you two don't need me anymore, then?"

They both chuckled, and Rebecca stood to her full height. "Of course I do. You, I don't mind accompanying me to the ladies' room."

Before she knew it, Rebecca was pushing her toward the bathroom. "Hey, slow down."

Rebecca stopped and released Megan's arm. "Sorry. It's just . . ."

"He's driving you nuts?" Megan laughed.

"It's not funny. You'd think I was terminally ill or something, instead of pregnant."

Although she knew Gage's attentiveness was probably getting to her overly independent sister, she also knew that Rebecca loved the attention. It was something Megan and Rebecca had lacked growing up—Rebecca especially. "You know you love it." Megan paused. "And him."

It took a few seconds, but then a soft smile brightened Rebecca's features. "It's sad, but I do. I know I shouldn't, but to know that he'd drop everything for me and the baby, no matter what, is a pretty amazing feeling."

"Yeah, I bet. I mean, we didn't have that growing up. He's going to be a great dad."

Rebecca glanced back to where Gage was now talking to his father and Trent. "He really is."

The talk of dads sent Megan's mind drifting back to Paul, and she immediately began searching the crowd for him.

"Looking for someone?"

Megan turned back to face her sister. "Huh? What?"

"I asked if you were looking for someone." Rebecca had a strange look on her face, and Megan knew Rebecca was going into big sister mode. It was the last thing she wanted.

"Not really."

Her sister frowned. "Is something going on I should know about?"

Now Megan was confused. "Like?"

"I don't know. I mean you've gone four months without chasing after a guy. That's a record for you."

Megan rolled her eyes. "Thanks."

"I didn't . . . I didn't mean it like that. I worry about you. I want you to find a nice guy—someone who will treat you well. I don't want to see you hurt again."

"I know. And when I find him, you'll be the first to know."

Rebecca reached up to brush a strand of hair away from Megan's face. It was something she'd done since Megan was little—a motherly gesture from the only real female authority figure Megan had ever known. "Come on. Let's get to the bathroom before I burst. I think I drank way too much water earlier."

Following her sister, Megan took one last look around trying to spot Paul, but she didn't see him anywhere.

Available now!

About the Author

Sherri spent most of her childhood detesting English class. It was one of her least favorite subjects because she never seemed to fit into the standard mold. She wasn't good at spelling, or following grammar rules, and outlines made her head spin. For that reason, Sherri never imagined becoming an author.

At the age of thirty, all of that changed. After getting frustrated with the direction a television show was taking two of its characters, Sherri decided to try her hand at writing an alternate ending, and give the characters their happily ever after. By the time the story finished, it was one of the top ten read stories on the site, and her readers were encouraging her to write more.

Since then Sherri has published several novels, many of which have hit the top 100 in their category on Amazon. Writing has become a creative outlet that allows her to explore a wide range of emotions, while having fun taking her characters through all the twists and turns she can create. You can find a current list of all of Sherri's books and sign up for her monthly newsletter at www.sherrihayesauthor.com.

Made in the USA
Middletown, DE
19 January 2019